Brass Knuckles

A Dave Haggard Thriller

By

Larry Matthews

\

Argus Enterprises International, Inc.
New Jersey***North Carolina

A-Argus Better Book Publishers, LLC

For information:
A-Argus Better Book Publishers, LLC
9001 Ridge Hill Street
Kernersville, North Carolina 27285
www.a-argusbooks.com

ISBN: 978-0-6157179-7-5
ISBN: 0615779-7-7

Book Cover designed by Dubya
Printed in the United States of America

Author's note

This is a work of fiction. The stories and characters I have created in Brass Knuckles are fictional and are not based on actual persons or events with the following exceptions:

Three real journalists have graciously agreed to appear in cameos as part of the story. Each of them interacts with Dave Haggard.

Neal Augenstein is a well-respected street reporter for WTOP, the top rated radio station in Washington. WTOP is an all-news station and Neal is a veteran journalist who is well known to the station's many listeners. In Brass Knuckles, Neal teaches Dave Haggard how to file radio reports from the field using his smart phone. Neal has been a pioneer in the use of new technology for radio field reporting.

Jim Russell is a public radio guru who was part of the team that created All Things Considered on National Public Radio, Marketplace and The World on other public radio outlets. He was a war correspondent during the Vietnam years. Today he is, as he says, "chief cook and bottle washer" at The Program Doctor, a consulting service for public broadcasting outlets. He is also an old friend. In Brass Knuckles he offers Dave Haggard career and personal advice.

Jim Bohannon is host of The Jim Bohannon Show and America in the Morning. The shows are heard on hundreds of radio stations by millions of Americans every weekday. Jim is one of the most well liked people in broadcasting and is a member of the National Radio Hall of Fame. He is another old friend. In Brass Knuckles, Dave Haggard appears on the Jim Bohannon Show to answer questions about the story that is the subject of this book.

I am grateful to all three of these outstanding broadcasters for their appearances in Brass Knuckles.

Chapter One

Federal Judge Alexander Beechum was a man of habit and routine. He believed that spontaneous acts were a sign of a cluttered life that had no meaning or order. His day was precise. Each day was planned in accordance with its needs, meaning, of course, his needs. His office in the federal courthouse in Washington was a tribute to his ordered mind, with a place for everything and everything in its place, including his well-groomed clerks and minions. "Let justice not be ill served by a misplaced fact or file," was one of his frequently issued slogans. And so it was that Judge Beechum went to lunch each day at precisely 12:30PM, walking through the front doors of the courthouse after a brief wave to the marshals who staffed the security point.

It was early April and the cherry blossoms were at peak bloom. The blossoms bring hundreds of thousands of tourists to the city to gaze upon the fragile flowers and spend money in local hotels and restaurants. Most years the blossoms are at peak for only a few days before a front blows through with wind and rain, sending the petals into the Tidal Basin and leaving the tourists with the taste of disappointment. Not so on this day.

Judge Beechum noted that the Mall area was crowded with smiling families, all of them taking pictures of each other with the Capitol building in the background. It was Wednesday, so the judge was having lunch at Sammy's, a sandwich shop on 4th Street. He would order, as on each Wednesday, a turkey and swiss on French bread with a light smear of mayo and a handful of sprouts. The sprouts were a nod to the health concerns of his wife, to whom he had been married for thirty-four years. He had eaten the same lunch every Wednesday for eleven years. Thursdays were soup and salad.

He stood in the sunshine and enjoyed the warmth it offered after a cold, wet and rainy March. He looked up at the monument to General George Meade, the Union general credited with defeating Robert E. Lee at Gettysburg. Meade's monument is on the plaza at the courthouse complex and it comforted the judge to see such a tribute to victory. As he stood facing west with a smile on his face a loud crack bounced off the stone skins of the buildings, making it sound as though several shots had been fired, but it was only one. The 7.62 millimeter round hit Judge Beechum just above his right eye. It exited behind his left ear, leaving a wound as large as an orange, sending much of the brain that had so impressed legal scholars spewing onto the stone image of General Meade.

A lawyer who was stuffing papers into her leather briefcase nearly tripped over him before she saw the body and the carnage around it. She screamed for help but it was several minutes before the scene was secured and U.S. Marshals from the courthouse began to assess the situation. By then the gunman was gone and so was the M14 that had killed the man known as Maximum Alex. It was a nickname given to him by defense lawyers in recognition of Judge Beechum's belief that public officials who are convicted of crimes against the people be locked up for as long as the law allows. The judge had sent a good many such officials away after a subjecting them to his infamous tongue lashings about the responsibilities of those elected to serve the people. Former members of Congress were sitting in their cells at that very moment, along with a few Cabinet officers and lobbyists, unaware, of course, that the man who had sent them to long stretches at Allenwood or Cumberland or Petersburg was facing his own eternity.

One man, a sitting Representative from Tennessee, was aware. He was facing his own legal challenges and his friends had taken action in an attempt to slow the wheels of justice. He was waiting by the phone for word that the problem had been solved. As he would learn, it wasn't as simple as a quick assassination.

Radio reporter Dave Haggard was sitting at his desk in his new office in a high rise building overlooking the Potomac River in Rosslyn, a section of Arlington across the river from Georgetown. "High rise" is a relative term. In Chicago or New York it means skyscraper. In the Washington area it's anything over ten stories. The D.C. region is a decidedly "low rise" area because the Washington Monument, at 555 feet, is as high as it gets. Rosslyn, with its steel and glass modernity, was a contrast to Georgetown, with its 17th and 18th Centuries store fronts and townhouses. Dave was happy to be looking back in time. He thought Rosslyn was hideous.

His employer, a Washington-based news service called Now News, had recently moved from smaller offices near Dupont Circle in the city to the high rise on the strength of its increased visibility and wealth created by the publicity of its involvement in the story known as The Priest Killings, a string of grisly murders of Catholic Priests. Dave had been at the center of the story and had, in fact, been part of the capture of the killer and the rescue of his then-girlfriend. The publicity had brought a rush of clients and funds to Now News, thus the new digs.

Dave was restless and bored. The tourist season had begun and it was difficult to get around the city. He was stuck covering the Justice Department and its newly installed and painfully boring leader, the aptly named Attorney General Jubal Gray, who spoke in sentences designed to suck the energy out of every moment. But Dave had to admit to himself that he liked the view. He could see the Kennedy Center, Roosevelt Island and its semi-wildness, the Georgetown waterfront, and, in the distance, the Washington Monument and the Capitol.

Two high school rowing teams were on the river, the four-man teams were racing each other in the long, thin boats in practice runs for the spring season. The boats went under Key Bridge and emerged heading north to Three Sisters Islands, a group of rocky protrusions in the middle of the river. The young men were powerful and the boats moved with amazing speed. Dave watched and had a moment of admiration for the boys who were on the river in the middle of a school day. The idyllic scene was interrupted by a scull being rowed by one man who pulled past the high schoolers and sped up the river by the rocky islands and disappeared behind the trees along the Virginia shore.

Dave saw powerful shoulders and arms and a white man's head under a Washington Nationals baseball hat. Later, when he was asked to describe the man, that is all he could recall. The moment was nothing more than an interruption in an otherwise idle day. He was killing time before yet another of the AG's news conferences about a legal issue relating to land rights in the West. Even the folks in Montana wouldn't be interested in this story. He wanted to press Sid for some street assignments around the city but that was not possible at the moment because Now News was still reeling from the priest killing story and Sid had made a deal with the F.B.I. to keep Dave out of harm's way. I'm a house cat, he thought, gazing down at the traffic on Key Bridge.

His phone rang. "Yeah," was his usual answer.

It was Sid, his boss, an old news lion who liked to keep the cubs in line. Dave was no cub but Sid still growled at him from time to time. "Get your ass down to the District Court. Somebody just shot Judge Beechum."

"Where?"

"Right in front of the statue of General Meade. All hell's breaking loose."

"I'm on it." Dave had his coat on and was out the door before Sid could change his mind. The taxi situation was always dicey in Arlington. Most of the cabbies wanted to drive in D.C. where there was more business. Arlington cabs mostly went to Reagan National Airport and the drivers spent a lot of time in line waiting for fares, unlike the city drivers who dropped off and picked up anywhere. Dave went out the lobby door and saw a cab dropping off a fare at the door and he raced to grab it. The driver was a Somali who had perfected the art of having no facial expression whatsoever. The man nodded when Dave told him he wanted to go to the federal courthouse at 3rd and Constitution and proceeded to head for Key Bridge.

"No, don't go that way. Loop over to Roosevelt Bridge and go down Constitution. It will be faster."

The driver kept going. "Are you aware of the Cherry Blossom Festival?" he asked in a formal, British public school manner. "There are many, many tourists here for that. It will take an hour that way." So he drove to Georgetown and headed down M Street to Pennsylvania and made it to the courthouse in twenty minutes. Dave felt foolish but he was grateful that the driver knew the city and its ways.

The courthouse is officially on Constitution Avenue at Third Street Northwest, within sight of the United States Capitol building. In fact, it is on Pennsylvania Avenue in a clot of intersections which, in high-tourist seasons, are packed with out-of-towners gawking at the

Capitol, the Mall, the Newseum, or the Embassy of Canada, which is arguably the most impressive embassy in Washington and is next door to the courthouse.

Pennsylvania Avenue was blocked by police cars with their lights flashing. The area was closed for blocks as federal agents searched for evidence and clues. A press pen had been established near the courthouse and Dave could see reporters frantically calling out to every cop and agent they knew, pleading for some crumb to report. Television reporters were the most intense because their bosses were yelling at them through the small earphones they had embedded in their heads. Newspaper and other print reporters were the most serene and detail-oriented because their deadlines were longer. Online bloggers tweeted out morsels of information that had no context and no one seemed to care. Press pens are areas where cops and other officials herd reporters during breaking stories to keep them from running around like a bunch of cats out of control. Loose reporters can be risky to people who are trying to control a narrative.

Dave saw a reporter from the Associated Press with whom he had shared information in the past and walked over to him. The man's name was Peter Deutch and he was a solid but conventional journalist. He could gather facts as fast as anyone but he was conservative in the conclusions he drew from those facts, unlike the cable television types who drew conclusions first and then went in search of facts to back them up.

"What are they saying?" Dave asked.

"That's him under the tarp. One to the head. I hate to say it, but this is good news for Congressman Prewitt." Deutch looked sad.

Chapter Two

F.B.I. Special Agent Milford "Bud" Ossening was watching the search for evidence and keeping an eye on the reporters who were penned up on the sidewalk. His primary concern was that one or two of them would slip under the yellow police tape and get close to the body of Judge Beechum and pollute the crime scene. Ossening hated reporters. He saw them as jackals and carrion eaters who cared about nothing but their own sensationalist interests. He believed that any one of them would publish the nation's nuclear secrets without regret for the simple glory of a scoop. He did, however, find some of them to be more interesting than others. Dave Haggard fell into the interesting category. Dave had a knack for coming into information best left hidden. He had come into such information in the search for the priest killer and certain actions had to be taken to control him, although the outcome in that effort was far from clear. Regrettable, that's how Ossening saw it. Regrettable.

There was Haggard now, talking to that AP fellow, no doubt plotting to uncover anything and everything about the tragic murder of Judge Beechum. Well, there's a lot to uncover, Ossening admitted to himself. Let's see how this plays out. He caught Dave's eye and waved him over.

"Hello, Dave. How goes the battle?" Ossening had his best F.B.I. smile, the one taught to him by the instructors at Quantico. The smile is intended to put the other person at ease. It's a generic I'm-a-nice-guy smile.

"It goes. How about yourself?" Dave's expression was not as friendly.

"Too bad about the judge. What are you hearing?"

"I'm supposed to ask you."

"You know I can't comment on an ongoing investigation and this one is certainly ongoing, given that the victim is still at the scene."

"So why wave me over?"

"A couple of reasons, really. One, of course, is to see if you're honoring our deal." Ossening looked at Dave and raised his eyebrows.

"I haven't reported a thing about it," Dave said. He was referring to an unofficial telephone monitoring operation he had come across while he was working on the priest killing story. The monitoring appeared to be government-sponsored but nothing official had been stated either way. Ossening had pressured Dave into keeping the information to himself and the U.S. Attorney's office had made Dave a material witness, effectively shutting him up. "What's the other reason?"

"If I say something, will you keep me out of it? Deep background or something like that, know how this works?"

"I don't break confidences."

"Tell that to Captain O'Neil." O'Neil was a D.C. police captain who had been burned by Dave during the priest killing story, or so O'Neil believed.

"We've squared that away," Dave said.

"Well, that's between you two. Here's the deal. We think this was a hit. It looks like a pro. Clean shot. Nothing left behind. You do know that Beechum was about to get the Prewitt case that Justice is building over that missing money down at Oak Ridge. Justice is looking for a way into the Congressman's files and thought Beechum would be a sympathetic ear. We hear word got out and the next thing we know, the good jurist is lying dead with a big hole in his head. Now, if I were an enterprising reporter I might want to look in that direction. Just a thought and you didn't get it from me." Ossening enjoyed tossing tidbits at reporters just to watch them scramble around like dogs after meat scraps. He kept his activities within a small group of reporters he believed he could control and it had served him well. All of his contacts with journalists were approved by his supervisor.

Dave did not trust the agent's motives but experience had shown him that Ossening's information was good. "And if you were such an enterprising reporter would you be sniffing around Washington or Tennessee?"

Ossening offered his most sincere smile. "That depends where the scent was coming from. Right now, I'm afraid, it's coming from over there." He nodded in the direction of Beechum's body. "We'll be moving it soon. Tell your friends in the press pen that I didn't give you anything and was just saying hello." He turned and walked toward the body, leaving Dave standing where he was, holding his smartphone, which had recorded everything Ossening had said. Dave would not use the recording on the air for his reports but he would listen and transcribe Ossening's comments and parse through them for meaning.

Deutch was scribbling on his note pad when Dave was hustled back into the press pen. "Anything?"

"No, he just wanted to say hello. He's kind of my minder on the priest killer witness issue."

"Anything new there?"

"Not yet. Has anyone said anything about the judge? Have you found any witnesses?"

"Chanel Five got a statement from the lawyer who almost fell over the body and some tourists are talking to anyone who'll interview them. Some people are saying they heard multiple shots but the cops are saying it looks to be only one. We're expecting something from the White House later but it will be the usual we-decry-this-senseless-act-of-violence statement."

Dave walked around and got a few tourists to talk about where they were when the judge was shot and how awful it was to be in Washington on such a nice day and be a witness to a murder. The folks back in Peoria will sure be eager to hear about this. Nothing like this happens in our town, no sir.

Dave hailed a cab and went back to Now News to put together a piece for the evening feed to the hundred or so radio stations that subscribed to the news service. The lead was the murder of Judge Beechum but Dave's piece was a backgrounder on the judge and his reputation for toughness. He did not mention a possible tie-in to the Prewitt angle, which was still too early to report.

While Dave was writing his story and preparing to record it, a fifty-ish man was waiting in a line near the main post office next to Union Station. He was carrying a small valise but no suitcase. The man was wearing a red Washington Nationals cap, khaki pants, and a brown canvas jacket. He wore wire rimmed glasses. To a casual observer he appeared to be just another middle aged man waiting for a cheap bus ride to New York; a bit thick around the middle, average height, with no outstanding features. The man displayed no outward anxiety and only a trained eye could detect that he was on high internal alert for any signs of threat. There were no trained eyes on him at that moment, but a security camera was recording the activity on the block.

His name was Edward Segal. He was known in his small, specialized community as Brass Knuckles, a nickname derived from the metal device he carried and used in hand-to-hand combat and street fights. Brass knuckles are designed to limit the damage to a fighter's hands when he punches another person. The "brass" knuckles, often made of steel, inflict what is known as "significant tissue and bone damage" to the person on the receiving end. Segal was a born scrapper. He was a former army sniper who had shown extraordinary skill in Iraq in 2005, when he was a minor celebrity in the sniper community for his skill at making head shots at great distance. He had long ago lost his sense of sadness at the death he caused. Now, wearing a prosthetic lower leg, he worked for a small, exclusive contract outfit that paid in cash. His only conditions were no kids, no women. Female terrorists were an exception. Segal had no qualms about sending Judge Beechum to his final reward.

He had scouted the city and the judge and determined that the job was laughably easy. The judge was always at the same place at the same time. Tens of thousands of tourists crowding the area where the judge would be shot made escape child's play. He rowed a single-man scull to the Watergate, a bicycle to the target area, and reversed the process after the hit as marshals, F.B.I. agents and D.C. cops tried to secure the scene. The river was smooth and he enjoyed rowing up to the drop point off the George Washington Parkway on the Virginia side of the Potomac, where he left the scull and drove away in a nondescript rental sedan, leaving it in the parking lot at Union Station. The M-14 was at the bottom of the river.

He preferred cheap inter-city bus lines because they picked up and dropped off on city streets instead of at bus stations where police and other security agents could set up surveillance. A government attempt to shut down the cheap bus lines in the name of safety had produced a new fleet just as suspect as the old one but with better public relations and drivers who were more or less conscious. His plan was to be in Ocho Rios on the Jamaican cost by midnight, enjoying a Plantation Punch and listening to the waves come ashore. He would spend two weeks there and he would return to Tampa, pick up his truck, and drive home to East Tennessee, where he would return to his farm near the town of Harriman, and work on his bass boat. And await his next job.

To the outside world he was just another good ol' boy who used his government check to fund a modest life of hunting and fishing. But Ed Segal was no ordinary redneck. He seethed with rage over what the government had done to his beloved hills and rivers. He shot up every sign he saw that warned him not to eat the fish in Tennessee River because of the pollution. He raged at the Tennessee Valley Authority and its foul treatment of the land and the people. The pot ash spill in December 2008 that fouled the river system sent millions of cubic feet of toxins downstream. That wasn't all. He was white hot with anger at the Oak Ridge facility where nuclear weapons were made. Decades of radiation had done God-knows-what damage to the land and thousands of pounds of mercury were still seeping into groundwater, even as the government tried to hush it up and assure the mountain people that it was okay to drink the water. No, he had no regrets at the killing of Judge Beechum. Ed Segal had no way of knowing that he had killed the wrong man. The bad guy was Congressman Prewitt, who at the moment was lighting a cigar in celebration.

Chapter Three

John Prewitt, Jr. had never worked for anything in his life, including his seat in the United States House of Representatives. He was the son of a prominent Knoxville lawyer, his father, and a tenured professor at the University of Tennessee, his mother, who was also a best-selling author of books about the Old South, the gauzy antebellum period of manners and grace. Messy details about slavery and general misery of the time were pushed aside. The books gave the family a certain cache among those who believed that what was wrong with America was entirely due to Yankees and their bad manners.

His father, John Sr., was a rainmaker for a prominent law firm and his specialty was land and development. It had occurred to the father that land was the source of all wealth and that zoning was the key to all land, and so he had developed a system of zoning through litigation. He used his considerable financial and legal resources to sue the various zoning boards in parts of East Tennessee to obtain the zoning he was after, either on behalf of his well-heeled clients or himself. He had managed to gain control or ownership of significant sections of land where now stood shopping centers, office parks, highways, or various other commercial interests. John Sr. had no other interests. He did not play golf and he did not hunt or fish, although he did attend occasional hunting weekends at country estates to promote himself or his clients and he had been known to shoot down the odd goose or quail. In all, he felt most comfortable in an expensive suit behind his hand-carved desk, surrounded by precious American art he had picked up here and there. His best moments were spent savoring outrageously expensive cigars in celebration of victory over someone else.

John Jr. had lived a life of privilege and indulgence. His father's self-discipline was lost on him. He had attended the finest schools and was an indifferent student, graduating only after his father had pledged funds for new buildings or athletic fields. He had impregnated several young women, all of whose families were paid generous settlements. He had once stolen a car on a lark, was caught, and escaped jail because his father was a secret business partner with the county attorney, who dropped the charges.

John Jr. was not well liked but he was well known and, in his community, that was enough to move him up the social and official ladder of the small town where the family was headquartered in a plantation house that had been rebuilt following the War. All of the family servants were black. John Sr. made a point of paying them generously and making that fact known to everyone who would listen. He had never been known to use the "N" word but the general feeling in the community was that the family held opinions that were no longer in vogue, not even in the South.

The Prewitt family was used to getting what it wanted and no one had succeeded in challenging the family on any matter of importance, not even the federal government. And so it was not surprising that John Jr. had turned to the darker elements of his world when word reached him that the Justice Department was sniffing the air for the scent of corruption in the billion-dollar cleanups of Oak Ridge and the T.V.A., in which Representative Prewitt was intimately involved. He was nearing his fiftieth birthday and was in his fourth term in the

House, which gave him enough seniority to chair a sub-committee that oversaw appropriations for things such as environmental cleanup and energy research. He enjoyed a well-appointed, if smallish office in the Canon House Office Building and use of an office in the Capitol, a perk that was precious in the arcane world of Congress.

Dave had a passing relationship with Congressman Prewitt and had interviewed him about one thing or another on several occasions and had once had him as a guest on a live radio show. Dave saw Prewitt as a martinet who used rules and social tradition as a way to control others and avoid criticism. Prewitt always had a smirk on his face that projected an attitude of superiority to whoever was in the Congressman's sight. His expensive suits and his sugary Southern accent reminded Dave of his own East Tennessee roots, though those roots ran to the scruffier, poorer communities where grits for dinner was common.

Prewitt always addressed Dave as "boy", as in "What can I do for you, boy?" The term was used to address inferiors, although some Southern communities saw it as a Jim Crow-era put-down for blacks. Where Dave and Prewitt came from, "boy" was well understood to mean a male inferior. Dave responded by referring to Prewitt as "John," a sign of disrespect for a member of Congress. Prewitt hated all members of the press and saw Dave as just another uppity reporter, but one who should know his place, given his background.

And so Prewitt took a deep breath when an aid told him Dave was on the phone. "Hello, Mr. Haggard, how are you this fine day?"

"Hello, John. Do you have a minute?"

"Always a minute for you, Mr. Haggard. What can I do for you, boy?"

"I'd like to buy your dinner tonight."

"I didn't know you people made enough money to buy even your own dinner, boy." Prewitt issued a small chuckle at his little joke.

"Well, we eat at greasy spoons and order the meat loaf, but we get by. Are you free?"

"What's the old joke? I'm not free but I'm reasonable."

Dave could imagine the saccharine smile on Prewitt's face. "Or I could come by for a little chat. There's something I'd like to talk to you about. Something private. Something I'd rather not go into on the phone."

Prewitt was picking up warning signals. "What's this about?"

"Like I said, it's a better left to a private conversation."

"Meet me at four-thirty in thirteen-ten Longworth. I'll be sitting at the press table near the back window." The line went dead.

Thirteen-ten was a committee room Longworth House Office Building is one of three that house members of the House of Representatives and their committees and staffs. Thirteen-ten would be empty in the late afternoon. A subcommittee chairman could order that no one enter while he was having a private conversation and such a venue would avoid the rumor mill that could come to life if the meeting were held in his office where staff members and constituents were going in and out.

The days were getting longer and that gave tourists more sunlight in which to clog the Mall and the afternoon rush hour was adding to the congestion along Constitution Avenue when Dave hailed a cab for his meeting. Truck vendors were packing up their t-shirts and souvenirs and moving on for the day before the police could ticket them. A police tow truck was pulling away from the curb hauling an SUV with Indiana plates. A visiting family from America's heartland was getting a lesson in rush hour parking restrictions. It was a lesson they wouldn't be aware of until they left the Museum of Natural History. By then the SUV would be in a police impoundment lot that accepted cash and credit cards in an amount the family would consider criminal.

The cab let Dave out near the Senate office buildings and he trudged across Capital Plaza to the House side and across Independence to the entrance to the Longworth Building, where he went through security with a gaggle of other reporters and other late afternoon visitors. He took the stairs to the hallway that led to thirteen-ten and his shoes made a clacking noise as he walked across the stone floor past offices and hearing rooms. Members, lobbyists and staffers were huddled along the walls, making deals or reviewing legislation. The Speaker came out of a men's room, zipping his fly and whispering to an aid. A movie star was followed by an entourage as he made his way from office to office seeking support for more funding for the arts.

Thirteen-ten was dark when Dave opened the door. "Over here." Prewitt's voice came from the other side of the room and Dave could see him silhouetted by the light coming through a tall window behind him. Dave walked over and offered his hand, which Prewitt ignored.

"So, what's so important that we have to meet like this?" Prewitt's expression was sour.

"I have received some information about a possible investigation involving you and some of your constituents. I suppose that's what I'd call them."

"What sort of investigation?"

"I'm told that Justice is seeking permission to search your offices here in Washington and in your home district. Any truth to that?"

Prewitt sat up and slapped the table. "What sort of crap is this? Who told you about this so-called investigation?"

"You know I can't reveal my sources. I wanted to give you a chance to comment before I run the story." Dave was bluffing. If he had been a poker player he wouldn't even have a pair of twos. He hoped Prewitt could not smell the bluff and realize that Dave didn't have anything close to enough information to run a story.

"Sources? What sources? You don't have any sources. You're making this up to see what I'll say, aren't you." Prewitt was sweating and Dave realized that the Congressman was also bluffing and was scared.

"I know that Justice went to Judge Beechum for authorization before he was shot. You have anything to say about that?"

"I know what's going on here. Somebody's pissed off about something and they're trying to screw me. If, and I emphasize if, the government is looking into anything involving me I want you to know that I have done nothing wrong. Nothing. You got that?" Prewitt's hands were shaking.

"I'm just trying to give you a chance to tell your side of the story. What can you tell me?"

"Let me ask you something. Did you get this tip from someone in Tennessee or here in Washington?"

Tennessee? Prewitt was admitting to something but Dave didn't know what it was. He had given Dave new information. Someone in Tennessee was aware of the investigation. Was that someone a target or a prosecutor? "I can't say, Congressman." Dave showed respect in his use of the formal title. "It's all confidential. You know how it works."

Prewitt looked at his shoes. "I need you to do me a favor. Keep this under wraps until I have a chance to get my ducks in a row. I'm being blindsided by this. I'll tell you something off the record. Off the record only and only if you agree to hold this for a while. Agreed?"

Prewitt was playing for time, it was clear, but Dave had no cards to play at the moment, so he paused for effect. "I'll agree on condition that I go with it if I have any reason to believe another reporter has it or is about to break it. First whiff of that and I'm on the air with everything I have." It was like a man with no gun threatening to shoot someone, but Prewitt didn't know that.

"Okay, yes, I have been targeted. It's some horseshit about money that I don't know anything about other than I pushed for funding to cleanup Oak Ridge. It's an environmental disaster and the federal government has a responsibility to clean it up." Dave hoped that Prewitt wouldn't go into a stump speech about it.

"So, what have they told you?"

Prewitt looked up. "That's about it. They want to come up here and search my office and my office in Tennessee. Trust me when I tell you there's nothing to find. Nothing at all." Dave's neck hair stood up whenever a politician used the words "trust me". Prewitt leaned toward Dave. "Going with this will just cause trouble and smear my good name. I promise that I will give you everything you need if you'll give me some time to clean this up."

Dave thought it was an interesting choice of words. Clean up what? "Here's my card. It has my cell number. Call me when you want to talk." This time Prewitt shook Dave's hand and the two men left the room. Prewitt walked to his office stewing about the meeting and its possible consequences. He was not a man who had experience with such things as consequences for his actions. He had always found ways around the trouble he caused and he assumed that this was just another small issue to be resolved with money and influence. He sat behind his desk and picked up his office phone. The man on the other end of the call picked up after one ring but did not speak. "Call me. We have a problem," Prewitt said, and hung up.

Chapter Four

It could never be said that Sid was a sentimental man. He had spent too many years in the news business to be sweet on much of anything other than the people who worked for him. He liked to compare himself to the old French philosophers who believed that, in the end, it was all bullshit and nothing much really mattered. What he cared about was matching fact with truth, which was not as easy as it sounded. Washington was awash in fact, true or not, and the daily grind of the news cycle spewed facts in all directions, every one of them subject to spin. The old joke, "Who are you gonna believe, me or your lying eyes?" was not funny in a city where the question was asked, in one way or another, in all seriousness.

He sat at his computer and read the summary Dave had sent about his meeting with Congressman Prewitt, whom Sid believed to be pompous, lying ass of the first magnitude. He sent a top-of-the-line message to Dave over the in-house text system. "Come in to my office."

Dave arrived carrying a coffee mug and a laptop computer. "You should spring for us to get tablets, you know," he said by way of greeting.

"At five hundred bucks each, dream on. I'm wondering what you're thinking about Prewitt."

"There's fire under the smoke. That's what I think."

"You got him to confirm it. That's good. Too bad you agreed to hold it."

"I agreed to hold it because I don't have anything I can go with."

"You have that he's under investigation for stealing money from the Oak Ridge cleanup and you have a tip that Justice was going to Judge Beechum for authority on it and Judge Beechum is now deceased in a very public way." Sid was just throwing out words knowing that there was not enough to use in a news story that Dave would quickly be asked to justify by the public.

"That and a cup of coffee, or whatever the saying is. I'm gonna go back to Ossening and see what he can add. Maybe he can send me to a good source in Tennessee. I'll see if I can get him to agree to meet me."

"Quite a relationship you two have. Did he ask you about the book?"

"No, he just reminded me about our so-called deal." The book Dave was writing would, in concept, detail the priest killing story and Dave's involvement in capturing the killer. He had also been involved in the rescue of Elena, his girlfriend at the time, who had been kidnapped by the killer. The information about a secret government-sponsored but suspect telephone monitoring operation in the Virginia countryside was, under agreement, off-limits until further notice, even though Dave had seen it for himself.

"I say write what you want and let Ossening raise hell about it later."

"Easy to say if you're not the one facing jail time." Dave tried to put a chuckle in his voice.

"Do you ever hear from Elena?" Sid knew he was stepping on rocky ground.

"Not directly, no. I don't even know where she is."

"She's coming back to work, you know. She's left the nunnery or whatever they call it and she's spending a few days in Ocean City. I talked to her this morning. She'll be in on Monday." Sid watched for Dave's reaction and saw him take a breath and look out the window.

"Maybe I'll call her over the weekend."

"Like I said, she's in Ocean City. Maybe you can catch her on her cell."

"I have to get back to work." Dave got up and went back to his desk. There was a message on the top of his computer screen. Call Capt. O'Neil, it said.

Warwicks had been on upper Wisconsin Avenue for over fifty years. For most of that time it had serviced the thirsts of reporters, engineers and camera operators at a string of television stations that had set up shop before the area had become home to upper income retailers, back when the blocks bordering Maryland were as cheap as land got in Northwest Washington. Now, Friendship Heights harbored some of the priciest stores in the world and the well-shod trophy wives who shopped in the establishments claimed the stores were actually in Chevy Chase, a tony community due east down Western Avenue along Connecticut. Chevy Chase was considered a much better address than Friendship Heights. Nevertheless, the block of Wisconsin just north of Western was known as the Rodeo Drive of Washington, even though, technically, it was in Maryland. In Washington, image is everything. Except in a place like Warwick's.

The saloon was a few steps down from the street, the steps being well-worn bricks that have known the footfalls of many drunks, some of them household names. The place had the appearance of an establishment that was decorated and furnished a long time ago and left to age in place. The bar was the first thing a patron saw at the bottom of the stairs and it ran the full length of the back wall. The full mirror behind the bar would have display the reflection of the incoming customer except that the mirror was all but covered by booze bottles, old posters, and artifacts of bygone eras. The varnish on the wood bar had been worn away for decades and no attempt was been made to polish it. The high-backed stools were wide enough to accommodate the enlarged asses of modern patrons.

It was dark in the bar, even at mid-afternoon. The bartender was a middle-aged white man with the friendly face of a fellow who has been serving liquor in such a place for many years. He was wearing a white shirt and tie but the tie was cut off halfway down the shirt front. Two men were sitting at the bar drinking shots and coffee. They were telling the bartender a story about Shaker Heights, Ohio, something about copper drain pipes.

The bartender looked and smiled up as Dave walked in. "Looking for something to eat or do you want to sit at the bar?"

Dave looked around and didn't see O'Neil. "I'm meeting someone. I'll wait."

"Get you something?" The bartender pointed to the bottles behind him.

"I'm okay." Dave was not okay. He was nervous to the point of being light-headed and had a moment of feeling that he was in a dream and would wake up and be in his own bed. He stood with his back to the wall and tried to smile as a young waiter walked by with a puzzled look on his face. He and O'Neil had a history that puzzled Dave. O'Neil was not someone who fit into any ordinary category.

Daniel O'Neil was a captain in the Metropolitan Police, the formal name for the D.C. police department. Until recently he had headed the Homicide Division and in that capacity had been a lead investigator into the priest killings and had sent Dave and Elena to a farm in Virginia when the killer was stalking them. Things went sour and the killer not only found them but kidnapped Elena and nearly killed her. It was Dave who saved her and it was O'Neil who was taken into custody by the F.B.I. in the official what-went-wrong phase of the after-action investigation into the whole sorry mess that the case became. What transpired after that was hidden in the jargon of "national security" but O'Neil had emerged with a new job under the umbrella of "homeland security" and was now ensconced in offices on upper Wisconsin Avenue in a building paid for with some of the Homeland Security money that was washing over the capital city like a high tide.

The priest killings had left Dave and O'Neil with bitter feelings about each other. Dave felt that O'Neil had put his and Elena's lives in danger and O'Neil felt that Dave had repeatedly violated his trust and had used information that should have been considered confidential between a source and a reporter. They had barely spoken since the F.B.I. had proclaimed O'Neil guiltless.

O'Neil was a red-faced Irishman who had dreams of becoming Chief. His dreams were dented by his reputation as a cowboy and he had clawed his way to captain by accepting jobs no one else wanted and he had made enemies. In fact, he was in one of those jobs now, sifting through the odds and ends of intelligence rumors for signs of threats to the capital of the Free World. He missed Homicide and the back and forth of life on the street. His new job was a gift from Justice. At least, that's how his "rabbi" at Justice saw it. "You could be in prison," is how the man had put it.

O'Neil parked on 44th Street near the Mazza Gallerie and dodged the upscale shoppers who were carrying their bags from the shopping mall's chichi stores and boutiques. He stepped aside as an older woman wearing oversized sunglasses and knee-high boots maneuvered her overstuffed shopping bags around a homeless man who was holding out a cup as she passed, tossing him a withering glance that said vermin should be shot on sight and not allowed to clutter the sidewalks in stylish shopping districts. He crossed Wisconsin and walked a half block to Warwick's. Anyone with any interest in cops would notice that O'Neil had it written all over him, from the way he walked to the suit he wore to the get-out-of-my-way expression on his face. He walked down the steps, opened the door, and came face to face with Dave, who felt a mixture of fear and rage.

"So, Ace, how's life in the news business?" His face reflected a smile from the nose down and a wary stare from the nose up.

"How are you, Captain?" Dave's East Tennessee accent asserted itself when he was uncomfortable.

"Never better. Let's get a table." O'Neil waved to a waiter and followed the man to a table in an area of the bar known as The Greenhouse, a glassed-in area that fronted along the sidewalk. It offered a clear view of a high rise parking lot across the street and an entrance to the Friendship Heights Metro stop. Two men in suits were eating burgers and tossing down Scotch at a nearby table but otherwise the room was empty. O'Neil pulled out a chair and sat, looking up at Dave, who felt awkward and unsure of what to do next. "You gonna sit or just stand there?"

Dave sat across from O'Neil and removed the napkin that was wrapped around the silverware. "To what do I owe the honor?"

"I'm simply wondering how you are doing." O'Neil offered a steady gaze without a smile.

"I'm still under wraps, if that's what you mean. I can't write about the surveillance operation at the farm and I haven't had any contact with Elena, but I'm working and that's a plus. How's your new assignment?"

"Boring. I was buried. That's what happens when they want to get you out of the action. I spend my days looking over pieces of paper that don't say anything. Speaking of Elena, I hear by the grapevine that she's doing all right and is going back to work. Is that what you hear?"

"Yeah. She's been at a convent recovering."

"Some place in West Virginia?"

"The church offered her some time there. After Father Darius kidnapped her and nearly killed her she needed some time to feel safe, I suppose." Dave offered O'Neil a cold stare. "That would be where you came in, as I recall."

"We've been over that, Dave. We thought we were keeping her safe, that's why we got you and her out to the farm. We didn't think he'd find you and we certainly never believed that he'd get at you. I'm sorry." O'Neil wore his most sincere face. "Did you ever open the flash drive I gave you?"

"It was locked. You didn't give me the password." O'Neil had given him the flash drive in the minutes before Ossening had taken him away in the aftermath of the arrest of Father Darius.

"So you don't know what's on it."

"Not a clue. Maybe you can give it to me now."

"The Warriors of Mary have been quietly vacuumed up. They've been hidden away or retired. They're on the drive but it's not important anymore. But here, open it with this." O'Neil passed Dave a business card with some numbers written in pencil. "You working on anything these days?"

"I'm working the Judge Beechum thing. Is that something you're looking at?"

"I'm officially in an analysis unit under Homeland Security. They grabbed a bunch of people from D.C., F.B.I., D.E.A and anywhere they could find them and set up units to spend all the money they've been given. 9/11 did two things. It sent us to war and it released billions of dollars to spend on anything that had law enforcement written on it. So, to answer your question, no, I'm not officially chasing the killing of the judge but I get to look at lots of stuff that has "maybe" written on it."

"What about Congressman Prewitt of Tennessee? You hear anything about him?"

O'Neil's face broke into a smile that spread all the way up to his eyes. "You have good sources."

"One of your old friends, as it turns out."

"Our good friend Bud Ossening. He's taken on the role of my minder. He gets reports about whether I'm being a good boy."

"Are you?"

"It's a little late for that." O'Neil chuckled and looked at the menu. "Crab cakes are good here. They still use the crabs from the bay and not those horrible things that come from China or wherever."

"So, Congressman Prewitt?"

"I've heard what you've heard."

"And that would be?"

"Justice is after him. I'm not in the loop on this one."

They ordered the crab cakes and sat in silence for what to Dave seemed like a long time. He watched people on the street and could tell when the trains arrived by the crowds exiting the Metro station. Rush hour would begin soon and the trains would come at shorter intervals, disgorging commuters heading home to the apartments, row houses, and single family homes in the streets near Wisconsin Avenue. He wondered how long he had to stay and talk to O'Neil.

"Tennessee." O'Neil broke the silence. "Tennessee. I'd go there if I were looking for something."

"What?"

"You asked Ossening if the leads on Prewitt were in Washington or Tennessee. I'd go to Tennessee."

"Ossening sent you to give me that message?"

"We talk. He mentioned your conversation."

"What else did he mention?"

"Well, and this comes from both of us, you might want to keep your head down."

"You gave me that advice once before."

"That's behind us."

"Jesus! You guys crack me up."

"Listen, I'll help where I can and with what I can. That's all I can offer. I will say this. Prewitt has some very nasty friends and you should be very careful if you go after this. My advice would be to ignore anything he tells you, especially if he's friendly."

Dave put a twenty-dollar bill on the table and left. He went to his apartment, found the flash drive and inserted it into his computer. He used the password O'Neil had given him and waited for the file to open. Instead, he watched the timer wheel go around and slapped his table when the screen displayed a message that said "file deleted."

O'Neil had used Dave and the drive to protect himself if the Warriors of Mary, a religious group with upper level government members, ever threatened him. Now that he was feeling safe, it was time to erase the file. Dave would never know how high the priest killing plot went.

Chapter Five

Elena Romona-Cayo stood on the balcony over-looking the beach near 140th Street in Ocean City, Maryland and watched the Atlantic Ocean pound its way ashore. She was fifteen stories above the sand dunes that taxpayers had funded to keep the waves from damaging the high rise buildings along the Gold Coast, a Mecca for summer visitors who came, spent money, and basted themselves on the beach. There were few visitors mid-week in April, even though the sun warmed the sand and the sky was bright blue. An older couple walked along the shoreline with the Golden Retriever. The dog jumped into the waves and ran out, shaking salt water, and ran back into the surf. A man with a metal detector scanned the sand for treasure, even though the pickings were all but nonexistent in the off season.

Elena lifted her face to the late morning sun and breathed the ocean breeze as it came in from the east. The soft air brushed against her copper skin. Her right cheek showed a long, thin scar where Father Darius's butterfly knife had cut her in the moment when she was rescued. A skilled plastic surgeon had repaired most of the cosmetic damage but her smile would forever be un-balanced because of the damage to the nerves in her face. She had been told repeatedly by counselors and psychiatrists that she was lucky and that the priest's other victims did not come close to surviving, but in her worst moments these assurances were empty.

She had spent weeks in prayer and meditation at the convent in the mountains, trying to understand what had happened. She had no clearer understanding now than before but she knew it was time to get on with her life and the *after* part of it. Her problem was not the wound and it was not the fact that she had been kidnapped. It was her feeling that Dave had betrayed her by convincing her that she should join him while he was hiding from Father Darius, who was stalking him. The drama had brought her into Father Darius's homicidal insanity and it had nearly cost her life. What should she do about Dave? Any healthy person would drop him and move on but she felt powerless to walk away from him and it saddened her to see herself as addicted to another human being.

She went for a walk along the beach, hoping it would clear her head. She did not return to her room until late afternoon and the air coming off the sea was cold as she walked into the elevator. She was lost in thought and missed her floor and rode all the way down, then back up again, before she got off and walked along the outdoor hallway that looked out over Assawoman Bay that lay to the west between Ocean City's barrier island and the Eastern Shore. The sun was setting and it reflected off the small waves where the last of the day's boaters were heading for home. It was so peaceful, she thought. She could stay here forever.

Ocean City was coming to life to prepare for the summer season and the tee-shirt shops and all-you-can-eat buffet joints were open, but there were few customers. By late May high schoolers would be throwing up beer and then the college kids would arrive and the serious partying would begin. By mid-summer families would take over the resort and Ocean City would have another rhythm, one not dominated by drinking and excess, but by kids and their parents. But all that was weeks away as Elena pondered her return to work at Now News and a face-to-face meeting with Dave.

She tried to analyze her feelings, something that had never really worked for her. She loved him. She admitted that. But she was scared. Could Dave ever settle down enough to keep himself out of trouble and give her a feeling that she was safe with him? Or was he a cowboy who would run wild until he was destroyed, taking her down with him?

Three hours to the west, in his office overlooking the Potomac, Dave was on the phone with Ossening, trying to pry some information out of the F.B.I. agent. It was not going well. Ossening prided himself on his ability to say nothing of importance to people like Dave.

"I talked to O'Neil. He said I should go to Tennessee. Is that what you told him?"

"Did he say I told him that?"

"He said you two talked and then he advised me to head south."

"That doesn't mean I told him to tell you to head south."

And so it went, round and round. "Okay, let's say Justice is actually going after Prewitt. There has to be a strong D.C. angle to this. Can you confirm that?"

"You know I can't discuss an ongoing investigation or even speculate about whether there is an investigation."

"We've already established that there is."

"That's your interpretation."

"I don't suppose the PIO at the Hoover Building will have anything to say about this."

"Why don't you give them a call. I wouldn't count on them having a ready press release but you never know." Ossening had the ability to sound like the friendly boy next door even as he was being uncooperative and nasty.

Dave stared out at the storefronts of Georgetown and pondered his options. He decided to go fishing. Not with a rod and reel, but with coffee. He called Peter Deutch at the AP and suggested that they meet at a coffee shop near Dupont Circle, not far from Dave's apartment. Deutch understood that such meetings are not entirely social and that Dave had something he wanted to talk over in private. It was a classic I'll-scratch-yours-if-you'll-scratch-mine arrangement. He assumed it had something to do with Judge Beechum's murder and the Prewitt investigation. He, too, had run into roadblocks and was eager to hear what Dave had, if anything.

The coffee shop was in a triangular-shaped building that came to a point at the circle near Connecticut Avenue and 19th Street and offered a panorama of the pedestrians who offered what in Washington passed for stylishness. The city was not known for its fashion but the Dupont Circle neighborhood had a reputation for alternative lifestyles, at least as defined in a city known for boxy suits and ambition. The coffee shop's ceiling speakers spewed out fashionable music produced in far more creative locations. The baristas were working for minimum wage and hoping for internships on Capitol Hill or even the White House in the way starving actors in Los Angeles wait for parts in movies. When asked what they do for a living they were likely to say they were involved "in public policy", not espresso.

A young woman who appeared to be Indian took Dave's order and recognized him from the priest killing story, when his image was all over the mass media. "If I give you my resume do you think you can pass it on?" she asked. "I'm looking for a job in media. I have a master's from Georgetown." Dave was used to the question but it still amazed him that media jobs had become so fashionable. "Sure," he said, folding her resume and sticking it in his pocket.

Deutch arrived a few minutes later, looking very Ivy League in a light blazer and tight pants. Deutch was the kind of person who could find a way to tell you he was a Yale graduate while you were shaking hands with him for the first time. "Hi Dave." He was all wide smiles and friendliness, which Dave knew meant he was on the hunt for information. "How's life at your shop?"

"Boring. How about you?"

"I'm working on this Beechum follow-up and Prewitt. I'm not getting very far. I was hoping you had something and we can sort of share." Dave was trying his best to match Deutch's friendliness.

Deutch smiled and leaned forward, opening his mouth to speak. He moved toward Dave as if to whisper in his ear, causing Dave to pull back. Deutch's forehead exploded as the window next to their table shattered. He fell back against his chair and toppled onto the floor, spewing gore onto a young man who was surfing the Internet on his laptop at a nearby table. There was a moment of quiet and shock, followed by hysterical screaming from the young barista, who was carrying a tray of lattes. Dave was covered with small bits of glass that had flown onto the table when the round came through. He moved to Deutch, whose eyes were open but focused in different directions. There was no doubt that he was dead. The noise level in the place rose to a full-throated scream as patrons and wait staff ran out onto Connecticut Avenue. The young man who was covered in Deutch's gore ran into the traffic, waving his arms and yelling, drawing the attention of a D.C. police patrol car that was parked a half-block away. The two officers in the car were chatting with a young woman whose bright blue hair and thigh-high boots had drawn their attention until the gory man ran into the street.

An hour later the Dupont Circle neighborhood was locked down. Connecticut Avenue, Massachusetts Avenue, and the streets feeding into the circle were blocked by yellow police tape and drivers trapped by the police action were honking their horns. A drum line in the park was evicted to hoots and shouts and television news crews were raising their booms to do live shots for the late afternoon news shows. The police chief had been at a meeting at the Wilson Building, the District's city hall at 14th and Pennsylvania, and had come up to the scene of the shooting to take a look, creating an even greater circus atmosphere.

Lieutenant (Acting Captain) Alden Jefferson was heading the homicide division now that Captain O'Neil had been transferred. Jefferson and two of his detectives were examining the crime scene and watching forensics people photographing, dusting, and looking for anything that would tell them about the shooting. Deutch's body was still on the floor and would not be moved until the scene had been processed. Jefferson and Dave Haggard knew each other but they would not be considered friends. Jefferson had driven Dave to the farm in the rush to protect him from Father Darius while the priest was on his killing spree and the two men had spent a few hours together in the Virginia countryside.

Jefferson was large, something over three-hundred pounds, black, and had a permanent expression of anger and disbelief on his round face. He wore suits that appeared to be two sizes too small. Nevertheless, he buttoned the jackets over his massive chest and stomach, stretching the fabric and causing those in his presence to wonder if he was going to pop the buttons or strain to breathe. "Let's go over this again, Dave. Why were you in this place with the victim?" Jefferson and Dave were seated at a table on the far wall from the shattered window.

"We're working on the same story. We got together to talk it over." Dave went over the story one more time.

Jefferson stared at his notes as Dave talked, looking for inconsistencies. Dave read from his own notes, which he wrote in his attempt to calm down after the police arrived.

Jefferson's expression was disbelief. "Here's how I see it. Either this guy Deutch was very unlucky and just happened to catch a bullet randomly fired by somebody or he was targeted by a very good shot who followed him here and picked him off just as he leaned over to talk to you or, and this is my personal favorite, somebody was trying to shoot you and got him instead. Where do you put your money?"

Dave looked over at Deutch, who was still on the floor waiting to be taken to the medical examiner's office. "Do you think it was an assassination?"

"Assassinations happen to presidents and people like that. Everyone else is just murdered. Why don't you come with me and we can talk about who might be pissed off at you."

Here we go, Dave thought. Another ride downtown to have a chat with the chief of homicide. He called Sid to tell him what had happened and Sid, of course, demanded that he file a report for the stations, leaving no detail unreported. Dave sat in silence in Jefferson's unmarked car and used his new tablet to write a two minute account of the murder of Peter Deutch. He did not report what the two men had been discussing when the round came through the window and into Deutch's head.

Chapter Six

Edward Segal rode a Metro bus to Union Station and walked three blocks to the line that had formed for the discount bus ride to Newark. He paid his fifteen dollars and found a seat in the rear on the aisle. Most of the other passengers were Hispanics who did not make eye contact with anyone. The men appeared to be frightened and Segal assumed they were wary of immigration agents. The women appeared to be trying to hide inside their clothes. It was not a group that would take much interest in others, although they would all note that a Gringo was aboard.

The bus was old and was one of the cheap-fare lines that had grown in number to service the travel needs of people of questionable immigration status and little money. The passengers were the faceless ones who cleaned houses and cut grass for the more fortunate. They were not seen by the well-dressed and self-important who occupied the best addresses near the U.S. Capitol and paid no attention to those who were viewed as lesser beings. Segal was satisfied that he would not turn up on a surveillance recording, despite the cameras that were becoming common in the capital city. His slight limp was the only remarkable quality he displayed as he mixed with others on the street as he made his way to the bus. He wore cheap clothing and a dirty baseball cap.

The bus pulled away from the curb and headed up North Capitol Street to New York Avenue and points north. Segal closed his eyes and went over the details of the shooting. He was disappointed that he had killed the wrong man but he did not allow himself the luxury of deep regret. He never allowed himself more than one shot and this one had gone into the wrong head, but he would have other chances, if it came to that. One shot was hard to identify in the confusion that followed a job and that confusion offered an opportunity for escape. Two shots would cut the odds of escape in half, in his estimation. And, he reasoned, if he could not get a kill with one shot, why would he be in the business?

Another M14 was at the bottom of the Potomac. He idly wondered what else was down there after two hundred years of intrigue, murder and treachery in Washington. This time he had used a canoe from the boathouse in Georgetown and had posed as a tourist from Arkansas, beaming at the opportunity to visit Washington. The rifle had been hidden in a cloth bag and Segal had told the woman in the boathouse that it contained a tripod which he would use to take pictures of the Kennedy Center from the middle of the river. The woman paid no attention to what the hillbilly tourist was saying and paid no notice when he returned without his tripod. She had long ago lost interest in the customers who came to paddle around on the water. Segal knew the type and was happy to factor them into his planning. Most people, he believed, paid no attention to what was going on around them.

He looked forward to a few days in Jamaica. He hoped his plans would not be interrupted by another phone call. But, he reasoned, the target was still upright and that presented certain problems. Also, he would not be paid until Dave Haggard was dead. But Edward Segal was not a man to indulge in emotions or anxiety when it involved the work he did. Dave Haggard's moment would come. Segal slipped into a light sleep and awoke near a transit stop in Newark. He took a bus to the airport and was in Ocho Rios before midnight.

Captain O'Neil's day had been spent pouring over nearly unreadable documents produced by the federal government's policies regarding inter-agency cooperation. Despite all of the talk following 9/11 about the need for transparency and the sharing of information, the truth remained that government agencies had no desire to cooperate with any other government agency. Information was hoarded like so many gold coins kept in locked drawer and the policy of sharing was masked beneath the strange language that bureaucrats use to speak without saying anything. This was especially true in Homeland Security matters around Washington. At least that is how O'Neil viewed it.

The District of Columbia and its suburbs are home to dozens of federal, state and local law enforcement, security, defense, and murkier organizations that spend as much time monitoring each other as they do gathering whatever information they manage to scoop up. For many of these agencies the mission is not the gathering of threat information as much as the gathering of budget information about the other agencies. Who has planes? Who has the best computer system? In the military this is known as "inter-service rivalry". On the civilian side it's commonly defined as "screw those guys."

It is understood to be the reality but rarely addressed openly and usually in the aftermath of a disaster that might have been mitigated by agency cooperation. Such was the case after 9/11 when it was revealed that the F.B.I. and the C.I.A. rarely exchanged more than a polite nod at official meetings and never any important information, even threats to national security.

But appearances must be accommodated and the various agencies and units charged with protecting the nation's capital were required to dump information into a pool so it could be sifted for this and that and one of the readers of this material was one Daniel O'Neil, who was parked at his desk as a form of exile.

He poured over pages of nonsense about mission definitions, threat motivations, tribal characteristics, port vulnerabilities and so on until he felt that he was developing severe narcolepsy, so strong was his urge to close his eyes and sleep. The language of saying nothing had been developed to the point where it was impossible to follow and remain focused. Federal agencies had it down to a fine science. The D.C. police department struggled with it and often sent in reports that contained real information. One such report was on his desk. It was a twenty-four hour summary of gunshot and explosion sensors in the city.

Officially called Gunshot Location and Detection Systems, the monitors were attached to cameras around D.C. and were programmed to detect gunshots and explosions and capture images in the area to aid police in identifying suspects. There were thousands of cameras in the city but not all of them were equipped with the gunshot location capabilities. The ones that could were in critical downtown areas or in high-crime areas where gangs and drug thugs settled their differences with drive-by shootings.

O'Neil was familiar with the system because he had helped develop it while he was heading Homicide and he knew how to read the reports and what to look for. He could call up the gunshot locations and scan the images taken by the cameras mounted on poles and buildings around the city. He had mixed feelings about such capabilities. The cop in him appreciated the efficiency it offered law enforcement. The citizen in him feared the potential harm to civil privacy and its potential for abuse.

He looked at the reports and the images as a way of relieving the boredom and senselessness of the agency reports. In fact, he quite enjoyed it and spent hours watching video of people on the street, going about their business. Now and then he would spot someone he knew, either a colleague or a criminal, and on occasion he had seen someone who was wanted for murder and he would telephone his friends at Homicide with the tip. He had a well-developed capacity to remember faces. It was a game he played at night when he was in the space between awake and asleep. He would try to recall every new face he had seen that day and put a name to it. If the faces were strangers on the street he would try to recall them in order. He could keep certain faces in his mind for months.

There were two shootings that day in Washington. One was at Barry Farm in Southeast D.C., an area of public housing projects and little hope. Violence there was common. A teenage suspect was in custody. The other was at Dupont Circle and was the murder of Peter Deutch by an unknown shooter. O'Neil had wanted to telephone Dave Haggard to talk to him about it but put it off in deference to Arlen Jefferson, who now ran Homicide. O'Neil believed that the shooter might be the same actor who killed Judge Beechum, given the single-shot-to-the-head scenario and the disappearance of the shooter. Both murders appeared to be the work of a professional.

He scanned the images around Dupont Circle in the moments following the shooting. He was looking for someone who seemed out of place, someone running or scanning the area in front of or behind him. It was a typical incident in that most people were unaware that anything had happened until police began to arrive, so the men and women near the circle stood in the sunshine or moved at a normal pace to wherever they were going.

People in the circle sat on the benches or near the fountain and enjoyed the sunshine. A young man and woman played Frisbee on the grass. A half-dozen men banged drums. A jogger ran through traffic in the circle and gave the finger to a driver who honked at him. Everything was normal.

O'Neil brought up the camera images that were captured following the shooting of Judge Beechum and saw the scene unfold as the U.S. Marshalls and the professionals at the federal courthouse secured the crime scene. He watched the pedestrians who see if anyone acted strangely. He knew that the F.B.I. had viewed the images many times, looking for the same thing, and had not found anything of value to the investigation.

He selected both video files and clicked "look for match," engaging a program that would try to find the same image in both files. The wheel on his screen slowed and nearly stopped and O'Neil was certain that the program had frozen and he was about to reboot when the screen displayed "match." A man wearing a baseball hat had taken a moment to look up at the security cameras in both locations. At Dupont Circle he was on 19th Street. Near the courthouse he was on C Street. At each location he looked up for only one second, but it was enough to capture his image. O'Neil brought the images together. The hats and clothing were different but there no doubt it was the same man. He walked calmly and carried what appeared to be a long clothing bag. He walked with a slight limp.

O'Neil captured the images and opened another program that would search hundreds of files for a match. Less than a minute later the screen displayed the photo of a soldier and a name. Staff Sergeant Edward Segal. Silver Star. Purple Heart. Instructor at Sniper School. Two tours in Iraq. Honorable Discharge. Hometown: Sevier County, Tennessee.

He sat back and smiled. I've still got it, he said to himself. And I've got you, you son of a bitch. He created a new file with the information he had found and saved it. He savored the moment before he picked up the phone and called F.B.I. Special Agent Bud Ossening.

"I've got your judge killer. He's the same guy who picked off the reporter today. I'm sending the file. You owe me." He hung up, put on his coat, and went to a bar.

Chapter Seven

Dave Haggard was trying to sleep but his mind kept presenting him with the image of Peter Deutch's brain on the floor of the coffee shop. He understood that the bullet was meant for him and only the random act of one man leaning forward and another man leaning back had meant death for one and life for the other. Lieutenant (Acting Captain) Jefferson had made him go over his story a dozen times, each telling drawing Jefferson's scowl.

Dave had called Sid, had filed two reports on the shooting and had done a Q and A with an editor at Now News about it. Question and Answer sessions were a cheap and easy way for broadcasters to use reporters. They required little if any writing or preparation and the answers could be edited or cut up for later use, thus offering more reporting time for the broadcaster. In this way a single reporter like Dave could effectively file a half-dozen voice reports if the Q and A material was added to the two formal, written and recorded reports he had prepared. Because of this, Dave's voice was in virtually all of Now News's outlets every hour. It was also on everyone else's newscasts, radio and television, and the cable outlets were bloviating about "why this one reporter in a city of thousands of journalists repeatedly turns up in the middle of these kinds of things." These kinds of things being murders. Fat, overpaid and underworked pontificators were filling air time speculating about a reporter who actually went out on to the streets to get news. At least that is how Dave saw it.

His cell phone rang with its dobro ringtone, a reminder of his East Tennessee heritage. He listened for a few bars and picked it up. O'Neil's name was on the screen.

"Yes, my captain, what can I do for you?" Dave was feeling friendly.

"Are you home?"

"Yes, given that it's the middle of the night. Aren't you supposed to be wrapped in the warmth of your suburban home with the wife and kids?"

"I'm working late. Actually, I'm a little drunk. I'm out front. If you'll call the desk I won't have to show my badge to get in and we can avoid loose talk."

"I think the desk guy already knows who you are from previous visits, Captain. I'll call down." Dave picked up the house phone and told the Cameroonian who was working the overnight shift that he had a visitor. "I see the captain now, Sir," said the young man. "He is on his way to your apartment."

O'Neil looked like hell. His tie was loose and set off to one side of his collar, which had turned under. His suit jacket appeared to have been balled up and dumped on a dirty floor, then put back on. His hair was mussed and he had an off-center smile on his face. "Well, Sir Scribe, how the hell are you?" He walked in and flopped down on Dave's couch.

"Better than you. How about some coffee." Dave went into his small kitchen and made two cups of espresso, handing one to O'Neil, who appeared to be in a daze.

"I have news, my friend." O'Neil drank the strong coffee in one gulp. "You have any more?"

"What's the news?"

"Coffee, then news." O'Neil had the silly grin of the truly drunk. He looked happy and pathetic at the same time.

Dave produced a second cup and handed it to O'Neil, who stared into it, then drank it. "Damn! What's in this?"

"Coffee. Now what's up?"

"Can you keep a secret?"

"I'm not in the business of keeping secrets, Captain. But if you tell me something is off the record, then I will keep it between us?"

"That's not what happened last time."

"Is that where we're going? We can spend the rest of the night talking about the last time." Dave stretched and yawned. "I need some sleep. You can crash there." He walked toward his small bedroom.

"Okay, okay. Let's say we're starting from scratch. You don't screw me and I won't screw you. How about that?"

"I'm listening."

"The guy who shot the judge is the guy who shot your friend today." O'Neil stared at Dave with a sad, drunken face.

"How do you know?" Dave pulled a chair away from the dining table that doubled as his desk and sat on it.

"I have my ways."

"Meaning?"

"Technology, my friend. All those goddam cameras around here must be good for something."

"You matched photos? You have photos of the shooter?"

"It took a little work, but I'm pretty sure it's the same guy, so yeah."

"Do you have a name on this guy?"

"I can't give you that, not right now."

"Do you know where he is?"

"Our friends at the F.B.I. are working on it."

Dave's phone was on the table, plugged into its charger. Its screen was dark and it appeared to be off. Software that cost less than one-hundred dollars had been installed on it without Dave's knowledge. It allowed certain parties to listen to everything that was said either during phone calls or while the speaker was within ten feet of the phone. One such party was located in what appeared to be a small grain silo on a farm in Rappahannock County, Virginia. It was an unofficial monitoring site that Dave had once seen and even reported on before he had been muzzled by the feds.

Dave's number was flagged and a voice recognition program identified Captain O'Neil, alerting a man on duty that a "red zone" monitor was active. Thirty minutes later a call was placed to a number in Tampa.

"You've been made." The line went dead.

Chapter Eight

Ocho Rios is a tourist zone on the north coast of Jamaica; its sole purpose being the separation of foreigners from their hard currency. Nearly all of those foreigners are white. All of those who serve them are black and overwhelmingly poor by American and European standards. The tone and amenities in the resorts are as foreign to the native Jamaicans as a whale is different from a chipmunk. There is a natural tension between those who visit and those who serve the visitors and that tension is what appealed to Edward Segal, registered under an assumed name in an aging resort that attracted aging Europeans, mostly Brits with some Germans thrown in. He was there with a very good false passport identifying him as a businessman from Belleville, Illinois.

Segal sat under a palm tree, enjoying the shade while he watched overweight couples wade in the clear blue water, their flabby white skin looking like fat bubbles in a bathtub. A scruffy wooden skiff trolled just off the beach piloted by a skinny, very black older man wearing dreadlocks under a knit hat. The aging motor on the skiff chugged and issued puffs of smoke in time with its pistons.

"Ganja! Ganja! Very good, mon. Ganja!"

A German woman who appeared to be in her late fifties giggled and whispered to her husband, who shook his head. A young equally black waiter in black pants and a white coat stopped on his way to deliver a tray of high-alcohol fruit punch to some Brits on beach chairs. "No, mon. No. You cannot sell here. Go away!"

The man in the boat waved and laughed. "Ganja! Very good. Ganja mon."

Edward Segal grabbed two twenties from his wallet and waded into the soft Caribbean water. His government-issue prosthetic lower leg was metal with a running shoe at the foot. Segal's natural foot was bare. He walked with a near-normal gait on land and had no difficulty in the water. The physical therapist who had worked with Segal at Walter Reed would have scolded him for walking the prosthesis into the salt water. Segal didn't care. The ganja man waited until Segal was chest deep before he brought the skiff closer to the beach.

"One hundred. Look. Very nice. One hundred."

"I'll take forty dollars worth. I won't spend one hundred."

"I don't break the bags, mon. One hundred or I go away." The Ganja man was waiting to see how eager Segal was to obtain some of the strong Jamaican marijuana, which was for sale all over the island at widely different prices and quality.

"Okay, no deal." Segal turned to wade back to his spot on the beach.

"I got a half bag. Fifty for a half bag." The ganja man smiled and leaned back against the motor of the skiff, which was idling and coughing smoke.

"Forty." Segal offered the twenties and the ganja man sat up and snatched the money, handing over a plastic bag that contained brown buds. "No seeds. Very good."

"If I like it I'll buy more," Segal said.

"All white people say the same thing, mon. Nobody buys more." The ganja man turned the throttle handle on the motor and the skiff moved away down the beach to the next resort where college kids were lined up at the water line waiting for him.

Segal moved back to his chair and ignored the stairs of disapproving Europeans who believed that what they had just seen confirmed their worst suspicions that Americans are depraved and reckless. He propped his metal foot up on the chair and watched as the cool Caribbean water dripped from the running shoe. Marijuana was his comfort, the escape to peace. He had been through the pharmacy of pain killers. Oxy, Percocet. He had even tried heroin. The trip back was too arduous, too painful, so he settled for a pleasant buzz now and then. He sat back and turned to his punch, wondering whether he had the energy to go to his room and roll a joint. He decided to close his eyes for a moment. A shadow appeared over him and he opened his eyes to see the smiling black waiter.

"I have a new drink for you, suh. I can get you some rolling papers if you want me to. Good price." The young man's teeth were very white as he smiled the smile that the servers offer the served. "And you have a message at the front desk."

"I don't need the papers." He handed the young man a dollar. "Thank you for the drink." He looked at his bag of marijuana and knew that the fleeting feeling of peace he was looking forward to was not going to happen. A message at the desk was a bad sign, like a telegram in the night. He briefly wondered if people got telegrams anymore or whether bad news just came in an email. He decided to finish his old drink and the new one before he checked the desk.

It was an hour before he walked into the open-walled lobby and approached the smiling young woman who stood proudly behind the guest relations counter in her pert blazer and straightened hair. He gave the woman his name and waited as she flipped through a small box that contained messages for guests. There were not many, this being a place where guests were either too old to be important enough for emergency messages or too important to bother while on holiday.

"Ah, yes, here we are." She handed him a sealed envelope with the logo of the resort stamped on the upper left corner. "Is there anything else I can do for you?" Her smile was vacant of an invitation.

He muttered "No" and walked up a flight of open stairs to his room, where he closed the door, walked past the bed, and sat at a small table on the balcony overlooking the beach. Shit! he thought, as he stared at the envelope. He opened it and saw a short message. "Plan B."

The message contained as many questions as answers but its import was clear. Return to Tampa for more information and don't go home to Tennessee. He knew what it meant. He had been identified. His face had been tied to a job, probably in Washington, but he wouldn't know for sure until he returned to Tampa and met with his contact. It could have been other jobs, of course, but Washington was the latest and the hit on the reporter had been botched. Maybe that was it. Maybe they were pissed off about that and wanted to talk. He considered taking another day to get stoned and stay that way but he knew he was expected to act immediately and, in any case, another day here would just offer more time in which to stew about possibilities. He called the front desk to ask for a taxi and was headed to the airport at Montego Bay fifteen minutes later. He had left the ganja in a hotel envelope marked "maid" as a gift, assuming she would turn it into cash by selling it to another tourist.

As the sunset brought the tourists to their beachside tables for grilled fish and steel band music the skiff touched the shore two miles east Dunns River Falls and the man with the dreadlocks stepped out of the boat and onto the warm sand. Waiting was a light skinned man wearing an elegant tan suit and expensive sunglasses. The man's shoes cost more than the ganja man made in half a year.

"Did you see him?"

"Yes, mon. He was there. I saw the leg. He bought a half bag for forty dollars."

"Was anyone with him? Did anyone talk to him?"

"No, mon. He was alone. My son is a waiter there. He told me the fellow had a message at the desk and left in a taxi for Montego Bay."

The man in the suit took a moment to absorb this information. "Very good." He handed the ganja man a hundred dollar bill. The ganja man returned to his boat and motored to his home, where he sat in the dark enjoying a large spliff and pondering the strange ways of white people.

Segal had managed to bribe his way onto a chartered flight to Miami and spent the sunset in the company of white haired Midwesterners who were showing each other photographs of their week in Jamaica. A chubby woman next to Segal spent the entire flight telling him that she was never comfortable around black people. He smiled at her and said he had contracted a "bug" in Jamaica and was too sick to engage in a conversation. "Probably the water," she said, leaning away from him.

In Miami he caught a commuter flight to Tampa and was removing the cover from his truck by midnight. There was a note on the windshield.

Chapter Nine

Judge Beechum's funeral was scheduled for ten o'clock on a gloomy, misty morning. As with all such events, this one was a media circus of television trucks and their "live shot" masts, cameras lined up on the sidewalk like so many seals on a beach, reporters jostling and shoving each other, motorcycle cops chuckling at off-color jokes, and the grieving family in black. The church was built during the administration of Franklin Pierce and it was small by current standards, holding less than three-hundred people. It had a Calvanist sturdiness to it, despite its Episcopal affiliation. Many presidents had worshipped there, some with more earnestness than others.

Judge Beechum and his family were long-standing members of the congregation primarily because he enjoyed the predictability of the worship service and the never-changing atmosphere of the spiritual experience offered by the building and its thin, gray and very sincere pastor, one Ellington Davies, who could recite the works of Homer in Greek and had memorized all of Shakespeare's plays. Reverend Davies had never been known to offend anyone in all his years at the pulpit, now well into his third decade.

A pool had been chosen from among the eager journalists gathered to observe the sendoff for the murdered jurist and Dave Haggard was one of two radio reporters selected. The other was Neal Augenstein, a veteran street reporter for WTOP, an all-news station that sat atop the radio ratings in the news-crazy city. Dave didn't know anyone who did not listen to WTOP at least once a day. The news community being a sort of cult, he didn't know anyone who didn't know Augenstein.

Dave carried his bag of recorders, cords, microphones, mike stands, clips and other gadgets into the church to find the mult-box that provided audio from the pulpit, where a single microphone had been installed to capture the words of Reverend Davies and those who would offer words of condolence, one of whom was the Attorney General himself. Another was the Chief Justice of the United States. It would be a banner day for speeches about the value of a free judiciary.

The television pool reporters were up in the balcony next to a camera that was one of four in the church, the others having been placed where the weeping mourners could be broadcast to whatever audience the funeral produced, which, as it turned out, was small. Several print and online reporters were standing against the walls.

Augenstein, a dark haired newsman who had the appearance of someone who had seen it all, carried only his smartphone, which he plugged into the mult box using a cable and adapter. Dave set about using his standard-issue cables and recorder.

"Where's your stuff?" Dave asked, pointing to Augenstein's phone.

"What stuff?" Augenstein had a small smile on his face.

"Aren't you going to get some audio from this?"

"Right there." He pointed to the phone.

"The phone?"

"Yeah."

There was a stir as the pastor walked to the center of the altar.

"Let's talk later," Dave said, as the congregation rose for the opening hymn.

The service was as dry and emotionless as Reverend Davies and the Attorney General could produce, with funereal platitudes and clichés filling the air about "a better place" and "closer to the Almighty" and "his work here is done." It was as if Judge Beechum had died peacefully in his sleep at an advanced age instead of at the hands of a skilled assassin who had cut him down on his way to lunch. There was not a wet eye in the house, excepting the judge's widow, who seemed drugged and truly in another place.

As the final hymn was sung by an unenthusiastic congregation, the judge's casket was rolled down the aisle to the unemotional stares of the mourners who were by now wondering why they thought admission to the funeral was evidence of their importance in the legal and political community.

The Attorney General stood in respect as the judge's remains rolled by and then he headed for a side door followed by some aids who looked as though they could use some air. Dave unplugged his recorder and ran after the AG, waving his press pass at the protesting mourners, who were heading for the front door. The side door led to a small garden whose stone pathway offered a direct route to Sixteenth Street and, for the AG, freedom. Dave caught up to him on the sidewalk and angled past two security agents whose attention was focused on the approaching black SUV that would take the AG back to the Justice Department on Constitution Avenue.

"Sir! Sir! May I have a moment?" Dave had his recorder going and was holding his microphone in front of the AG's face. Augenstein had caught up with Dave and had his phone up.

"Have you found the killer?" Dave asked, expecting the AG to confirm that the killer had been identified.

"The F.B.I. and other federal and local law enforcement agencies are conducting a thorough investigation and we are confident we will identify and bring to justice the person responsible for this heinous crime." The Attorney General turned to leave.

"Isn't it true that the killer has been identified and has been linked to both the murder of Judge Beechum and the shooting of Peter Deutch?"

The AG stopped and stared at Dave. "Where did you hear that?"

"I can't reveal my source but I'm told it is a solid identification."

"And where did this so-called solid identification originate? I have not been informed about anything like that. To my knowledge the killer has not been identified and no link has been established between the two murders you mentioned." The AG's face was red. Dave saw it as a sign that the AG believed him and would pound his desk at Justice once he returned to his office.

Dave played a hand he didn't have. "I have proof that the gunman has been identified and has been linked to both killings. I have been told that a search is underway for the man whose arrest is imminent."

The AG turned to his aids. "Get me out of here!"

Augenstein watched the AG get into his SUV and speed away, with motorcycle cops flashing lights and sirens and traffic officers blocking traffic. "I can't hold this," he said. "Everybody in the city will be listening to hear what you have."

Dave sat on a bench in the garden and regretted cornering the AG in front of Augenstein. He needed some confirmation of what Captain O'Neil had told him, but he should have been more discreet. He had not planned to go with the story but now he was in danger of allowing it to run away from him. He listened to the recording of the AG and thought about how to package what he had without looking foolish or blowing O'Neil's cover. He took a notebook out of his bag and wrote a piece, a "wrap" in radio news jargon, with him doing a voice segment, playing a short piece of audio with the AG saying he didn't know anything about the shooter, and ending with another voice segment wrapping up the report. It took him about fifteen minutes to write it and he would go back to Now News to edit the recording, record the piece, and put it into the system.

Augenstein sat nearby with his smartphone. As Dave was standing to head back to Now News, Augenstein was hitting send on his phone. His piece was filed and ready to air. "I've filed."

"How's that work?" Dave asked.

"I can do it all on the phone. Interview, edit, voice my track, send it to the newsroom."

"On the phone?"

"I dump it online and the station pulls it down."

Dave had put off jumping into the world of smartphone journalism but it was clear the time was at hand. "What kind of software do you have?"

"There's lots of audio editing apps out there. I use Vericorder AudioPro. It's three track and lets me do almost everything I could do in the newsroom on Adobe Audition. Check it out." Augenstein held up his phone to display a WAV file. "You can adjust natural sound by just moving this fader up or down."

Dave was used to something bigger, a screen and a keyboard that fit his fingers. "How does it sound?"

"With the built-in mike I estimate it's 92-percent as good as if I were using a Shure SM63 with a digital recorder. I can send an entire news conference back to the desk."

Dave was only vaguely aware of what the technical terms meant and he had no idea what a Shure SM63 was, but he assumed it was a microphone. It occurred to him that he was well behind the curve on the issue and he felt foolish that he was still lugging a heavy bag of gear around when Augenstein was kicking his ass with only a phone.

His opinion was confirmed when he walked into Now News and Sid was yelling at him that WTOP had scooped him on his own story. "Have you heard Augenstein's piece about the Attorney General? Isn't that you asking the question? Did it occur to you to share that information with the rest of us? Into my office now!"

Sid pulled out the bottom drawer of his desk to use as a footstool as he fumed at Dave, who felt like a third grader being kept after school for misbehavior. "You know your problem?" Sid asked, using his softest, angriest voice. "You're stuck in the 1990s. You still think the Internet is an oddity that Al Gore talks about. Well, guess what. It's how the world works. I've been hammering you to learn how to file on your smartphone for months. You don't have the luxury of dragging your little kit bag back to the office and thinking the big thought anymore. The world is running off without you. Now file your goddam piece and spend the rest of the day learning how to be up to date." Sid waved his hand toward the door, dismissing Dave to the curious stares of the news folks who were looking up from their computer screens.

The door from the lobby opened and the attention in the room shifted. The staff stood and applauded and hardened news types dabbed their eyes. Dave turned and looked into the face of the most beautiful women he had ever known. Elena was back.

Chapter Ten

Captain O'Neil was back at the Justice Department building, the scene of many ass chewings in his past. He had come to see such sessions as badges of honor and daydreamed that each one would earn him a colored ribbon to wear on his uniform, on those rare occasions when he wore it. He could imagine himself with a train of ribbons nearly to his belt. His youthful vow to be a man who did something rather than nothing had resulted in years of scoldings and reprimands, even as his reputation as a man who got things done grew. He had spent more than a few periods in timeout assignments, like the one he had now, but he was always brought back to bring life and effectiveness to an office that was not performing. That is how he ended up heading Homicide. That is also how he ended up spending his days looking at useless paper.

The Attorney General had personally called him in for this session and he was prepared. He had the time in to file his retirement papers and if it came to that he was ready, although he would rather have a street assignment. Anti-terror. That's where the action was these days. That's where the money was flowing, whether it was well spent was another issue, one that O'Neil didn't worry about. The AG's office fronted Pennsylvania Avenue and, given its place on the Washington pecking order, bespoke the prestige the job required. Other, lesser beings at Justice slaved in government-issue chairs over government-issue desks, but the AG was a potentate and his office reeked of privilege.

Jubal Gray had the look. He was tall, thin, and graying in an expensive way, wrapped in a fine and well-cut blue, pin-stripe suit, custom shirt, three-hundred dollar tie, and a haircut whose cost would feed a family for a month. He had no known legal accomplishments outside his years of being a toadie for various powerful men and women who seemed to think he had something wise to say now and then. Jubal Gray had learned as a young man that most people think you're smart when you complement them, so that became his currency, which he spent freely. And now, here he was, standing regally as Captain O'Neil approached, wearing his cop face over a cheap suit.

"Captain, thank you for coming." O'Neil tried to hide a smile. It seemed silly to thank someone for doing something they could not refuse.

"Glad to be here," O'Neil said, offering his hand, which the AG ignored. There were several others in the office, including Ossening, who was standing against the wall.

"Well, let's begin, shall we?" Gray sat behind his large, historic desk and unbuttoned his suit jacket. "I hear you have something to tell me."

"I'm not sure what you mean."

"Please, let's not beat around the bush. I'm told you have identified the assassin who shot Judge Beechum."

"I believe so, yes. I have passed that information on to the F.B.I." O'Neil nodded in Ossening's direction.

"Hmmm. Yes. So I hear. I'd like to hear it from you. How did you arrive at this conclusion?"

O'Neil explained how he had matched the photos from the street cameras using the gunshot monitors. He offered a condensed version and wondered why the AG didn't just ask the F.B.I. for information.

"And so you think you know that this fellow Edward Segal is the doer, as the cops say. This man who is a decorated veteran and who has no known criminal record. You think he's the one?" Gray raised his eyebrows.

"Yes, sir, I do."

"Very interesting. You are aware that there is no forensic evidence to tie him or, at this point, anyone else to the shooting of either Judge Beechum or this reporter fellow."

"I wouldn't say that. It's the same type of bullet and the same method of execution. Long range shot fired by an expert marksman into the head of the target. Segal is an expert marksman."

"So are thousands of other military-trained snipers and I don't see you putting them on your list."

"I don't have their pictures near the crime scenes."

"Thousands of people were in the streets at each incident. Have you determined how many of them are good with a rifle?"

"No, sir."

Gray paused and made a pyramid with his fingertips. "Here's what we're going to do. Nothing. Nothing right now. If we get more evidence tying this man Segal to the crimes we'll move forward. Until then, we're not going to go chasing after a war hero on some specious assumption based upon faces in a crowd. Am I clear?"

O'Neil's bullshit antennae were picking up strong signals. He was being waved off Segal and told there was nothing to pursue. His years as a cop told him the real story was not Segal but the reason behind the AG's order. He looked at Ossening, who had no expression. The AG picked up the glance.

"The F.B.I. is on board with this order, Captain." Gray stood. "Thank you for coming. I hope you're enjoying your new assignment. I am told that it was a generous attempt to keep you around." Gray had a smirk on his face that O'Neil took to be the man's true nature.

"I'll see myself out."

O'Neil walked out onto Pennsylvania Avenue and climbed into his unmarked car, a rare benefit left to him from the department, and pulled away from his illegal spot at a hydrant. His "Official Police Business" notice was left on his dashboard. At that moment he would have welcomed a ticket if only to have the joy of tearing it up. He stopped at the light at 14th Street and made a call.

Dave Haggard's drobo riff ringtone cut through the noise of Elena's welcome and he saw that it was O'Neil. "Hello, my captain."

"Got time for coffee?"

"Any particular flavor?"

"Bullshit. That's the flavor. I can be there in ten minutes."

Dave had been sitting in a corner near a studio door watching Elena make the rounds of her colleagues, each one offering a hug and a welcome. She glanced in his direction a few times but never met his eyes. She appeared small and vulnerable and he wanted to hug her and love her. He missed her profane accusations that he was a shit and her "fuck yous" and the Latin temperament that had given him so much grief and joy. He was charmed by her off-balance smile that was the result of the knife wound from the insane Father Darius, the priest killer who had nearly killed them both. Sid had once described them as a cat and a dog. Elena was the cat, lithe, beautiful and clever; Dave was the dog, dense and slobbering. He felt like a dog at that moment, a mutt. His phone chirped. It was a text message from O'Neil. "I'm here. I have something."

Like a dutiful spaniel Dave got up and made his way to the door. Elena looked up and dabbed her eyes.

Chapter Eleven

The brass knuckles that Edward Segal carried were, in a sense, a family heirloom. They were issued to his father by the United States Army in 1953 in Berlin, where his father was a field agent for Army Intelligence during the height of the Cold War. The man had also carried a blackjack, lock picking tools, an ornate cane that was a cleverly disguised 20- gauge shotgun, and assorted other items including small cameras, handguns, and fighting knives. Segal was proficient in all of these things. He had learned to shoot as a boy and could have qualified as an Army expert marksman at the age of ten.

Segal liked the brass knuckles because of their past, but he was also partial to their special design. They were a lesson in functional simplicity. They were brass, for one thing, but had a special coating that made them black. They were unadorned with points, knobs, or anything that might add weight or volume. They had a professional, even industrial, appearance. They had smacked against many things, faces mostly, but showed no dents or any other signs of wear. They were easy to hide. Segal's father had instructed him on the proper way to hit someone with brass knuckles, how to sew a pocket for them in his pants, and how to slip them on his fighting hand and use them in the time it takes to smile.

He had also told his son that practicing in a mirror is no substitute for field work and suggested that practical experience in street arts was easy to find in the alleys of bad neighborhoods. That's why Edward spent time in the worst areas of every city he visited, exposing himself to street thugs, hustlers, and the scum that collects to take advantage of the weak. And that is how he found himself next to derelict railroad tracks behind an old warehouse off 5th Avenue in Tampa, hunched over and trying to look as weak and vulnerable as possible. He was wearing a short-sleeve, button up shirt, baggy khaki pants, and dirty baseball hat that sported a Cleveland Indians logo. He exaggerated his limp and tried to appear drunk as he walked along the old tracks, humming to himself. It was a cool night and he felt energized and eager to take out his frustration on someone whom he considered to be a shitbag.

Two drunks were propped against the warehouse, passing a bottle back and forth. One of them waved and asked if he had any change. He did not respond and kept walking. Two young men in hoodies were smoking cigarettes about a hundred feet down the tracks and Segal stumbled toward them, singing a song of nonsense and looking at the sky, which offered a thin view of some stars. He noticed that the men were glancing at him and gesturing with their cigarettes, taking faster puffs and making nervous moves with their shoulders. He knew they were going to make a move when he got closer and he got the same feeling a kid gets when he sees the circus coming down the street, a sense of joyful anticipation.

In his mind this was nothing more than a training exercise but it offered the added benefit of release of tension. He was high strung at the moment. He needed something to calm him down. And so he kept moving toward the men in a manner that suggested he did not notice them. When he was ten feet away one of the men moved to block his way.

"Hey, old man, you got some change?" The man's face was partially hidden by the hoodie and Segal couldn't get a good look at him. The man appeared to be Hispanic but he had no accent.

Segal didn't respond so the man put his arm on Segal's shoulder. "Old man, I asked you a question. You ain't disrespectin' me, are you? I don't like that."

The other man had moved behind Segal and was standing with his legs wide and his arms at his side.

The first man moved closer. "How much you got on you?"

"What do you want?" Segal asked, taking quick glances at both men.

"We gonna fuck you up then we gonna take what you got."

Segal straightened himself and pivoted on his good leg, bringing his right hand out of his pocket as he smiled at the man, whose face imploded with the force of the fist and the brass knuckles. Before the man hit the ground, Segal had turned to smash the second man in the nose, crushing it and sending forth a spray of blood that spattered onto Segal's shirt. The man was blinded by the blast to his nose and went down in a cascade of blood, snot and tears. It was over in seconds.

Segal was disappointed that it had not lasted longer and briefly considered finding another spot for another exercise before he decided that the blood on his shirt would attract too much attention, so he went back to his truck and drove to a room he had rented.

An envelope was under the door. "Washington" was the message. He showered, threw the bloody shirt into a plastic bag, packed, and left. He stopped near the Georgia line to drop the bag containing the shirt into a dumpster behind a strip mall. He got caught in the Washington rush hour traffic on I-95 at Dale City, Virginia and did not cross the 14th Street Bridge until almost noon. He sat in traffic and glanced at the lines waiting to visit the Holocaust Museum, idly watched tourists on the grounds of the Washington Monument, endured the backups up to K Street, where well-heeled, well-fed lobbyists sat in their offices plotting to skim money from the federal treasury, and made the turn onto Massachusetts Avenue at Thomas Circle, heading west through Dupont Circle and up to National Cathedral and Wisconsin Avenue, where he headed north. He was experienced at this sort of thing and knew the city better than many longtime residents. He found the building he was looking for and pulled into the parking lot of church, where he backed his pickup under a tree at the far corner and sat in silence, watching.

Inside the building, Captain O'Neil was at his desk, idly wondering whether it would be a good idea to get a little drunk in the middle of the day.

On Capitol Hill, Congressman John Prewitt, Jr. was sitting at a table in a private office in the Capitol building, enjoying a lunch of grilled wild salmon and salad. A glass of white wine was there to wash it down. Seated at the table with him was an older man in a five-thousand dollar suit and shoes that were hand made in London. Both men were smiling.

The man in the expensive suit put down his fork and turned to Prewitt. "Payback's a son of a bitch, ain't it." He forced a backwoods accent to cover his Harvard education.

"That's what I hear," Prewitt said, taking a sip of his wine.

Chapter Twelve

Elena retreated to a small studio to catch her breath. Her reception had overwhelmed her and she felt great affection for the staffers at Now News who had worked hard and long hours to help find her when she had been kidnapped by Father Darius. They had sent notes, flowers and even poems during her physical and emotional recuperation. She had to force herself to walk through the door and into the newsroom but she convinced herself that it was for the best and she had to get on with life. In her heart, however, she was afraid of seeing Dave again. To her, he was an addiction, unhealthy and out of control.

She had expected him to rush to her and embrace her, offering apologies for all that he had put her through and begging forgiveness. Instead, what she got was his standing back and staring at her like she was some kind of display item at a store. Goddam him! It was his default reaction to any personal encounter that bordered on intense and emotional. She sat and allowed herself a weepy moment, dreading returning to a work station in the newsroom and acting as though everything was fine. She had spent her recuperation away from the news, not reading newspapers and websites and not listening to radio or television news programs. She did not know about the assassination of Judge Beechum or the shooting of Peter Deutch.

She wiped her eyes and stood up. She took a deep breath and walked into the newsroom, waving to those who looked up, and sat down at a work station to log in.

As was the custom of everyone who worked at Now News, the first item of the day was scanning the wires to catch up on the day's news. The first story she saw was about Judge Beechum's funeral and Dave's statement to the Attorney General that he had been told a link had been made between the judge's death and the killing of Peter Deutch. The story explained that police believed the real target had been Dave Haggard. She read it several times. Then she fainted.

While Elena was being revived and comforted, Dave was sitting across from O'Neil at a coffee shop just off Pennsylvania Avenue, his smartphone recording their conversation. "Just background," he said. "I'll use it as background to make sure I get it right."

"I've heard that from you before," O'Neil said, offering his cop face.

"We either get past all that, both of us, or we don't. Let's talk about right now."

"The AG has told me in very firm tones to back away from this ID. The doer is radioactive to me. Ossening is on board with it. I smell something that stinks." O'Neil's Irish face got even redder and Dave wondered if some table pounding was coming. "I can understand if they want to protect somebody who doing some under-the-radar work but if a federal judge is shot, that's not in the game. You know what I mean?"

Dave pondered what he was being told. "You're sure you got the ID right?"

"I got him at the scene of both shootings and I got a hit on his face."

"How do you know the AG isn't right when he says all you have is the face of the guy in a crowd. Somebody else could be the shooter and his face is not in the picture."

"I'm a cop. I know how to put things together, how to connect the dots, as they say these days. You got two head shots that have pro written all over them. You got a pro at the scene. Hello? Anybody home?"

"Okay, let's make this about me for a minute. Am I hanging out there with my dick in my hand? I'm the one who went to the AG with this ID and it didn't take long to get back to you."

"It wasn't you. It was Ossening. All it took was one phone call to find out who was the source of this. I called Ossening when I made the ID."

"He apparently didn't do anything with it."

"I don't know what he did or didn't do. He won't do much now that we're all being waved off."

Dave stared out at the pedestrians on the sidewalk and wondered if their lives were as complicated as his, if they were aware of how much treachery was behind the smiles and expensive suits in the city. "So, in your professional opinion, what do you think is next?"

"The shooter is not going into retirement. If he was nobody would give a shit what happens to him. I don't know what's going on but I know this; he's still useful to whoever is protecting him. I'd keep my head down if I were you."

"I hate it when you say that." Dave got up and stared at O'Neil. "I'd keep my head down if I were you. I don't think I'm the only one around here wearing a target."

Dave took a cab back to Now News and was staring at his phone when he walked into the newsroom, checking his email. He looked up to see if Sid was in his office and saw a group of staffers comforting Elena, who began to weep when she saw him. His first instinct was to get back onto the elevator and leave but the staffers who were with her gave him angry looks and a young male desk assistant looked as though he wanted to punch Dave in the face, so he walked over to Elena, knelt in front of her, asked her how she was.

"You know, it was hard for me to come here today but I wanted to get back to my life. I even wanted to talk to you and listen to you ask me for forgiveness for what happened to me. You didn't even look at me. You just left. Then I read that somebody is trying to kill you. How do you think I am? Do you even know how other people feel? Do you know what you do to other people, Dave?" Her face was contorted in her hurt and anger. She shook her head back and forth, staring at him. "I need you, Dave. I need you to help heal me. Do you understand that? I need you to take me home right now and comfort me. Can you do that, Dave? Do you have it in you to do that?"

Dave emotional circuits were shorting out. The staffers were staring at him with looks that said he had only one option and if he didn't act on it they would throw him off the building. "I'll be right back. I'll take you home."

He walked to Sid's office and knocked on the door, opened it, and walked in. "I've got a situation I have to deal with. I need to talk to you but it will have to wait. Maybe I'll call you later."

Sid was behind his desk with a smirk on his face. "Buddy, you sure do have a situation to deal with. Call me later. Be very nice to the lady. She's fragile and there's only one person who can fix her. If you fuck this up we're all going to kill you, you won't have to worry about that other guy." Sid waved at the door. "Get out of here."

Dave flagged a cab and sat in silence with Elena on the ride to Philadelphia House, a condo building near Dupont Circle, where he occupied a five-hundred square foot place on the third floor. The front desk was staffed twenty-four hours a day by Cameroonians who were students at Howard University. They all spoke several languages and were elegant in their manners and offered an Old World charm to the otherwise modern lobby. The young man behind the desk saw Dave at the front door and buzzed him and was surprised to see Elena walking in behind him.

The man, tall, thin, very black, and usually reserved and dignified, jumped up and opened his arms. "Oh my god! Oh my!" The man had tears in his eyes as he came around the counter and ran to Elena, hugging her. "It is so good to see you. I have been praying for you. You are even more beautiful." The man stood back and looked at Elena, who was crying and looking awkward.

Dave and Elena took the elevator up to his floor and walked in silence to his apartment. Inside, she walked to his small sofa and sat down. "Did you see how he greeted me? Did you see that? That is what I expected from you. Instead I got you standing around with your hands in your pockets and heading for the door. Do you see what's wrong with that?"

"I'm not an emotional person," Dave said, sounding weak by even his own standards.

"No shit, Sherlock. What a breakthrough! Well, Mr. Insight, I have something to say to you. You treat me like shit. You nearly got me killed. You owe me. She owe me big. Do you get that part? I expect you to make it up to me and if you don't I promise I will make your life miserable." She was crying again and wringing her hands.

Fifty miles away, in the silo at the farm, a middle aged man was listening to the exchange and smiling. He turned to another man. "Dave's fucked," he said, chuckling.

Chapter Thirteen

Edward Segal was a patient man. He had learned patience in sniper school, where instructors would scan the tall grass looking for any sign of movement from the students who were expected to remain motionless for long periods of time, hours if necessary, to wait for the perfect shot. It had taught him to control his mind, to let it slow, to concentrate on his breathing and allow his heart rate to drop. Had he been a spiritual person the state he achieved would have been sought through prayer or meditation. Segal did it through intense focus on his objective. His objective at this moment was Captain Daniel O'Neil, on loan to Homeland Security from the Metropolitan Police Department, commonly referred to at the D.C. police. Segal had been instructed to teach the captain a lesson. And so he waited in his truck, under a tree at the far end of the parking lot on upper Wisconsin Avenue. He was in no hurry.

O'Neil was at his desk, fuming over the AG's instructions. He stared at a stack of papers on his desk and moved them to the side, shouting "bullshit!" He pulled up the street photos and the readouts from the gunshot monitors and matched them again. There was no doubt in his mind that Segal was the shooter. There were two ways to play it. He could raise hell down on Indiana Avenue by demanding to speak to the Chief, who already saw him as a loose cannon who should be fired. She had never really explained why he was not already on the retired list of tainted cops who were told to take their pensions and leave town. Or he could keep his mouth shut and wait for further developments, which he felt sure were on the way. More killings? Maybe this wasn't about Congressman Prewitt. Maybe it was about something bigger. Or different altogether.

He resisted the urge to pull the bottle out of a desk drawer and pour himself a stiff drink. He locked his office and headed home to suburban Maryland and his wife and kids. The spring soccer season was beginning and he would help coach a team. That would help take his mind off the stink that coated his career at the moment. He looked forward to being with his family and watching some mindless television.

The elevator dropped him to the lobby and he saw that it was nearly dark. He dreaded the rush hour traffic but he had an oldies CD he could listen to that would help clear his mind and, he hoped, drain away some of his anger. His car was parked in the back of the lot and he was lost in thought as he opened the driver's door, unaware of the man who slammed a brass knuckled fist into the back of his head, forcing his face into the edge of the car's door, knocking him out and producing a cracked skull and a deep dent in his face. He saw nothing, he felt nothing, and he would remember nothing.

Segal looked around and determined that no one had taken notice of the attack. He quickly went through O'Neil's pockets, removing his wallet, his keys, and his phone. He wanted the attack to look like a common street mugging. He left O'Neil's police badge. He went to his truck and drove away, stopping in Bethesda to drop the wallet, keys and phone into a trash bin outside a French restaurant. A homeless man digging through the trash later that night found money in the wallet and left the credit cards and other items in it. He took the phone. He paid no attention to the keys.

Six hours later the dobro ringtone on Dave phone sounded. He was lying on his bed holding Elena and he ignored it. Five minutes later it rang again. It kept ringing at five minute intervals until there was a pounding on his door.

"Here we go," Elena said. "You're like a flashing light that does nothing but attract attention. Answer the door."

Dave picked up his phone on his way to the door and saw that Sid had been trying to reach him, which did not surprise him. That's why he ignored the calls. He opened the door to find Sid and Megan the desk assistant standing there, looking frantic.

"Why didn't you answer the damn phone?" Sid was pissed.

"I'm comforting Elena and I didn't want to be bothered." Dave said, stepping aside. "That didn't work, did it?"

"You're friend Captain O'Neil is nearly dead. Somebody jumped him outside his office on Wisconsin Avenue. He's at George Washington Hospital having his head put back together. I need you to get over there. Megan will stay with Elena."

"You don't need me on this. Elena does. Send somebody else." Dave sounded weary.

"I do need you on this. There isn't anyone else who can work this. The cops haven't released anything on it yet and when they do it will say it appears to be a street robbery. His wallet was taken along with some other stuff. Lieutenant Jefferson called me and gave me a heads up and he also said he thinks the attack was about something else, not a robbery. He's waiting for you at G. W."

"O'Neil going to live?"

"Who knows? He's in bad shape. His wife and kids are on the way in case goodbyes are in order. It's like that."

Elena stood by the bed wrapped in Dave's bathrobe, looking very tired and fragile. "Go ahead. Megan and I will have some tea and talk about what a dick you are."

Her comment cheered him up. Calling him names had always been her way of being close to him. Megan, a young woman with a permanent sad expression, looked on, sadly, and wrapped an arm around Elena and watched Dave and Sid close the door. "Well, fuck it," Elena said. "Let's get some sleep."

Dave and Sid drove to George Washington University Hospital just off Washington Circle in the Foggy Bottom section of the city. It's part of the medical school and its emergency room has treated the city's bums and the powerful, including Ronald Reagan after he was shot by John Hinkley and Dick Chaney during his heart emergencies. On this night the usual assortment of medical crises were on display. College students with high fevers, street people with rotting feet, chest pains here, breathing problems there.

O'Neil had been moved up to an operating room where surgeons were repairing his face and skull. His wife and children were in a small waiting area where the kids were driving their mother crazy with questions. She was on the verge of hysteria and was fighting off images of her husband's coffin being lowered into the ground while a police bagpiper played Amazing Grace. She was having trouble catching her breath. Sitting with her was Lieutenant (Acting Captain) Alden Jefferson, patting her shoulder. His expression exposed a desire to murder someone. He had the posture of a man waiting to spring to violence. Jefferson jumped up when Dave and Sid walked into the waiting room and for a moment Dave thought he was about to be punched in the face. Jefferson wrapped his huge arms around both men and steered them into the hall.

"We need to have a talk," he said. "We got some serious shit going on."

Sid had the air of a man who had seen too much serious shit in his decades in the news business and he looked at Jefferson with sympathy and nodded. "Talk to us."

"You know that he made the shooter in the Judge Beechum murder and the reporter killing." Jefferson faced Dave. "He told Ossening at the F.B.I., Dave here, and me. Maybe other people but if he did he didn't tell me who. He was waiting for somebody to move against the doer but nothing happened until Dave here told the Attorney General at the judge's funeral, then the hammer came down on him to shut up and go away. That's some serious shit right there but then somebody bashes his head in. The doer in this case took his wallet and his phone but left his badge. I see it as a message. We got something serious going on and I want you guys to know what I know because nobody knows what's going to happen next." He stared at Dave and Sid, waiting for a response.

Sid looked at the floor. "Am I hearing you say you think, as a professional investigator, that the Attorney General of the United States is involved in the killing of a federal judge?"

"I ain't saying nothin' like that. Officially. So I don't want to hear nothin' like that on the radio or anywhere else and Dave here should keep his fuckin' mouth shut when he's in public about whatever he knows or thinks he knows. I think somebody should know what I know." He offered the men his fierce and doubting face, the face that had produced dozens of confessions from the men and women who had been subjected to Jefferson's brand of interrogation.

"I'm not sure why you're telling us this if you want us to keep it quiet," Dave said.

"I told you. I don't want to be the only one sitting on this and I don't know who to trust right now."

"How are you going to play this attack on O'Neil?"

"I can get away with saying it appears to be a robbery but we are investigating all possibilities. That happens to be the truth."

"What do you want us to do?" Sid stood straight with his hands in his pockets and pressed his lips together in a tight line.

"You have sources. Work them. I know you've talked to Prewitt, Dave. Work him, run some possibilities by him and see if he squirms. We'll keep each other informed. Maybe I'll get what I want and you'll get yours. I need some help here." Jefferson's face softened.

Sid said nothing and steered Dave into the waiting room where both men sat in silence while surgeons did their work on Captain O'Neil's face and skull.

Fifteen miles north Edward Segal sat in a small seafood restaurant eating fried flounder and drinking the bitter bar wine. He had a notebook on the table and was outlining what had happened since he had been offered this assignment. He liked to diagram his work in much the way he planned and reviewed his life as a sniper. What went right, what went wrong. Who was where. He had learned in Iraq that not all of his targets were bad guys and not all of his colleagues were good guys. It was time to take stock. Things were not adding up.

Chapter Fourteen

Congressman John Prewitt, Jr. was feeling expansive and full of himself. He had consumed a fine meal at Blowfish Funhouse, the city's newest trendy restaurant where a typical dinner tab ran over five hundred dollars, not including wine, which, on Prewitt's tab, ran to nearly a thousand dollars. He had no concerns about the tab because he wasn't paying it. That duty ran to the man across the table, a Capitol rat who privately claimed to "own" every important member of the House, including the leadership. It was a claim no one challenged, if only to humor the fellow and enjoy an outrageously expensive meal or weekend.

The man, who bristled at the word "lobbyist", was adorned in nearly ten-thousand dollars' worth of fabric, gold, and grooming. His suits were custom made in London, along with his shoes; his shirts were delivered from a source in Hong Kong, and his watches from Switzerland by way of Dubai. He spent more on his haircuts than a mid-level government worker spent on rent. His tan was suspiciously even and deep. His fingernails glistened. His teeth were whiter than the napkin in his lap. A well-off family visiting Washington from Kansas City stared at the man and wondered if he was a Hollywood actor or a mannequin. He was neither. He was Arnott Banner Cole, a self-made dealmaker, unburdened by scruples or sympathy for other human beings. He was born Edgar Goldman in Brooklyn, New York and following his dishonorable discharge from the U.S. Navy, reinvented himself with a new name, history, and address. A chance meeting with a shady Washington source had brought him to the seat of power and he had made the most of it.

"Here's to the American taxpayer," Cole said, holding up his glass.

"God bless them, everyone," Prewitt chuckled.

"And don't forget the Chinese, who are dumb enough to send us credit cards." Cole took a sip of his wine.

"I don't mean to inject some bad feelings into this fine evening, Cole, but how's the cleanup coming along?"

"It's a little messier than we thought it would be but it's being handled. Lots of moving parts but we think it's being contained. Nothing to worry about. You do your job and we'll do ours. It's worked out so far, hasn't it?" Cole smiled but his eyes were piercing.

"Yes sir, we're good." Prewitt was in no mood to move out of his comfort zone. He had no doubt that Cole would make things right. Money could solve all problems.

"So here's what I need you to do," Cole said, leaning in and flashing his expensive teeth. "I need you go down to Tennessee and do some maintenance on the good folks back home. There might be some rumors or even newspaper stories that could cause certain people to get a bit edgy, if you get my drift. This Justice thing is beginning to leak all over the place and this Dave Haggard fellow is only the beginning. Lots of folks are sniffing around looking for this and that. We can contain it on our end but you need to make sure your folks, the ones that are your core, are ready to stand up for you if anybody comes snooping around down there. You get my drift?"

Prewitt was becoming edgy himself. "What do you mean leaks?"

"Nothing to worry about just yet. The Justice Department has folks who don't want to get in line with the program and they're talking. Nothing serious at the moment, just bread crumbs for reporters to follow. We have to make sure they run out of crumbs before they get where they want to go."

"Who's leaking?"

"I'm not sure. The Attorney General's been waylaid for the moment but he won't be for long if things don't get controlled. He thinks there's a big national security issue that Homeland Security won't tell him about and he'll call off the dogs until he figures out it's bullshit. We have until then to work out a plan to derail this thing for good. That's why I need you to go home and shore up your end."

"I was in a good mood until ten minutes ago. What I'm hearing you say is this thing ain't under control at all." Prewitt waved at a waiter and pointed at his wine glass.

Cole shook his head at the waiter. "You don't need to get loaded. You need to get going."

"We have a break coming up. I'll get down there and see what's going on."

"No, you tell them what's going on. You control the narrative. If you ask them they'll imagine the worst and believe any rumor that flies by."

"A hundred million dollars. Imagine that. Like taking candy from a baby." Prewitt was pouting.

"Pull yourself together. You could get ten years for each million." Cole had a cat-like expression on his face, almost as though he was mewing. "I don't have to remind you that this is the big league and you win big and you lose big. The lucky losers are the ones who make an apology and move down to K Street to be paid six times what they made up here. If this blows up there ain't no plan B, there ain't no K Street. And you can bet your ass the government will find itself another hard-nose like Judge Beechum to send us so far up into Allenwood we can barely breathe."

"Don't mention Allenwood. Stogis is up there on a seventy-eight month sentence. I remember when he was chairman of the appropriations subcommittee. Gives me the willies just thinking about it." Prewitt was fast losing his good mood.

"Stogis was stupid. We're not stupid. We just have to hold it together until all of this goes to the bottom of the pile."

"How are you feeling about this guy you hired to take care of it?"

"I told you, he's solid. He just needs to catch up to technology, that's all. No one knew how fast these cameras and these damned gunshot monitors or whatever they're called could put this together. The police captain's been taken care of. I need you to calm down and do some maintenance on your people. We clear?" Cole was worried that Prewitt would crack and run off at the mouth, producing a cascade of F.B.I. raids. Cole knew his office, his house, and his pied-a-terre at the Watergate would be high on the list. The beach house in Rehobeth would not be far behind. Too many bold names had too much on the line to let that happen. He tried to gauge Prewitt's weakness and wondered if maybe it wasn't time to call Segal about a new task. He'd give it another day or two.

"Listen to me. Normal is what we need from you. Just be yourself. People up here can smell fear and it gives 'em a hard on, so keep a smile on your face and a shine on your shoes, as they used to say."

"I gotta run. Some folks from Wall Street are looking for some favors." Prewitt was a bit shaky on his feet.

"Don't get too cozy. This ain't the time for anything but the straight and narrow."

"I know how to play the game. Thanks for dinner." Prewitt waved to a table of well-suited men and women who smiled at him as he left the restaurant and hailed a cab. His heart was pounding. He wasn't sure a trip back home was a good idea.

Chapter Fifteen

O'Neil was having trouble coming around. He could hear voices but he had no idea what was being said or where he was. He thought he was in a dream. It was dark. He had no sensation of being. The voices were nearby, male and female. He felt a hand on his wrist.

"His pulse is good." It was a woman's voice.

He felt something sharp on the sole of his foot, causing him to jump. "He's feeling his extremities." It was a man's voice.

"Captain O'Neil. Captain O'Neil. Can you hear me?" The man's voice was closer.

O'Neil tried to speak but something was in his throat. A strangling noise came out instead of the words he was trying to form.

"Don't try to talk. Move your hand if you can hear me."

O'Neil raised his right hand. Five minutes later a small group had gathered around his bed. Within half an hour the D.C.P.D. knew that O'Neil was conscious. It was the lead on the five and six o'clock local news programs. Edward Segal caught the six o'clock news on channel four and smiled. He had an odd attachment to O'Neil. He felt a kinship with the cop that he did not feel with the people who had hired him. He was glad he had not killed the captain. He took a drive to Antietam Battlefield near Sharpsburg, Maryland and sat in the dark on the ground where twenty-three thousand men fell in a single day during the War, ten thousand of them Confederates.

"This is what the sons of bitches will do," he said into the dark. "They'll send you to the grave without as much as a thank you. They'll poison your water and sicken your kids and not think a thing of it. All of you out there, all of you who fell here, you know the truth of it. They deserve to die just like you did not." Edward Segal fell forward onto his face, tears dropping onto the ground where so many were slaughtered on a warm day in 1862. It was the first time he had cried since the day he left Tennessee to avenge 9/11.

Segal spent the night there on the ground, allowing himself a moment of self pity and regret. He was sore and cold as dawn came over the battlefield and, most profoundly for him, he was confused. His hatred burned as intensely as ever but he didn't know where to aim it. He wondered if he was going insane. He felt as though he was losing control and he asked himself if he should be worrying about it.

A park ranger arrived to open the battlefield for visitors and saw Segal wandering over the fields and hollered that the park wasn't open yet and to come back in a couple of hours. Segal looked at the man and saw a uniform. He walked to the ranger and moved up close to his face, his eyes unfocused and his blood racing through his brain like water through a hose. The ranger was startled and opened his mouth to say something when Segal hit him with the brass knuckles, caving in the ranger's jaw and front teeth, sending him to the ground. Segal looked down at the man and walked away.

Seventy miles away Captain O'Neil was becoming aware of his own injuries. His face was wrapped in bandages that hid the stitches and surgical work that had put his skull back together. He was groggy and unsure of the moment but he knew he had been hurt but he had no recollection of it. He could hear activity in the hospital intensive care unit and an odd voice here and there talking about food or medicine or pain or comfort. He put himself into a mental drill to recall who he was. He knew his name and he knew he was a police officer. He knew the names of his wife and children and he knew what street he lived on but he could not recall the street number. He tried to recall the names of everyone he knew but gave up when it occurred to him that he had no way of knowing if he was getting the number right. He drifted off to sleep as he tried to put faces to the names of the men and women on the homicide unit, which he mistakenly assumed he still commanded.

Dave Haggard sat in the room with O'Neil and watched him fidget and make noises under his bandaged face. Dave wondered what O'Neil was thinking and if he was in pain and trying to ask for relief. Dave had slept in small naps during the night but his dreams were troubled and woke him up with a feeling of dread and anxiety. Jefferson had made clear his opinion that the attack on O'Neil was related to the killing of Judge Beechum and the mistaken murder of Peter Deutch, and his strong belief that higher ups in law enforcement were preventing the killer from being brought to justice. Jefferson had let slip his own desire to find the killer and deal with him in a "street way". "You have a right to remain silent and dead. That's how I'd read him his fucking rights," Jefferson had said, offering his meanest face to those who were watching his fury build.

Now, as the spring sun rose to warm the day over the world's most powerful city, Dave sat alone with O'Neil. The others had gone home to rest, gone to work, or were sleeping on the small sofas on the waiting room. He looked out the window at the rush hour traffic on Washington Circle. The most educated city in the world.

And the men and women who were sipping expensive coffee on their way to their cubicles had no idea what was happening around them. What chumps! He chuckled. It came to him that he was one of the chumps. He didn't know what was going on, either, despite being among the privileged "media elite" in Washington. *We all just pass around the same fairy tales and congratulate ourselves that we're on the inside*, he thought. *We don't know anything.*

Elena was sitting on a bench in the park inside Dupont Circle, watching the water flow out of the fountain in the center, sipping coffee and finding peace. The traffic around the circle was heavy in the rush hour and it was chilly, but the park was nearly empty except for a few pedestrians who were hurrying through to get to their jobs. A homeless man was sleeping under a tree, covered by a filthy sleeping bag. She liked the idea that she was back in the city and life was returning to normal. She was trying to decide whether to stay at Dave's apartment for a few days or return to her own place in Adams Morgan a dozen blocks away.

A scruffy-looking young man was strumming a guitar on the nearby bench and working through the words of a song he was writing.

I love you
I really do
But I can't stand you
Can't you understand me
I can't stand you
But I love you

Elena laughed and called out to the songwriter. "Breaking up?"

He looked around and saw her laughing at him. "It's just a song." He turned back to his guitar.

"Okay, whatever you say," she said.

"Love is hard," he said, not looking up.

"Let me know when you've figured it out. I kind of like the song, though. I feel that way about someone."

"Everybody does," he said, working through a chord progression.

"Are you writing about your girlfriend?"

"Girlfriend? I don't like that word. It's confining. We're all just moving parts. We don't need to be confined by words like that."

"How old are you?"

"Does it matter?"

"Well, tell me."

"Twenty."

"That explains it. You're right. You don't need to be tied down when you're twenty. Thirty, maybe, but not twenty. I hope you don't still feel that way when you're thirty."

"I'll never be thirty." The young man offered her what he imagined was his most serious, experienced face.

Elena looked at him and her heart softened. "Well, good luck with the song." She turned back to the fountain and watched the water splash down from the bowl over the three classical nudes that were said to represent the sea, the stars, and the wind. She felt at peace and it was a rare moment.

The young man with his guitar was still working out his crazy song.

I can't stand you
But I love you

She turned to the singer. "Any chance I can get you to record that for someone?"

Chapter Sixteen

Special Agent Milford "Bud" Ossening was at his desk reading reports about everything associated with Judge Beechum's assassination, Peter Deutch's murder, Captain O'Neil's fractured skull, and Edward Segal. Ossening was not a sentimental man and he devoted a considerable amount of introspection to hunting down and suppressing his own prejudices. He even questioned his own loyalties for tell-tale signs of weakness that might compromise his mission, as he saw it, at the F.B.I. As a result of the distance he placed between himself and others he had few friends, if any, and had two failed marriages behind him.

He liked the idea that facts speak for themselves and do not need interpretation by persons who have an interest in how any given fact falls into or out of an investigation. He believed that too many criminal cases were stained by the opinions of those bringing the case and that facts were seen as nothing more than ornamentation on the tree, to be moved, arranged, or ignored.

What he saw before him was confirmation that O'Neil was correct. Edward Segal was the shooter. He believed that Segal was the man who attacked O'Neil. After all, the man's street name was Brass Knuckles and Lieutenant (Acting Captain) Jefferson had been clear in his opinion that brass knuckles had done the damage to O'Neil's face and skull. It all added up.

So why was the Attorney General sitting on it? Why was he ordering a stand down on the link to Segal? What's the link to Congressman Prewitt? Ossening had been an agent long enough to smell the connection. What was it that he had drilled into him at the army's intelligence school? There is no such thing as a coincidence. They had said pretty much the same thing at Quantico. If it looks like a duck…

He took a cab to George Washington University Hospital and walked into O'Neil's room to find Dave dozing in a chair and a nurse writing down some numbers from the monitors next to the bed. The nurse looked up when he walked in and he flashed his F.B.I. credentials to keep her from ordering him out. "How's he doing?" he whispered.

"He's coming around. You should talk to the doctor." The nurse turned back to the monitors.

Dave opened his eyes, which were red and unfocused, and rubbed his face. He saw Ossening standing next to the bed and assumed there was bad news. "What's the matter?"

"Nothing. I'm just checking on him. Any news?"

"He's conscious, at least some of the time. He responds to commands and can feel everything. That's good news."

"When can I talk to him?"

"Beats me. Talk to the doctor." Dave the reporter kicked in. "Where's the investigation into the shooter? Get him yet?"

"Not yet." Ossening was not in a mood to share.

"Soon?"

"When we have something to release, we will." Ossening submerged himself in F.B.I. public information speak.

"You connect this," he pointed to O'Neil, "to the shootings?"

"You guys just never give up, do you." Ossening nodded in the direction of the nurse and mouthed "later".

The nurse left, giving Dave an angry look. She smiled at Ossening.

He smiled back and looked at Dave. "Law and order. Good guys, that's us, versus the bad guys, that would be you."

"The F.B.I. in peace and war," Dave said.

"So, Dave, how's the book coming?" Ossening had a curious look on his face.

"You know I can't write about that. You guys have the priest killing story pretty buttoned up. I had to wave the advance. A lot of money. People still ask questions about that little monitoring operation you guys have out in Rappahannock County."

"Who says it's ours?"

"Is it still up and running?"

"Like I said, who says it's ours and how would I know what, if anything is going on there?"

"So, what's really going on?"

"Some strange stuff, Dave. This is between us and not even within the unnamed source rules. Don't do anything with this until I say so. Deal?"

"So why are you telling me anything?"

"You'll see. Deal?"

"Deal."

"The AG called O'Neil, me, and a few other people to his office and told everyone, O'Neil in particular, to forget about the link between the shootings and Segal. He says there is no link and to drop it. O'Neil thinks Segal's the shooter and so do I. So why is the AG calling off the dogs?"

"You're asking me?"

"You didn't just get off the boat. You've been around. What's your read?"

"One of two things. Either he believes what he says or he has another motive." Dave watched Ossening's face for reaction. The agent had been trained not to react so he just stared back.

"Or someone is giving him orders which he's just passing along." Ossening said it as though he was thinking it over.

"Who has the authority to give him orders?"

"The White House, of course, but that's not where this is coming from, if it's true. The pecking order is the Oval Office, State Department, Pentagon, and, these days, Homeland Security. Let's rule out the White House. Even if it's them there won't be any footprints. There's nothing in it for the Pentagon and the State Department that we know of. That leaves Homeland Security, which is wagging a very big tail in this town. What's in it for them?"

"They're getting a lot of money, most of it under the table." Dave had done some stories about the secret facilities that had been funded and excavated under Washington area office parks. No one was quite sure what was happening in those places. Civil liberties types were convinced it was the government spying on everyone and everything.

"I don't know. Segal has a connection to the Pentagon through his war record. He's a trained army sniper and a decorated veteran. His file has him living on some farm in Tennessee doing part time work for anyone who'll hire him as a general worker, whatever that means. He travels a lot and his passport record has him spending time in Jamaica. That's usually code for somebody who likes to smoke a little dope now and then in a country where they won't be arrested. Maybe he's a part time pothead."

"Well, that narrows it down to half the country." Dave had been known to smoke a joint now and then, especially when he was younger.

"Have you ever met a professional hit man?" Ossening had his most gracious smile.

"Not that I'm aware of. I've met a few murderers, but they were of the street variety, not the action movie kind."

"My money is on Segal being one of those. Let's suppose he's the shooter. Who's he working for?"

Dave had given it some thought on his own. "Somebody who doesn't want Congressman Prewitt's bad deeds made public."

"Bingo. That's my read. Who's that?"

"Everybody who's skimming the Oak Ridge clean-up money."

"Now you're following the bread crumbs. I know you've talked to him. That's probably what got you shot at. Maybe you could think about another meeting to get his blood pumping. Do you think you're up for that?"

"Jesus! Do I get body armor?" Dave thought about his last meeting with Prewitt and looked forward to getting under the Congressman's skin again. "Give me something to get him going."

"You don't think you have enough right now?"

"Come on. You've got something in mind. Let's have it."

"It's always better to leave an unstated threat on the table. It has more of an effect on the mind. Leave him thinking you have more than you do and, if you can, convince him that he's already screwed and there's no way out. That will send him running to his masters, assuming he has some. We'll watch to see where he goes."

"Ah, now the truth comes out. You want me to be the game beater to flush out the quail so you can shoot them."

"Something like that."

There was a sound from bed and both men turned to see O'Neil's hands patting the mattress. "Captain, you okay?" Ossening asked.

O'Neil pointed fingers at Dave and Ossening and pointed thumbs up on both hands. He had been listening to their conversation and approved of the plan.

Ossening laughed and clapped his hands. "Once a cop…"

The monitoring station in Rappahannock County was, indeed, up and running, although Ossening's knowledge of it was minimal. The computer monitoring Dave's phone did not report anything usual and had, in fact, missed the conversation. Dave's phone was in the front pocket of his jeans and the only thing picked up by the monitor was some muffled voices that could not be understood.

Chapter Seventeen

Thirteen-ten Longworth was emptying as Dave arrived for his meeting with Congressman Prewitt. A subcommittee hearing had ended and the witnesses were still smiling and enjoying their moment in the limelight, shaking each other's hands and being admired by assistants whose only job that day was to tell the witness how wonderful they were. It was easy to tell the first-timers. They assumed that their appearance before Congress was an indication of their importance in the nation's affairs. Old hands knew it was all just theater and they got the hell out of there as soon as the gavel came down.

Dave knew he was looking at rooky witnesses and he waited patiently as they filed out, smiling and beaming. A committee staffer turned out most of the lights and the room went dark and quiet. Dave sat in a chair and waited for Prewitt. He looked up at the committee dais where the members' name plates were being removed from their assigned places by a young intern who looked to be about fifteen in a wholesome girl-next-door way, her modest blazer a bit too large. No doubt her parents back in Real America were proud that their daughter was experiencing the business of administering to the nation's welfare. It didn't take long to become cynical, he thought, as he watched her go about her duties. She looked very sweet. He hoped none of the wolves on Capitol Hill had any designs on her.

Prewitt entered the committee room through the members' door behind the dais and ignored Dave as he walked to the press table where they had met the first time. Prewitt sat and looked out the window. Dave walked over and sat down across the table. "Nice view," he said.

"If you like looking at government buildings," Prewitt said. "So, what's so important?"

"You're fucked," Dave said, startling himself. He had planned to save those words for later.

Prewitt turned to look at Dave. There was fear and hatred in his eyes. "Who do you think you are, talking to me like that, even as a joke?"

"It's no joke. This thing is leaking all over the city. People are putting two and two together and coming up with links to you and the guy who killed Judge Beechum." It was partly true. It was an exaggeration to say the link was being made all over the city. As far as Dave knew, the link was being made in a small circle, but Prewitt had no way of knowing any of it.

"What a crock!" Prewitt's eyes betrayed building hysteria. "I think you're having some kind of drug reaction. What have you been smoking?" His hands were shaking.

"I think the Justice investigation into whatever's been going on with the Oak Ridge cleanup money is the least of your problems."

"I'm a goddam member of Congress, you little piece of country trash! Your daddy took off his hat to my daddy. Never in your miserable life will you be able to talk to me like that. Now get out of here." Prewitt stood up and stormed out through the members' door into the committee offices.

Dave was shaking. He felt the fear that Prewitt's words produced, words grounded in truth about the class structure of the South, where powerful men lorded over lesser men, white and black. He accepted that Prewitt's family could have ruined his own in past generations by simply allowing them to starve. The South's lower classes, the families that did the hard work and got hands dirty, remember the days of pellagra and the swollen tongues, the lesions, and death, all from a weakness in the food. Food. The rich ate better. That was life's most important lesson, at least among a class of people where Dave came from. No one talked about it anymore. The rich still ate better but the poor don't suffer from pellagra. Now they're fat. They eat for volume. Maybe it's a natural reaction to the starving of their ancestors.

Dave stared at the door Prewitt had left open and felt weak. Dave's father had, indeed, lifted his hat to Prewitt's father. The South is an honor society and at that moment Dave felt as though his honor had been insulted and he fought a country boy's desire to grab a shotgun and blow Prewitt's head off. Instead, he took a few deep breaths, stood up, and walked out onto Independence Avenue, hailed a cab and went back to his apartment in the Philadelphia House, where Elena was waiting.

She was sitting on his small sofa, looking relaxed and beautiful. She still took his breath away and made him weak in the knees. She had been reading and she looked up when he opened the door and walked in. "So, how was your day?" She smiled her crooked smile.

"Long. How are you?"

"I'm waiting for something, Dave. Can you guess what it is?"

He fought his natural urge to freeze and stare or change the subject. He walked over to her and knelt on the floor. "I have something to say. I'm sorry. I am very sorry. I was stupid." He paused and saw that she was waiting for more. "I love you, Elena."

Her smile turned to tears and her face contorted. "You are a bastard, Dave Haggard. You are a goddam bastard." She balled her hands into fists and pounded on his shoulders. "You almost killed me and you didn't have the decency to chase me to where I felt safe and make me feel like you love me. You just went about your business. Mister big shot reporter. Do you think the others at Now News or the other newsrooms in this city admire you? They think you're an idiot, Dave! They don't say it to your face but not one of them would be so stupid as you've been."

Dave's first reaction was regret that he had come home to her anger and pain. He should have gone back to the hospital to stay with O'Neil, he thought. Then he wondered what was wrong with him. Maybe he should have stayed in the therapy Now News had arranged after the priest killing ordeal. It might have helped him come to terms with himself.

"You're right, Elena." His voice was weak.

"About what?"

"Everything."

"See! That's what I'm talking about. That's not validating my feelings. That's humoring me. I need you to say back to me what I told you so I'll know you heard me."

He was feeling trapped. He had no idea how to move this argument away from where it was. "I'm stupid. I was stupid. I'm sorry." He hoped it was enough.

"Go on." It wasn't.

"Okay. First, I don't really give a shit what other people think of me. I do care what you think of me. I am very sorry for what happened to you. In my defense, I got you away from Father Darius, not the cops."

Her face softened. "At least you expressed yourself. You get points for that. How's Captain O'Neil?"

"He's coming around. He hears what's going on and he seems to understand it. He has feeling in his arms and legs. I guess that means he'll be okay."

"Why don't we take a little nap and then we'll go visit him together. How's that sound?" She offered a smile.

Two hours later, hand in hand, they walked out of the Philadelphia House to hail a cab on Massachusetts Avenue. The sky was cloudy and dusk was early, giving the air a chill that cut through Elena's dress and light jacket. They looked very happy.

Across the street, Edward Segal watched and felt a pang of doubt. He believed that those who employed him were beginning to see him as a problem to be dealt with. He had seen it before with others who did this work and he had, in fact, been the instrument of their ends. There was only so much usefulness in the business of killing before the risks to the employers overcame the benefits they received from those who did the blood work. It was a mean truth that the U.S. military turned out highly trained killers in volume and a percentage of them became so emotionally insulated that they would take the work that Segal performed, even against their own. He felt it. His instincts told him the time had come. He also understood that his enemy was not this man walking with the woman. His enemy was his employer and those he served. He watched Dave and Elena and felt no desire to harm either of them. For a moment he envied them.

He turned and walked south on 17th Street in the direction of the White House and waited at K Street until it was dark. He slipped into an alley that led to the entrance of a parking garage and felt his heart pounding. He needed to blow off some steam.

A middle aged man wearing an expensive suit and carrying a high-end briefcase was on the phone and having an animated conversation with someone in his office as he walked into the alley on his way to retrieve his car.

He barely noticed Segal, who had his head down. The brass knuckles hit the man at the base of his skull, causing him to collapse. The man went into convulsions and died before EMS technicians could get to him. Segal was on a bus going up 16th Street when the man was pronounced dead. He felt much better.

Chapter Eighteen

Arnott Cole was getting nervous. His phone call with Congressman Prewitt had not gone well. The congressman was hysterical, that was obvious, but he was also careless. He came right out with what was on his mind, which was incriminating and a gift to anyone who happened to be listening in on the call. Cole assumed that all of Prewitt's calls were monitored. It was standard procedure for anyone under federal investigation, especially a probe involving a hundred million dollars in taxpayer money.

Cole's other problem was the council, the group of "partners" who had put together the scheme, men and women who had this or that connection to nuclear power, environmental policy, cleanup, water issues, and several other pieces of a puzzle that added up to a huge pile of cash that was fair game to those clever enough to go after it. Billions. It was almost too good to be true. Oversight of federal spending was lax, despite cries of overregulation from certain offices on K Street. But the scheme only worked if all of the parts fit. Prewitt was a key part and he was falling apart. Frankly, Cole admitted, Prewitt wasn't the only part that was failing. The thing was springing leaks. Soon the rats would be running for the door and all hell would break loose as everyone tried to save their own asses.

Humpty Dumpty needed to be put together again. He poured himself another snifter of the brandy that had cost as much as a car and drank it down in one gulp. He poured another and watched the flames in the gas fireplace dance over the fake logs. How much is too much? he asked himself. How much is enough? He idly wondered if the richest man who ever lived thought he had enough. Probably not. He thought about the families in the ticky-tacky developments in their three bedroom/two bath tract homes. Did they think they had enough? Were they less happy? Happier? Cole threw his crystal snifter into the fireplace and watched it send high-end shards in a spray against the firebox. "Chumps!"

He looked at his six-figure watch and judged that Prewitt had had enough time to calm down. He pressed a button and heard the congressman's phone ringing.

"This is Congressman Prewitt." It was his standard answer and sounded officious even to his friends.

"Get over here."

"What, right now?"

"Right now." Cole ended the call.

Thirty minutes later a cab pulled up in front of Cole's iron gate at the entrance to his three acre estate in Bethesda. Cole pressed the button that released the gate and he watched Prewitt trudge up the brick drive. He was waiting at the door when Prewitt walked up with panic in his eyes.

"Jesus! What's wrong? Why the late night meeting?"

"We need to talk. We need a plan. You need to get hold of yourself. Come in."

Prewitt was unhinged. His hair was uncombed, he wore no tie, his shoes were untied, his trench coat was buttoned in a lopsided way that made him look like a derelict at Farragut Square asking for spare change. His eyes were red. He smelled boozy.

"My god, man! You're a mess. Come in." Cole was beginning to think Prewitt needed a stint in a funny farm far away from Washington.

Cole's house was a model of poor taste and excessive income. He had hired and fired a succession of decorators, all of whom had a different "vision" for the house. There were rugs of all types and colors, mismatched but pricey art on the walls, an antique spinet upon which sat a clarinet said to have been played by Benny Goodman. One wall was covered by a large tapestry displaying a scene from 17th century Belgium, when it was known as the Austrian Netherlands. The tapestry was, to Prewitt's eyes, hideous, given that a modern stone table had been placed against it. The room had the feel of a storage area.

The gas fire was still dancing and the flames illuminated the shards of crystal from the shattered snifter. In Prewitt's hyper-mood, the whole place seemed like something from Hell. He stood before the fire and tried to catch his breath. "What's going on?"

Cole was drunk and growing mean. "You're a goddam idiot. You call me and spill the beans to the whole world! Didn't it occur to you that your phones are monitored. You can't take a piss without the F.B.I. knowing about it. My god! What the hell is wrong with you?"

"I'm a member of Congress, goddam it! The F.B.I. can't just snoop on me. Separation of powers and all that."

"Jesus, you're dense. Don't you think they've managed to obtain a warrant? Do you think that murdering Judge Beechum calls off the dogs? The idea was to trade up to a better deal. You're giving them all the ammunition they need to put you and the rest of us away. Pull yourself together." Cole poured himself a stiff round of brandy and gulped it down. "Some of our friends a getting concerned. We need you to call in some chits around town and water this thing down."

"What kind of chits?"

"Do I have to spell it out for you? You're a sub-committee chairman. That has to count for something. Look at it this way. You're the engineer on a runaway train. Pull the goddam brake handle."

Prewitt sat down and rubbed his face. His hands were shaking. "This guy Dave Haggard says I'm fucked. It's over. What do you think?"

"I think he's been told what to say. He's not making this stuff up. Somebody is feeding him information. That's where the problem is. If Haggard's getting it, so are other reporters around town. That's how it works. I wonder why nobody else has contacted you to get your read on it."

"I'll tell you what I think. I think Haggard's the only one with this right now. He told me it's all over town but I'm not getting any feedback except from him. Maybe we should deal with him." Prewitt had an evil look on his face, a smirky smile and dead eyes.

"And accomplish what? Whoever is feeding this to him will just feed it to someone else. I think he went to you to see what you'd do, how you'd react. And what you did was call me and tell everyone at the F.B.I. what's going on. You're doing what they want you to do. Now stop it. Try to backtrack. Maybe spend some time at a resort and claim you're suffering from exhaustion and a problem with sleeping pills that makes you say things you don't mean. Damage control." Cole was grasping at any idea that came to him. "There are some nice resorts in West Virginia. Quiet, private, isolated. I'll make the arrangements."

Prewitt sat back and closed his eyes. "I thought you wanted me to stroke the folks in my district."

"We can put that off for a couple of weeks. Right now, you need some rest. I like the exhaustion story. It can help explain a lot."

The computer program monitoring Cole's home recognized Prewitt's voice and alerted a technician at the farm in Virginia. The conversation was automatically recorded and transcribed and sent to an interested party where it was analyzed and filed with other information about the two men and others who were involved in the issues at hand, including Dave Haggard. The touch of a key would bring up a screen pinpointing each man's location.

Chapter Nineteen

Dave and Elena were in a state of relaxed anxiety; the warmth that envelops the moment when two people have agreed to be close with the knowledge that a hard moment is only a matter of time. They were lying on Dave's bed, stroking each other's face. For Dave it was a visit to another reality, one far removed from the craziness of his life. He looked into her brown eyes and saw beauty and gentleness and he felt guilty and stupid. This is what his life should be about, not chasing stories around Washington. This is what it's all about. Love. Peace. Gentleness. He ran his fingers over her beautiful copper skin and thought how good life would be if he had moments like this every day. *I can give up the street reporting and edit or produce. That will get me away from the craziness.*

Elena had forced herself to think in the moment and not about what was real outside these walls. She willed away thoughts about bad men with guns and knives who wanted to harm Dave. She willed away her fear that Dave was like a skittish deer and would run away at the first hint of a threat to his life as he knew it. She pushed back her belief that he could never change. Right now, in this moment, she needed this peaceful, loving reality, however brief it might be.

"I'm going to talk to Sid about a new job. Maybe work the desk or edit. Maybe it's time for Dave Haggard, Ace Reporter, to come inside." He smiled at her, expecting a grateful smile in return.

"Don't," she said. "Don't say anything." She felt the edges of the good mood beginning to fray.

"I mean it. I'll talk to him."

"Don't say anything like that right now. Let's just enjoy this and worry about other things later."

"You don't believe me."

"I think you believe it right now and I think you'll have second thoughts the minute a fire engine races by and you run after it. That doesn't mean we can't have this." She kissed him and hoped it would shut him up.

He pulled back. "You need to give me some encouragement."

"I'll give you this. You follow up with a talk with Sid and let's see what happens." The air was changing and it was colder. They lay in silence and fell into a shared sleep. The darkness outside the window gave way to gray and then a spring sunshine.

Dave made espresso and they began the day in the relaxed manner of people who are comfortable with each other. They shared a cab to Now News in Rosslyn and offered each other a brief kiss as they walked into the newsroom. Elena wondered whether the good feeling was coming to an end. *Not to think about that now.*

Dave knocked on Sid's door and heard, "Yeah," from inside, so he opened the door and walked in. Sid was behind his desk talking to a man Dave had never seen before.

"Come on in," Sid said, waving Dave inside. "Dave, meet Jim Russell, an old friend from way back."

Russell smiled and stood. "It's very nice to meet you, Dave." Russell had a soft, cultured voice and Dave pegged him at around Sid's age. He was a large man and had an easy smile. Dave saw him as a man who made friends easily. "You spend as much time in the news as the people you cover," Russell said, "Not always a good thing in a street reporter." He said it with a smile.

"We're doing a little strategic thinking," Sid said. "The world is changing and we want to make sure we'll have jobs next year. We can't count on you to bring us attention and funding."

"I need to do some strategic thinking of my own," Dave replied. "It might be time for me to come in from the cold, as they say."

"I'd be happy to offer whatever advice I can," Russell said.

"Jim knows as much as anybody about public radio. He helped create some programs you may have heard of. All Things Considered, Marketplace, The World. He was Vietnam bureau chief for UPI Audio during the war. I've asked him for some ideas about where we go from here." Sid had the look of a man who was comfortable with an old friend. "He's a consultant these days and runs a company called The Program Doctor."

"Are we sick?" Dave asked, hoping it sounded like a joke.

"The world is changing, Dave," Sid said. "That means we have to change with it. It also means opportunity." He turned to Russell.

"This is a difficult period for anyone in broadcasting," Russell said. "There are, in fact, people who think radio is on its way out." He chuckled. "I have to say that ninety-two per cent of all Americans tune in to radio at least once a week. The interesting thing, though, is that there is a hell of a future, perhaps a better future than ever before, in producing audio. I deliberately use the word audio instead of radio because radio seems to be dependent on an increasingly arcane notion of going from a tower to an individual radio. There are so many ways of transmitting, why would anyone want to be locked in by an old technology."

Sid offered a wide smile. "New ideas! That's what we're talking about, Dave. We have a hell of a news operation here but we're still thinking about old technology. Jim here is going to draft a plan for us to move into the future. Hell, Dave, you could be here for the rest of your life."

Dave thought about his promise to Elena. "Well, I don't think I want to be on the street much longer. What's the chance of something inside?"

Sid glared at Dave. "Maybe this is a conversation we can have later."

Russell offered a friendly smile. "Why don't I get a cup of coffee and you two can have a talk."

"No, stay here. Dave and I can talk another time." Sid waited for Dave to catch the cue to leave.

"I'll look you up on my way out and we can chat about your options," Russell offered his hand. "Nice to meet you."

An hour later Dave and Jim Russell were sitting at a small table in a studio. "So, I gather you have some personal reasons for wanting to get off the street."

"My life is out of balance. My girlfriend, if she's even that, says I don't have a life. I'm thirty-three. I work and work some more. I love this job but I don't want to end up as some worn out newsman alone at the bar at the Press Club."

"If you follow your own star, there is a price. It's a very high price. You need to know that. Don't be as blind as I was. I dragged my family all over the country following my star. One of the things I hear more and more in thinking about this kind of subject is balance; living a life that is in balance. We, meaning guys like Sid and me, never used that word. We weren't seeking balance. Balance seemed dull, homogenized, white-breadish. The last thing in the world I wanted was balance. Hell, I wanted the excitement. I wanted the high highs and I even benefited from the low lows. It made me a much better writer. People have asked me, after I went into management, did it replace the excitement of being a street reporter? The answer is it never, ever did." Russell offered a small chuckle but his eyes were serious. "It's about choices." He paused and a look of sadness came over his face. "My wife of forty-three years decided she'd had enough. I'm divorced. Think about it."

Dave stood up and offered his hand. He left the studio without responding. He walked into Sid's office and waited for him to look up. "We can talk when the Prewitt story and Beechum assassination are wrapped up."

"It could be awhile and it could get messy again, especially for you. Your life could be on the line again."

"It's a hell of a story, Sid."

"I thought you'd say something like that."

Chapter Twenty

Captain O'Neil was sitting up when Dave walked into his room. His face was heavily bandaged but his eyes were uncovered and he was watching a cable program about guns. "Uhh. Shiii dnnn." His jaw was wired shut and his speech was labored as he motioned to a chair.

"You're looking better," Dave said, trying to smile. The effect was the greeting an adult might give to a toddler.

O'Neil grabbed a note page and wrote in small letters, "fuck you."

"Same old cop, I see."

O'Neil wrote "how's things?"

"Well, the bait's out there. Prewitt got pretty pissed. Have you seen Ossening?"

O'Neil nodded and wrote "rabbit's running."

"I wish you could talk. I'd like to know what that means."

"Call him."

"Have the doctors told you how long you'll be here?"

"Couple weeks. Face fucked up."

"Nothing new there." It got a painful laugh out of O'Neil.

"Can I get you anything?"

O'Neil shook his head. Dave sat in silence watching the television with O'Neil for an hour and left. He found a bench in a small park and called Ossening's number, which was picked up after one ring.

"There's a coffee shop at 7th and Pennsylvania. One hour." That was all Ossening said and he ended the call.

One hour. George Washington Hospital is on 23rd Street at Pennsylvania. It was a nice day so Dave decided to walk. The usual protesters were outside the White House, ranting about war and drugs and oppression and something that happened in El Salvador a couple of decades ago. At Freedom Plaza, across from the Wilson Building, aka the District Building, aka City Hall, police were hassling some kids on skateboards. Tourists mixed with government employees on crowded sidewalks. The tourists wore their new shorts from Wal-Mart and the government workers wore their bargain suits from Macys. Everyone looked stressed. Dave laughed at a family from God-knows-where, strung along an entire block, with Dad in front, holding a map and pointing at something while Mom tried to calm a teenage girl who was whining that she had never been so bored, and younger brother was moping along and complaining that he was tired. Welcome to Washington! Dave thought.

The coffee shop was crowded and a line stretched out the door as Dave approached. Ossening came up behind him and touched his shoulder. "Fuck this. We'll be here all afternoon. Let's head over to the Navy Memorial and find a seat." The U.S. Navy Memorial runs from 7th to 9th streets along Pennsylvania and its centerpiece of the statue of the Lone Sailor, standing watch. Dave covered the dedication of the memorial years earlier and watched as hardened Admirals teared up at the statue. The fountains contain water from the Seven Seas gathered by navy ships. It's a popular daytime spot to lunch, watch the crowds, and daydream. There's an amphitheater at the memorial and Dave and Ossening found a spot on the steps away from others.

"I went to see O'Neil. He's looking better," Dave said.

"He told you to call me, I take it."

"Yep."

"Prewitt seems to be taking the bait but he hasn't swallowed it yet."

"Why not?"

"I can't go into it."

"What can you go into?"

"These things can take time. They tend to move at their own pace. You know that."

"Why do I get the feeling that I ran an errand for you and you're not going to reciprocate?"

"You'll get what you want but I can't give you a play by play, Dave. There are too many moving parts right now."

"Let's play twenty questions. Yes or no. Prewitt is not in this alone, yes or no."

"The way you phrased it I could answer either way and be right and wrong."

"So he is not alone and you're watching the other players."

"Yes."

"Justice is still going after him about skimming Oak Ridge cleanup money."

"Yes."

Dave's heart was beating. He had thrown it out on a guess.

"Prewitt is linked to the assassination of Judge Beechum."

"Looks like a duck, yes. No firm evidence."

"We already know who the shooter was."

"We've gone over that."

"So, how long before everybody is vacuumed up?"

"We stop here."

"You know this is going to get out. My guess is newsrooms around the city are already sniffing this out and it's only a matter of time before it turns up in the

Post or the Times. There are too many odors coming off this."

"I'll give you a tip. Prewitt's going away to get some rest for a few days. Some place in West Virginia. Then, tanned and rested, he will go home to Tennessee to do some maintenance on the good folks who keep him in office. You won't see him until then. His people are putting him on ice to keep him from going off the deep end which, I might add, was where he was headed after your very successful visit." Ossening had a big smile on his face.

"I assume, and you don't have to confirm this, that you guys are watching and listening at his every move."

"We don't talk about such things."

"You don't have to. Everybody knows."

"If you say so."

"I need to file on this. I need something to advance the story. I'm spending too much time in shadows having meetings like this. If I reported what I know the lid would blow off this town, to use a cliché from the thirties."

"You'd get your ass sued and you know it."

"Maybe, but the suit would force the suers to offer some evidence that I'm wrong."

"How hard to you think it would be for the F.B.I. to do that? For God's sake, Dave, Oak Ridge is a national security facility. Probably the highest value real estate we have. We make the bomb there. You won't get far with an open records request, I'll tell you that. Hang tight. You'll get what you want." Ossening offered Dave his best F.B.I. face, the one that's supposed to be both reassuring and dominating.

"You guys are a piece of work. How much psychology do they teach you at Quantico?"

"Nothing you can't handle." Ossening laughed. "Listen, how about this? You can report that investigators believe they know the identity of the shooter and are pursuing all leads to his or her whereabouts."

"Her?"

"Why not? The guy might have had a sex change in the last day or so."

"You want me to help flush him out, don't you. If that's the case, why the "her" bullshit. I'll say you know the identity of the man and he'll know you're on to him and make a dash for safety or whatever you want him to do."

"Hey, it's your story. Just don't report how we know and where he lives or anything like that."

"Where does he live?"

"Off the record? He's one of Prewitt's constituents. That's all I can say. One more reason to be careful when you make your little trip south. You might want to pass that on to your boss, otherwise, mum's the word, as they used to say." Ossening stood up, dropped his coffee cup into a receptacle, and walked away.

Dave took his phone out of his shirt pocket and checked to see if it had recorded the conversation. He played back a portion of it to check the quality. He would not use any of it on the air but he would listen for cues as to what he could use in his reporting. The playback was picked up at the monitoring station on the farm and within minutes Ossening was aware that his talk with Dave had been recorded. He remembered the slogan of his field intelligence unit in the army: *Savoir C'est Pouvoir*. Knowledge is power. He smiled and went to see his boss.

Chapter Twenty-one

Washington news was thin. Capitol Hill reporters were churning angles on the Congressional gridlock that kept the people's business at bay. The Pentagon was pushing press releases about how well the new policy toward gays was being received by the troops. The State Department was doing its diplomatic contortionist best to avoid saying anything of substance. The White House was attempting to suck up whatever air was left in the press room. A normal day.

Dave's report that the federal and local investigators working to solve the assassination of Judge Beechum had identified the shooter became big news, if only because it was the only thing that could reasonably be classified as "news" from Washington. Dave was careful not to identify his sources but everyone assumed it was either the D.C. police department or the F.B.I. Maybe both. He was also careful not to go beyond his agreement with Ossening, which meant he didn't say that the shooter lived in Tennessee or might have a link to Congressman Prewitt and the ongoing Justice Department investigation into Prewitt's sticky and crooked fingers.

He filed several versions for radio, did a television interview with the public TV service that fed Now News stations, put up a Q and A on the website with links to Facebook. And, new to him, he tweeted a link to the Now News site where his picture and video were waiting to be viewed. He missed the days when a radio reporter filed for radio and went home. But, as Jim Russell, the Program Doctor, had said, it's not radio anymore, it's "audio". And video. And digital. Maybe next would be standing on a corner and yelling it out.

It wasn't long before the phones rang with calls for Dave, either to be interviewed by other news services or from other reporters wanting to pump him for information about his sources. He did the interviews and blew off the attempts to get him to betray himself.

Elena had spent the day getting back into her work routine, doing telephone interviews, editing them, calling news sources and doing the work that makes news desks run. She began the day with a good feeling about her relationship with Dave and ended it feeling miserable and defeated. He was being Dave and she felt sick about it. So much for coming in from the street. She could see on his face the thrill of the hunt and the joy he felt at being the center of attention on a big story. Despite herself, she agreed to wait for him to share a cab back to his place. She didn't know if she had the stomach for a fight. She still felt tender.

Captain O'Neil saw Dave on the television news program he was watching in his hospital room and knew what Ossening was up to. He sent a text to him. "keep me informed." Five minutes later his phone beeped and he read, "roger that."

Congressman Prewitt watched at home as he was packing for his visit to the Greenbrier, the storied West Virginia luxury resort where the U.S. government was to be housed in the event of a nuclear attack in Washington during the Cold War. Members of Congress were regular visitors and were always eager to take their guests through the fabled bunker where eleven-hundred people could be sheltered in relative comfort following a nuclear holocaust. These days it's a tourist attraction. No one believes anymore that there would be any comfort after a nuclear attack, but in the 1950s, as school children were being told they could survive a nuclear bomb by hiding under their desks, the bunker seemed like a good idea.

Prewitt had been there many times and was known by the staff. He would be flattered and catered to and given all the privacy he wanted. He looked forward to the golf, the luxury, the hiking, and the peace. He was in a good mood until he saw Dave on television telling the world that the F.B.I. and everyone else knew who shot Judge Beechum. Did they also knew who hired the man? Prewitt ran to the bathroom and threw up. He grabbed his bag and went to his car. He stopped at a convenience store and threw his cellphone into the trash and bought a prepaid phone and stuck in his glove compartment. He didn't plan to call anyone but if there was an emergency he would have a phone. He felt better. At least the F.B.I. wouldn't be listening in on his calls.

Edward Segal was at a dumpy, low rent motel in Hagerstown, an independent that accepted cash with no questions about license plate numbers and IDs. The place was one step above homeless. It was a place where the down and out, the out of control, the mildly criminal and the boozed-and-drugged out could get some rest, if they were still up to it. He asked for a got an end room that backed up to some woods that led to a trailer park two hundred yards away, where other low renters were holed up higher on the pole. The dumpster was just outside his door but he didn't mind. It was still cool enough at night that the trash didn't have much of an odor. The location would give him a decent escape route if he needed it.

He walked around the motel building looking for signs of trouble. Most of his fellow residents were old and worn out. The men hadn't shaved or paid much attention to their appearance in some time and the women didn't seem to care. They were balloons that had lost their air. They sat in plastic chairs outside their rooms and smoked and drank fortified wine out of paper bags. When Segal looked into their eyes, he didn't detect much going on inside. Their faces were blank. It was what he was hoping for. He was just another face in the crowd. He didn't say anything to them and none of them offered so much as a greeting.

He stayed outside until the chill raised the pain level in his stump. He hated small motel rooms and he felt trapped in them. His had only one way out. He cleaned and loaded an M9A1 nine millimeter Beretta, the army's standard-issue handgun. He oiled the fifteen rounds he inserted into the magazine. He had learned to minimize the risk of the gun jamming when he needed it. It had served him well. He cleaned and loaded his M4 carbine. It would not be good for distance but it would be lethal in a close combat situation. He had a thousand rounds of the new M855A1 bullets, designed for combat in Afghanistan, where accuracy and lethality were the currency of the day. He opened his bag and removed his U.S. Army body armor, put it on, and lay down on the bed. He turned out the lights and waited in the dark for his senses to kick in. He mind would not calm. He saw the heads of those he shot exploding. He saw his friends blown apart by IEDs. He felt the shock of looking down and seeing his foot gone and feeling no pain. He felt the bed spin and knew he had to find a way to calm himself.

Segal turned on the light and searched for the remote that would bring the television to life. He pressed the power button and saw the introduction to the eleven o'clock news and there was the face of Dave Haggard.

"A Washington-based reporter for a public broadcasting service is reporting tonight that investigators have identified the man who shot and killed Federal Judge Alexander Beechum. Dave Haggard, in the news earlier this year for his role in the hunt for the serial killer of Catholic priests, is reporting tonight that the killer of Judge Beechum is being sought by the F.B.I. and local police. The suspect's name has not been released." The anchorwoman played a short clip of Dave offering some background on the judge's murder.

Segal lay back and took deep, slow breaths. He had been tipped that they knew who he was but this was a new wrinkle. They were going public to flush him out. Next, they would identify him and put his picture on television and ask anyone who has seen him to call the police. It was all so predictable. Segal had to admit that it usually worked. Even the zombies who resided at this seedy motel would recognize his photo if they saw it on television five minutes after he walked by.

The question he faced was whether to leave now and hope his face had faded by the time it went public or wait until then and make a run for it. Where would he go? He had been warned not to go home and even if he did the meth lab guys in the hills near his house would sell him out for a dime. His passport was still good so maybe he could head for Costa Rica. Maybe the cops were waiting for his passport to be run by a scanner so they could pick him up. He needed to think. He rolled a joint and waited for it to hit him, then he slipped into a shallow sleep.

Sometime before dawn he was awakened by yelling in the room next to his and a pounding on the wall that separated the two rooms. Two of the low-end residents were having sex and fighting at the same time. He wondered how low a man had to get before he would have sex with the woman in that room. He guessed that she had less than a half dozen teeth and most of her hair was gone, along with whatever sense she might once have possessed. Her man wasn't much better. His eyes looked in different directions and one of his ears had been torn off. He tried to imagine them locked in a sexual embrace and burst out laughing. Would they remember the man in the next room? Shooting them would cause more problems than it would solve, so he tried to go back to sleep, which took a while, given the noise through the wall.

Chapter Twenty-two

"A name! We need a goddam name, Dave!" Sid was loud but he wasn't red in the face, so Dave understood that there was some theater in it. "It's great that you got a nice little scoop on a slow news day but every reporter in this city is knocking on every door looking for a name."

"Ossening's not budging on this, not right now. He's sitting on it, like a fisherman letting out his line."

"Jesus, what a crappy metaphor. You're a better writer than that." Sid laughed and took a sip of coffee. "Try O'Neil. He might offer it for public consumption. This idea that just by reporting that the cops know who did the shootings won't shake this guy out of the trees. If he's a pro he'll know what's going on and he won't be flushed out until his picture is on television. Even that won't do it if he's holed up in some backwoods cabin eating squirrels. I don't like Ossening and this thing has a smell to it. See if you can get him in here for a meeting. If he doesn't want to come here I'll go to him. I need to talk to this guy in person."

There was a knock on the door and the news desk manager, a man named Gabriel, opened it a crack. "Dave, you have a call. You might want to take it. It's a guy at AP."

Sid pushed his phone across the desk. Dave picked up the handset and pushed the blinking light. "Dave Haggard."

"Hey, Dave. It's Bill Adams at AP. I worked with Peter Deutch on D.C. stuff. I've got his story files to see what needs to be followed up. Any chance we can grab a cup of coffee today?"

Dave wanted to say something to the effect that the last time he had coffee with a reporter from AP the guy had his head blown off, but he thought better of it. "I'm open."

"I'm in the lobby of your building. I'll meet you in the shop down here."

"Yeah, I'll be right down." Dave put the receiver down and looked at Sid. "Bill Adams at AP wants to meet right now. He's downstairs."

Sid waved at the door and turned to his computer screen and scanned the wires.

Bill Adams was younger than Dave, who pinned him to his mid twenties. That meant he was smart, probably an Ivey Leaguer, a good writer, and knew someone who knew someone at AP. He had the eager I'm-pretty-smart expression of young men who believe they are going someplace in life. He had a smooth face and was showing early signs of male pattern baldness. He wore khaki pants and a blue blazer, which identified him as a group thinker in Dave's mind.

"Hi, Dave. Nice to meet you."

"Yeah, you too." Dave thought Adams had a weak handshake.

They stood in silence while they waited for their lattes and found a table along the wall.

"What's up?" Dave asked.

"I heard your report about the cops identifying the killer of Judge Beechum and, I assume, Peter Deutch. As you no doubt understand, we have a special interest in this guy at the AP."

"We all do."

"I don't suppose you got a name out of your sources."

"Is that why you're here? Every reporter in the city is after the name, including me."

"Does the name Edward Segal ring a bell?"

Dave looked at Adams and took a moment to gather his thoughts. "Who's he?"

"I thought you might be able to help me on that."

"Doesn't ring a bell. Where did you get it?"

"I believe from a mutual acquaintance."

"Feds?"

"Yup. Peter had Milford Ossening's name in his file of sources. He kept it under lock and key, meaning in a locked file on his computer. Our IT guys got in and it was handed to me. I started calling them and most of them said they didn't know why Peter had their name anywhere. Not unexpected, I suppose. But this guy Ossening wants to meet me face to face. He doesn't say much but he gives me the name of Edward Segal and tells me to call you for the background. Here I am."

"Like I said, I never heard the name."

"But you know who he is, don't you." Adams got a frat boy grin on his face. "He's the shooter."

"I have no idea. Do you have any proof?"

"I can connect the dots, if that's what you mean."

"Maybe you have something you can run with but a name thrown out by Ossening or anyone else doesn't link this name to anything. Hell, he could be Ossening's brother in law."

"We'd like to work a deal with you. My editor wants to share the story. We work it together and we break it together."

"Maybe he should call my boss this deal."

"She. It's a she."

"Okay, she should call my boss."

"Who will ask you what you think. So, what do you think?"

"Not much. I'm ass deep in this and I've a lot of time into it. It's a little late to play sharesees."

"We have a lot in this, too. One of our guys got killed."

"So I understand. I worked with Peter on some stories and it worked out because we knew each other and trusted each other. I don't know you."

"Think about it." Adams got up and tossed his cup into a trash can. He walked out without looking back.

Arrogant prick! Dave thought, throwing his cup away.

Sid was waiting when Dave returned to the New News newsroom and waved him into his office. "So?"

"I think this guy Adams is an asshole."

"His boss is nice. I met her at a Press Club thing. She's sharp and she knows he's a young buck who's got lots of ambition. I told her we'd leave it open and keep in touch."

"I told him to go fuck himself."

"Take a deep breath. The AP got you a name that you can try out on your sources and the AP won't do anything with it because they don't really have anything to tie it to. But the clock is running, Dave."

"I'll go see O'Neil. Maybe somebody here can work the Web for something on Segal."

"Elena's on it. My guess is the AP will have a profile of the guy by the close of business."

"Elena's good. So will we. All we have to do is pin him to the shootings."

"Then there's Ossening. He's playing you and Adams and probably a half dozen other reporters, throwing out bread crumbs here and there and laughing his ass off while everybody scrambles around like kids after candy."

"You've got some shitty metaphors of your own, Sid."

"Fuck you. Get out."

O'Neil was sitting up sucking on a straw when Dave walked in. He looked alert but drawn and exhausted. His eyes revealed he expected a visit from Dave.

"Well, enjoying some find hospital nutrition," Dave said, sitting on the side of the bed.

O'Neil made an animal noise through his wired teeth, put down his cup and picked up his notepad. "Segal?"

"You're ahead of me."

"He's the guy," O'Neil wrote. "Army. Iraq sniper. Pro."

"Tennessee?" Dave asked.

O'Neil nodded.

"Do you know where I can get a photo?"

"Search online. I can't." O'Neil was writing fast and Dave had trouble reading the words.

"Can I use you as a source?

"No name."

"Now that we have that out of the way, how are you?"

"Going home tomorrow. Six weeks." He pointed at his mouth.

"May I visit you at home?"

O'Neil nodded. "I have more. Come to my home."

Dave was back at Now News by five o'clock and was at a work station writing his story when Elena sent him a top-of-the-line message on the in-house text system. "I have a photo of Segal."

An hour later Now News Television was feeding stations the photo with Dave's report. It was on every news outlet in the country a half an hour after that, along with Dave's picture. The AP ran a long story on the wires that claimed the ID and credited Now News with some background material.

Cole was at his office watching the news and threw a glass at his television, shattering the flat screen. Prewitt was on his way to West Virginia and was listening to a Beach Boys CD, so he missed the news until the next morning, when he picked up a paper and saw Segal's face on the front page.

Edward Segal saw it on the late news, packed, and left.

The couple in the next room did not remember what he looked like other than he was a white guy with a limp. Or maybe a Mexican. It was dark.

Chapter Twenty-three

Segal was having one of his spells. He was confused and angry and had to fight to concentrate on the road and the lane lines. He was travelling south on I-81, a north-south route running from Upstate New York to East Tennessee. Segal picked it up at Hagerstown and headed south, crossing the Potomac River into West Virginia for twenty-six miles before travelling into Virginia and the long, three hundred mile journey down the Shenandoah Valley and into the mountains of Southwest Virginia and Tennessee.

I-81 is primarily a truck route moving products and produce and travelers are advised to be alert as they weave in and out of caravans of tractor-trailers loaded with everything from parts to pigs. Segal began to panic as he imagined the dangers lurking in the big rigs. In Iraq he had seen the enemy attack the supply trucks, blowing them up, shooting the drivers, and dying bloody deaths with their parts all over the road. He was breathing hard as he fought to control himself, imagining jihadists disgorging from the tractor trailers and killing everyone they found. He drove onto the shoulder and nearly ran into the muddy median while another driver honked at him. He managed to pull off at a rest stop and sat in his truck as he composed himself. His hands were shaking and he needed to go to the bathroom to empty his bowels. A young boy with a plastic rifle ran by making "bang bang" noises and he dropped his head to the passenger seat, shouting for everyone to get down. The boy walked over to stare through the window at him and said, "There's something wrong with this man," to his father, who came to get the boy.

"He's just tired. Leave him be."

Segal managed to get to the bathroom and do his business without attracting more attention and he was outwardly composed when he stepped out, lighting a cigarette. He watched the families and the truckers taking their breaks from the road and felt his breathing return to normal. A truck driver walked past him and brushed up against him.

The driver gave Segal a dirty look. "You're in the way," he said. "You're blocking the door." The driver was a bear of a man, taller than Segal, with a shaggy beard and a big belly. He wore a baseball hat backwards and looked like a man who was used to bullying others. "What the fuck is wrong with you?"

For Segal it was a blasting cap that set him off. "Fuck you," he said, waiting for the big man to move in. The driver obliged, leaning in to say something. The brass knuckles connected where the man's nose met his upper lip, caving in the middle of his face, sending blood and snot into the air. The big man fell, moaning and still. A man and his son were walking to the men's room and stopped to look at Segal and the driver. "This guy tried to rob me. I'm going to call the police," he said, going back to his truck. He drove to Route 11 and found a road heading east and was in the Washington suburbs by dawn. His trip to Tennessee would wait. He had some business to attend to.

Wisconsin Avenue through Bethesda was backed up at the Walter Reed National Military Medical Center, a merged version of the old Walter Reed, once located on Georgia Avenue in D.C., and Bethesda Naval Medical Center, the Navy's premier hospital. The new facility was created as a cost saving measure but overruns and the usual miscalculations had long since thrown any savings away. Now, an explosive increase in staff and visitors to the new, larger medical center had made traffic a nightmare. Segal was stuck in it and his panic had returned.

It took three cycles before he could move through the light at Jones Bridge Road and down to Bradley Boulevard, where he turned right and drove into a residential area that gave way to large lots, mansions, and gates that kept the riffraff at bay. Partners at big law firms, heads of defense contractors, developers, media stars, and lobbyists lived in the grand houses surrounded by hundred foot trees.

Cole's house was tucked up a long, curving drive and was approached by navigating terraces that allowed a series of fountains to flow into a koi pond at the bottom. Spring flowers added color and the budding trees provided a gauzy green backdrop as Segal approached. He had left his truck in the parking area of a private boy's school with a handwritten note on the windshield that said "grounds cleanup." No one would bother the truck, assuming he was part of the seasonal effort to spruce up the place.

Getting over Cole's fence, even with a prosthetic leg, was not a problem. The fancy wrought iron fence was along the street and was intended to make a statement to those driving by. The back of the lot, heavily treed, was marked by a four foot chain link fence that had begun to rust. Segal moved through the trees along the property line to the house next door and made his way through the evergreen bushes that were part of the landscaping for the fountains. He knew that Cole had an alarm system but he guessed that it would be off as Cole went about his morning routine. He saw him sitting in his kitchen, wearing a silk robe, drinking coffee, and reading the Post. His picture was on the front page above the fold. Cole was staring at it.

Segal sat on the ground against the house and re-viewed his options. He could wait until Cole walked out and take him then, or he could knock on the door and smash his face in when he answered. He did not want Cole to have a chance to call the police or anyone else. The key was surprise. One quick look into Segal's eyes for a moment of panic, then the blow from the brass knuckles and oblivion. He smiled. He wanted a cigarette but he didn't dare light up. Cole might smell it and be-come alarmed. Segal wanted him to feel safe and secure in his nice, big house.

He had a moment of doubt when he realized that he could no longer remember why he was there, but it passed when he imagined his pleasure when Cole's face caved in. He had lost the reason for it but not the sense of mission. It was like Iraq. Go there, kill him, get out.

Cole was looking at Segal's picture on the front page of the Post and reviewing his options. Segal's use-fulness was over, past, done. He had made some calls. It would not be easy. Segal was too well respected to make it easy. Even men who had no qualms about taking lives balked at the assignment. No, he had to find someone who had never heard of Segal and wouldn't care if they had. Such men were out there. He knew that soon he would hear from them. Prewitt was another matter. *What an idiot. How did this guy get elected to Congress?* He laughed out loud. The place was full of idiots. It was easy to manipulate them. Wave some money wrapped in the flag and they would do anything he asked. Prewitt would be a touchy move. People ask questions when a member of Congress is killed. It is better to find ways to send them to jail. In Prewitt's case, that was easy. Get-ting him to keep his mouth shut would be harder, but not impossible. Everyone has something they want to pro-tect.

The day was going to be nice, he could feel it. The sun was coming through the French doors and warming the kitchen. Tulips were abloom in the garden. The grass was green again. *Life is good.* He poured a fresh cup of coffee and walked out onto his stone patio. He had imported the workmen from Italy and the intricate stonework was the envy of his neighbors, who noticed such things. The songbirds were back with their music in the trees. A small dun colored bird was building a nest in the awning. He looked to the sky and allowed the sun to warm his face. *Life is a balance. For every dark moment there is a lighter one.* His money made him popular among a certain class of ladies in the capital, those who were excited by power. Even as women rose in influence and power on their own, these ladies were interested in other things. Things from expensive stores. Cole had his pick of them. He shied away from commitment and confined himself to arm candy. He was a man who indulged in a deep and gratifying self-congratulation at moments like this.

He opened his eyes and shouted, "I am hot shit!"

Then he looked into the eyes of Edward Segal, who was smiling. Cole opened his mouth to ask why Segal was there but the brass knuckles cut short his question. Minutes later Cole's shattered skull lay in a large puddle of blood on the expensive Italian stonework. The blood followed the drain lines designed to channel rainwater to the flowers.

Segal wanted to spit on Cole but worried that it would give police easy access to his DNA, so grabbed a handful of dirt and threw it down on the body.

"This is for everybody who can't be here to piss on you," he said.

He used a garden hose to wash the blood off his boots and walked through the woods to his truck. An hour later he was stuck in traffic on the Beltway at Tyson's Corner, where construction had caused backups for years. *Who can live in a place like this?* he wondered.

Cole's body was not discovered until the next day, when a woman from a cleaning service arrived for her weekly duties. Montgomery County police issued a press release theorizing that Cole had interrupted a burglar. It would be two more days before Ossening got wind of the details and asked an F.B.I. forensics expert to examine the body. Cole's wounds were consistent with an expert using brass knuckles. The expert also opined that it could have been another object such as thin metal rod. Ossening put the killing file into his thickening folder on Edward Segal. He had the link to Prewitt and Segal. It was coming together.

Chapter Twenty-four

Congressman Prewitt was fighting hysteria. He lay on the bed and tried to catch his breath. He thought about grabbing a plastic bag from the waste basket and putting it over his head, either to calm himself or smother, he didn't care which. It had never occurred to him that something like this could happen. After all, it was just a little caper, a skimming, a small piece of a very big pie. How could it come to this? Prewitt had never put much effort or risk into anything in his life, given the status he had been born into. He made whimpering noises, like a small child in a closet, hiding from monsters. His legs shook and made the bed vibrate. At that moment he was like a toddler throwing a tantrum.

He remained on the bed for most of the morning, making his strange noises and flapping his hands and feet. A housekeeper knocked on his door and he calmed himself enough to tell her he didn't need his bed made or any clean towels. That small connection with another human being gave him enough presence of mind to sit up, which led to a bathroom break and a drink of water. That was enough to get his mind working, although he could not have been described as rational.

Cole was dead. Cole was murdered. Cole had hired a murderer to kill Judge Beechum, who was also dead. Dave Haggard was not dead. The killer had gone after Cole, not Dave. What did that mean? Was the killer coming for him? How could that be? He was a member of Congress. People don't kill members of Congress, for God's sake! Okay, there was that incident in Arizona but the shooter was nuts. This shooter is a professional kill-er. He knows how to find people.

Prewitt paced his room, ignoring the glorious mountain views out his window. He no longer had the stomach for a stay in this beautiful place. He could barely stand to be alive. He needed a plan. He grabbed a notepad with the Greenbrier logo on it and a courtesy pen. He sat at the desk and wrote "situation" at the top of the page. Then he wrote the number "1" and quickly added "life threatened". He added "2" and wrote "how to get the money". He sat back and stared at the page. Nothing else came to mind. He was probably being hunted by a professional killer and he had no idea how to get the money, his share, of the scheme to skim the Oak Ridge cleanup.

He occurred to him that they had all been too clever for their own good. Cole had insisted that he be the only one who knew the names of the others on the "council", the group of men and women who would implement and benefit from the scheme. "If they grab one of us they can't get the rest of us," he had said. "People inform on everyone else when the feds grab them. If you don't know who to rat out, you can't do it. We're all safer that way." No one bothered to ask what happened if the only guy who knows everyone else gets killed.

Did the council know about Cole's hiring of the killer? Maybe the killer is one of the council members! His thoughts ran wild with possibilities. He had to get the list. He had to get to Cole's house and find the list. *Yes! That's it! I'll go there and look around until I find it. I'll contact the others and we can move ahead without all this trouble.* He believed that Cole had been the source of their problems and now that he was gone it was good news, not bad. *This whole thing will go away once we get back on track.*

He felt better. He felt in charge again. *I'm not where I am because I'm stupid. I'm a member of the ruling class and I should never forget that.* He showered, dressed, and went to lunch in the dining room, enjoying a fine glass of wine with his fish and salad. After lunch he checked out and drove back to Washington. As he approached the Roosevelt Bridge from Arlington into the city he felt elated and it was all he could do to keep from shouting with joy as he drove onto Constitution Avenue past the Lincoln Memorial. Tourists were snapping pictures and disappearing down the walkway to the Vietnam Veterans Memorial. He drove past the statue of Albert Einstein where children were sitting on his lap, laughing as their parents snapped souvenir photos. *All is right with the world. It's going to be fine.* He went to his office and joked with the staff. He met with several aids and discussed legislation and party issues. He went home and watched the news and learned that Cole's home had been sealed by police. He could wait. He gave no further thought to the assassin Cole had hired. He drank an entire bottle of Tennessee whiskey and passed out in his chair.

Edward Segal was in a cheap by-the-month motel in Front Royal, Virginia. The clerk, a kid wearing a "Shit Happens" tee-shirt, didn't even look up as Segal paid in cash. Now, Segal was watching the news on the set in his room. He, too, was experiencing a moment of peace. He wanted some time to think.

Ossening was at Cole's house with an F.B.I. forensics team when Dave arrived. "Hello there, Ace." The agent had a smile on his face.

"Finding anything?"

"We don't comment on ongoing investigations."

"Then why did you invite me here?"

"I wouldn't call it an invitation. It was more of a suggestion. There's a difference."

"If you say so. Any other reporters on your suggestion list?"

"Not that I see at the moment. Come with me." Ossening motioned for Dave to follow him into the woods behind Cole's house. "The guy came in from over there." He gestured to the corner where the rusty chain link fence's top bar was slightly bent. "He came over the fence, probably from the school."

"Okay. Then what?"

"Cole was drinking coffee in his bathrobe, so he was outside on a beautiful spring morning taking the air when Segal hit him. That's how I read it."

"So it's Edward Segal."

"Looks like it. Just between us girls, I'd say Segal has changed teams, probably because he's figured out that his usefulness is over and they'll be after him next. Taking out Cole means he went after the guy who hired him and who would, presumably, be the guy who would hire the hit man to go after Segal. Live by the sword, as they say." Ossening watched Dave's reaction.

"Where does this leave Prewitt?"

"Well, if I were the good gentleman from Tennessee I'd be looking to take a vacation in Bora Bora."

"Are you protecting him?"

"You can assume we are keeping an eye on him."

"In more ways than one."

"Very clever. The real question for you is what Segal's change of plan means for Dave Haggard. He tried to shoot you once and missed. Will he try it again or has he lost interest. We've got some of our behavioral people at Quantico trying to figure this guy out. I'll let you know if they come up with bad news for you. Right now I'd say he's very dangerous and unstable. That means he could do anything. We're getting calls from all over the place after the media coverage but so far we don't have, ah, what's the current term? Anything actionable, that's it. We don't have information that's actionable."

"So you're chasing a bunch of limping bums that might look like Segal."

"Yeah, that's it. Limping bums. America is awash in them, as it turns out."

"Are you getting anything in there?" Dave pointed to the house.

"He kept everything on flash drives and he had them stashed all over the place. We're sending them to the lab in West Virginia. It will take a few days. We'll have to separate his porn from his client lists." Ossening offered his best F.B.I. chuckle, the one that contained no mirth.

"So, why was it suggested that I come by here?"

"We'd like you to get Segal's face out again and maybe suggest that sources close to the investigation now believe that Cole was not the victim of a burglar. His killing has been linked to the assassination of Judge Beechum and the murder of Peter Deutch. How's that for a scoop?"

Dave was stunned. "You're going public with this? Beechum to me to Cole? Same guy. Prewitt's fingerprints on the story?"

"I didn't say anything about Prewitt. I said Beechum and Cole with the Deutch sidebar, as you call it."

"May I ask why you're doing this?"

"Same old thing, Dave. You're the beater who gets the quail to fly. And for that you get the journalistic glory."

"I'm feeling like the whore whose client is saying 'I'm about to have the best sex of my life'."

"I wouldn't describe myself as your client, but the rest fits, in my view. It's very important, and I can't stress this enough, that my fingerprints are nowhere to be found on this. As far as I'm concerned we're both getting something out of this. If you fuck me, it's a new ballgame. Are we clear?"

"You're a source close to the investigation."

"I want you to use the words sources, not source. And if you've recorded this on your phone I'll know about it before you hit playback."

"How do you know that?"

"We're the F.B.I., Dave."

"Is that a threat?"

"We don't make threats, Dave. It's just a bit of information." Ossening walked back to the house, leaving Dave at the tree line. He took his phone out of his shirt pocket and wondered how to erase the voice memo he had just recorded without bringing the F.B.I. down on his head. He would ask the Now News IT department to look at it.

Chapter Twenty-five

Arnott Cole had been known as a kingmaker in Washington and had become a political legend after he told a national television audience that campaign finance reform had lowered the cost of "buying a member of Congress." He added, for good measure, "and once they're bought, they stay bought." That, he said, was why he was against term limits.

Cole was not well liked. He had few, if any, real friends in Washington and his death was met with relief in some quarters. He had spread great sums of dollars around the city and had received what he had purchased either in legislation or other favors, so his accounts were considered balanced by most of the men and women he dealt with. More than a few of his "clients" had a small laugh at the fact that he had been beaten to death.

Dave Haggard's report that Cole had been killed by a professional assassin only added importance to his legacy. After all, so the thinking went, if he was important enough to have been assassinated he must have been a very big deal indeed. In the twisted logic of such things, a few well-suited types were envious. That Cole had not, in fact, been assassinated was a point missed. But clarification would come later.

The calls to Now News resumed with other news organizations asking that Dave appear for interviews or asking who his sources were. He declined them all. He did radio, television, Internet, and every other outlet presented to him that had a connection to Now News. The

Post ran the original image of Segal next to one from Dave on its front page above the fold.

Bill Adams at AP called and wanted to meet. Dave put him off. Congressman Prewitt's office called and passed along an invitation to have lunch with the Member. Dave accepted. Edward Segal watched the news in his cheap motel room and laughed.

Dave met Prewitt in one of Capitol Hill's A-list watering holes, a clubby, white tablecloth place with ancient wood paneling and photographs of long-ago power mongers on the walls. It was easy to crack the social code in such establishments. Those who were up had a look of self-satisfaction on their faces. Those who were down looked worried. A recently disgraced House member sat at a low prestige table and looked as though he would cry, even as his colleagues stopped to pat him on the back and tell him he'd be all right. Such assurances were seen as last rites.

Prewitt was all smiles at a table near the center wall, a mid-to-high prestige spot. Leadership got the best tables and freshman and disgraced members got the worst. Dave thought the pecking order was a lot like high school, with the leadership taking the role of football stars.

"Good to see you, boy," Prewitt said, offering his hand. "Have a seat, please."

Dave read the Southern code and recognized that Prewitt was offering the same greeting that would have been offered by a Jim Crow racist to a black man from whom he wanted something.

"How are you, Congressman?"

"Couldn't be better. Here, take a look at the menu. The crab soufflé here is something else. And it goes well with sweet tea for us Southern boys." Prewitt handed Dave a hand-written menu that contained a short list of the day's dining options.

"That sounds fine." Dave's alarm bells were going off. "What can I do for you?"

Prewitt sat back with a false look of alarm. "Why Dave, I didn't ask you here for a favor. I just wanted to mend fences after our unpleasantness in the past. I hope you don't think I have an ulterior motive. It's nice to get together with someone from back home now and then."

It occurred to Dave at that moment that everything that would follow would be a lie. "Why that's wonderful, sir. I would like that."

"Wasn't that awful about Mr. Cole. I surely hate to see something like that happen to any man." Prewitt offered a sincere look of regret.

"It sure was," Dave said. "Beaten to death like that."

"I wonder why police changed their minds about the burglar theory." Prewitt's voice had a false note of distraction as though he really didn't care but was just making conversation.

"I think once the F.B.I. got involved they had more access to forensic science."

"So, do you think Cole's killing was linked to the assassination of Judge Beechum?"

"That's what I'm told."

"Hmmm. I swear. What a world we live in."

They ate in silence, with each man waiting for the other to offer a direction in the conversation. Dave had to admit that Prewitt was right. The crab soufflé was excellent. A waiter removed the plates and the tea was replenished. The men smiled at each other. Lunch was ending and the men and women in the power suits were leaving and returning to the business of governing in a gridlocked Congress.

Dave recalled the old lawyers' saw that he who speaks first loses. He thought it was a load of crap. "So, any plans to go home to see the folks?"

"I need to get down there, no doubt about that. This place can change your thinking and pollute the mind. It's not like where we come from, Dave. Here there's treachery and deceit. Back home folks are honest and straightforward. I need some of that now and then."

"May I ask an unpleasant question?"

Prewitt put on a wounded face. "Aw, must you?"

"Have you heard anything from Justice?"

"Not a word. There's nothing there, Dave."

"Do you have a lawyer?"

"I am a lawyer."

"In this town even lawyers have lawyers."

"Off the record? I've had conversations that were the result of all of the vicious and unfounded rumors and, frankly, some of your comments. Nothing official."

"Who's your lawyer?"

"No, no. We're not going there." Prewitt's face returned to its natural arrogant state.

"Have you paid a retainer?"

"My financial matters are not your concern."

"So you have hired a lawyer."

"There are a thousand reasons why I might need legal counsel and not one of those reasons is any of your business."

"Have you or your attorney had any conversations with anyone at the Justice Department or the F.B.I.?"

"Again, none of your business."

"How well did you know Arnott Cole?"

Prewitt's face was red. "About as well as everyone else around here. He was well known. He had his picture taken with everyone in Washington. We were not friends, if that's what you're asking."

"When was the last time you talked to him?" Dave decided to go fishing.

"That's it! Lunch is over. It's time for you to leave!"

Bingo! Dave got up. "Thanks for lunch." He walked out and hailed a cab as it disgorged a gang of giggling businessmen and women who were in Washington lobbying for tax breaks. They seem excited to be there and happy to be eating in a place where "shit gets done", as one of them said. *Not really*, Dave thought. *Not the shit you think gets done.*

He walked into Now News and found a work station where he could listen to his lunch conversation with Prewitt and gather his thoughts. Prewitt wanted to pump him for his source on the link between Cole and the Beechum killing but he didn't have the guts to press Dave for it and that part of lunch went nowhere. On the other hand, Dave got Prewitt to confirm that he had hired an attorney, even though it was a roundabout way of doing it, and that was news, but he needed to work it through. The city's A-list defense lawyers, a very short list, would never divulge anything like that, so he had to work the edges. He'd start with Ossening, who, as usual, picked up after one ring.

"Our man has a lawyer," Dave said as an opening line.

"Who?"

"I was hoping you would tell me."

"Why would I know that?"

"Give me a break."

"Sorry. You'll have to do your own homework." The call ended.

He went through the computer system's phone list and called the top law firms in the city, beginning with Larson and Spang, home to Jerry Finegan, whose claim to fame was that he never lost a case in criminal court. Finegan was choosy and only took cases when he felt there was a reasonable chance of victory over the government and the client had at least a one-million dollar retainer. He had kept more than one member of Congress out of jail. He was a master of criminal law and had humiliated a small army of young federal prosecutors who went into court assuming that the government never loses.

"Hi, Dave Haggard calling Jerry Finegan."

The woman who answered the phone at Larson and Spang was used to reporters' calls. "Regarding?"

"It's personal."

"I'll connect you to his office."

There was silence on the line for five minutes and Dave thought the call had been cut off. He even wished Larson and Spang had cheesy music for callers on hold so they would know they were still there. He heard a click and a phone being picked up.

"Have you been arrested?" Finegan was on the line.

"You can't shoot anybody in this town anymore. How are you Mr. Finegan?"

"Never complain. Never explain. What can I do for you?" Dave heard other people in the room with Finegan.

"Congressman Prewitt says he has a lawyer. Anything to say?"

"Did he say it was me?"

"Is it?"

"I can't talk about my clients. You know that. Whatever you need you'll have to get it from him, not me. So I gather this is not a personal call after all."

"It is personal. It's just not personal for me." Dave hoped it sounded like a joke.

"Don't do this again, Dave. I have great respect for you and what you've been through and I've been following your reporting on what happened to Judge Beechum and all of these rumors, and they are just rumors, about Congressman Prewitt. But I can't be a source about anything for anyone. My clients are a sacred trust, Dave. All the best to you." The line went dead.

Dave was elated. It was as close to a confirmation as he could get without Finegan holding a news conference about it. But it was still unconfirmed. He was in the limbo that reporters enter when they know something to be true but they don't have the backup to use it. Sid's door opened and Elena walked out looking at a notebook. She passed his work station and he stroked her leg, causing her to look down, ready to slap him. She broke into her crooked smile.

"Well, look who's a pervert."

"Just for you. How are you?"

"Sid's given me a project. Got a lot of calls to make. How are you, Mr. Bigshot Reporter?"

"Busy. See you tonight?"

"Is there something in it for me?"

"That's what I'm thinking."

"Well, then, get to work."

He walked into Sid's office, sat down, and briefed him on the Prewitt story. Sid listened and stared at the ceiling. "You'll have to throw something at the wall to see what sticks. There's a risk. If you bounce Finnegan's name around town everybody will pick it up and somebody might get ahead of you on it. If you sit on it, it goes nowhere and sooner or later somebody will run with it. Call Ossening again and see if reacts to Finnegan's name. And try O'Neil. He's in everybody's loop. Maybe he's heard something."

Chapter Twenty-six

O'Neil lived in Charles County, a fast-growing outer suburb in southern Maryland. The county dates back to the 1600s and is best known as part of John Wilkes Booth's escape route after he shot Abraham Lincoln. New developments spread during the real estate boom that collapsed in 2008 and growth stopped for a time. Families moved to Charles County because housing was cheap by Washington area standards. Government workers liked it because they could afford the houses they wanted. Police officers liked it because it was cheap and still rural, meaning it was not gun shy.

O'Neil had lived Waldorf for ten years in a standard-issue Colonial with a two-car garage. He had an acre lot with a swing set and a metal storage shed in the back and a bald spot on his lawn where an above ground pool had been. He had planted some bargain bushes from a local nursery in the front of his house and they were scraggly and hidden by weeds as Dave walked up to the front door. He had rented a car from a company that provided a members-only service in D.C. It was cheap and convenient but the cars were a bright yellow/green and bore a company logo that was impossible to miss, even at highway speeds. Dave was embarrassed by the stares from other drivers.

O'Neil's wife was a pleasant-faced, red haired woman named Maureen who had gained a few pounds since her younger days. She had the look of a woman who accepted that one day she might get a visit from the police chaplain bearing very bad news.

"He's in the family room," she said by way of greeting. "Straight through."

Dave walked past the stairs, a small bathroom, a closet, and into a kitchen/family room area where O'Neil was resting in a recliner, watching Fox News on an oversized flat screen television. He waved at Dave to sit down on the sofa near him.

"Catching up on all the conservative news, I see."

O'Neil grabbed his notepad and wrote, "fair and balanced."

"Says you," Dave replied.

O'Neil tried to stifle a laugh. He wrote, "Finegan?"

"You're always ahead of me."

"Can't make official, yes. Unofficial." O'Neil's scratchy writing was messy and hard to make out.

"Let me take a stab at this. Prewitt's hired Finegan but it's still confidential until he needs him to step in and do what lawyers do."

O'Neil nodded and smiled.

"And certain law enforcement people know about it but they can't go public because they found out through unofficial means and it's not their job to make these announcements anyway."

O'Neil gave Dave a thumbs up.

"So we're on touchy legal ground here that involves wiretaps and other types of surveillance that get dicey under certain legal circumstances and might, one day, be grounds for appeal."

O'Neil write, "I'm not a lawyer."

"And if it became public knowledge that Prewitt had retained the city's top defense attorney it might be seen in some quarters as an admission that he's facing serious criminal charges which, in turn, could place him on the wounded list. In today's political climate the wounded are eaten. That would leave Prewitt as a carcass in the District without even a K Street lobbying firm to take him in. Stop me if I'm going too far."

O'Neil had a grin on his face. He wrote in small, hard to read letters, "I'm just a cop."

"Who knows everything about everyone."

O'Neil shrugged. "beer?" he wrote

"I have to drive back, but thanks."

"check court."

"Downtown?"

"maybe a filing. ?????"

"Will do. So, how are you?"

"bored."

"Are you going back to Homeland Security when you're well?"

"we'll see." O'Neil was smiling and Dave took that to mean he was looking forward to his days out of the wilderness.

The federal courthouse was closed when Dave got back to the city so he went back to Now News to brief Sid.

The sun was setting over the Potomac when Congressman Prewitt was escorted through the mail room of the 9th Street building where Jerry Finegan had his well-appointed office suite. Its corner windows faced south to the rooftops of the Smithsonian buildings and the Washington Monument slightly to the west. He was taken up the freight elevator to the tenth floor, where the hallway had been cleared. Finegan was waiting with a glass of Tennessee whiskey, neat.

"Good to see you, Congressman. Please, have a seat." He motioned to an overstuffed chair that was part of a grouping around an ornate fireplace that was cold. "We have some things to discuss."

Prewitt swallowed his whiskey in one gulp and held out his glass for another round. Finegan raised an eyebrow and poured about half an inch.

"The first question I have is what would you like me to do for you? The egg is going to crack, as they say. This reporter Dave Haggard, the one who's always in the news, called me to ask if you had retained me. Did you tell him that?"

"God no! He has sources all over the place and they tell him things he has no right to know. These so-called sources don't have the right to know either. It's disgusting."

"You know you're being monitored, don't you? Every call you make, probably your movements. I don't doubt that they have warrants to put GPS devices on your car. So, let me ask you, have you done or said anything to anyone that might have given the government ammunition in their investigation into your activities?"

"No, of course not."

"Allow me to be blunt. You have retained me as your attorney. I need to know the truth, all of it. The worst thing that can happen is a surprise that's very bad news because the client withheld important information, even if it's very bad information. Have I made myself clear?"

"What do you want from me?"

"Everything."

"I might have had a conversation with Arnott Cole recently when I was drunk and on sleeping pills. Maybe I said something things. They were just rants. I was not myself." Prewitt had the look of a dog in a corner.

"What kinds of things?" Finegan had been lied to by the very best and could smell a case going sour.

"Nothing important. I was acting, role playing, kind of like a guy who was under the gun and saying things just to get the guys on the wiretap excited." His right leg was shaking.

"Such as?"

"Jokes. Jokes about Judge Beechum and a hit man and a scheme to steal money from the government. Jokes. Nothing that was true. Just regular jokes, the kind you might hear in a bar."

Finegan sat back and studied Prewitt. He considered giving back the million dollar retainer. Skimming money, kickbacks, payments for access to power, these were all things that a skilled lawyer could maneuver and color. The schemes could be made to appear confusing and he-said-he-said before a jury, which could rationalize an acquittal. Murder was something entirely different. Murder of a federal judge was a ticket to the gurney and lethal injection. Finegan did not want a guilty verdict on such a charge to be on his gilded resume.

"So, if I were an F.B.I. agent listening in on this joke would I hear many details about this fabricated hit man?"

"I don't remember. I was drunk and out of my mind."

"And you have not heard anything official regarding this investigation other than what's been in the news?"

"Not officially, no. Like everyone else I've heard about this alleged investigation and the rumor that Justice went to Beechum for some authority, but, no, I haven't been notified that I'm a target."

"Frankly, I don't know what it means. It could mean the whole thing is nothing more than a rumor and it will die off. It could mean they came, they sniffed, they walked away. That might explain why you haven't been notified. My guess is they're being very careful to get their legal ducks in a row before they do anything to prevent me or anyone else from getting in the way. The federal prosecutors have almost unlimited power and leeway, despite what you hear about due process and all that. They can be quite nasty. They went after Senator Stevens of Alaska and nailed him before Brendan Sullivan got it overturned on prosecutorial misconduct. Most lawyers aren't as skillful as Sullivan. I like to think I am. But don't think that because you're a member of Congress they'll shy away from playing hard ball."

"What should we do?"

"We? You should stop this kind of joke-making, for one. Keep your mouth shut. Do not talk to anyone about anything other than normal Congressional business. Do not, for God's sake, talk to Dave Haggard or anyone else in the news media. Give me twenty-four hours to think about this. We'll talk tomorrow here. We'll see where we want to go." What he meant was where he wanted to go with the case, if anywhere at all.

Chapter Twenty-seven

Edward Segal bought oversized sunglasses, neglect-
ed to shave, and picked up a camouflage and orange
hunting cap with "Buck Fever" printed on the front. He
wore work boots and blue work clothes he bought at
Wal-Mart.. He looked like any other redneck with a
truck in that part of Virginia. Lined up, it would be hard
to pick him out of a dozen other men within two blocks
of the dump where he was living. That was the plan. He
would lie low while he tried to sort things out.

He spent his days walking in the nearby parks; the
Shenandoah National Park was a favorite, although he
was worried that one of the rangers would recognize
him. There were trails and riverbanks to explore and it
gave him peace. He liked the mountains because they
reminded him of his home in Tennessee and the people
had accents that rang true to his ears. They were solid,
Southern mountain people who were devoted to their
families, their churches, and their guns. Such people had
long provided America's wars with its best soldiers.
Segal felt bitterness at that, believing that it was Northern politicians who sent Southern boys to battle as cannon fodder.

The springtime was magical in the mountains. The
dogwoods and redbuds gave color to the hazy green of
the new growth on the trees. Cardinals and blue jays
added even more color and their songs made him smile.
As he grew closer to the land he grew angrier at those
whom he believed had soiled it and made it nothing

more than a money-making tragedy of sickness and death.

He went to an Internet café in Front Royal and spent an afternoon researching Oak Ridge, The Tennessee Valley Authority, and the history of Yankee crimes against the mountain South. Good intentions turned to poison. That's how he saw it. Why didn't they build the bomb up north? Let the Yankees deal with the mercury and the death. The hills of Vermont weren't poison, so why were the hills of Tennessee? His anger began to boil over and felt himself losing control again.

A college student out for a day of fresh air along the Appalachian Trail paid the price for Segal's blind anger. The young man died before he was found. His death was ruled a homicide but it was never closed. Segal spent the evening in his room, drinking beer and smoking weed, watching television. There was nothing on the news about anyone he knew or about him. The world had moved on.

It was two days before Ossening saw the report of the young man's death. The report crossed his desk because it occurred on a portion of the trail that is on federal land. Severe trauma to the face. Murders were not common on the Appalachian Trail but they were not unknown, either. The F.B.I. got the cases on federal land and worked with local authorities on evidence and identification. An F.B.I. forensics expert reported that the death was consistent with brass knuckles but other weapons could not be ruled out. Ossening took a trip down Interstate 66 to Front Royal.

The town is in the Shenandoah Valley seventy miles from Washington in the northwest corner of the state, not far from West Virginia's wildness. It is popular with retirees and people who either can't afford to live closer to Washington or don't want to. The town has something under fifteen thousand residents protected by a police force of thirty-seven full time cops and one part time officer, two police dogs, and some clerks. Within the ranks are five detectives who investigate crimes such as murders, rapes and assaults and the like. If things get out of hand, there's always the Warren County Sheriff's department, which has more resources. As with all organizations these days, the Front Royal Police Department has a mission statement which promises, in part, "We, the Front Royal Police Department, are committed to providing the highest caliber of police service through our partnership between the department and the community."

Ossening thought it was a lot like Mayberry in the old Andy Griffith Show. The town looks up at both the Blue Ridge Mountains and the Appalachians and a visitor from Washington could be excused if he felt like he had travelled a thousand miles from the capital. Power suits and expensive haircuts were rare in the town. Pickups and hunting rifles were common. Churches were filled on Sundays. The bars were filled on Saturday nights, although the patrons were not likely to be the same people who filled the pews the next morning.

Murder was a big deal in Front Royal and F.B.I. involvement was news. Local media were all over the story and ran a photo of the young victim, identified as a student at Shenandoah University in nearby Winchester. The student, a twenty-year old named Brandon Stein, was from Pittsburgh and was studying to be a pharmacist. One of the local weeklies did a two-thousand word feature on whether the area was still "safe" by historical standards. As with most such features, it raised questions that were answered by dueling experts in different ways. But, from the weekly's point of view, it was a better story than the city council's vote to fill the potholes left by the winter cold.

The chief was eager to work with Ossening and pointed out that, technically, the student was not killed within the town and that his people were providing assistance as a courtesy. He handed the file to Ossening and left him alone in a small conference room. He had seen the photos before and had read the file but he reviewed it again to see if anything new had been added. Nothing had.

He met with the chief again and handed him several photos of Edward Segal. "My hunch is this man killed Stein. If so, he's around here somewhere, or was. He's a pro, a trained army sniper with a good number of kills in Iraq. We believe he killed Federal Judge Alexander Beechum, a reporter named Peter Deutch, a Washington lobbyist named Arnott Cole, and others. We also believe he assaulted and nearly killed a D.C. police captain. If you have him in your town, you have an extremely dangerous and unstable actor to deal with."

"Holy shit!" the chief said. "You have any idea where he might be?"

"That's why I'm here. I think he's hiding in this area. If you were hiding out here where would you stay?"

"There's a thousand places. We have a lot of areas up in the mountains where somebody could hide for a while. Local people would notice you sooner and later and they might call someone. We have the usual assortment of low rent motels and campgrounds."

"Maybe we can take a little tour and see if anyone's seen this guy."

The photo Ossening chose was not recent. It was an army head shot that showed a clean shaven, serious-looking man with a short haircut. He and the chief visited several low end motels and no one had seen the man in the photo and most people who saw the picture had no desire to spend any time talking to law enforcement types, no matter the reason. These were places where people went to hide out for one reason or another. Only a few could reasonably be called law abiding citizens.

Segal was sitting in a lawn chair outside his room when he saw the police car drive up to the office. His instincts told him the visit was about him. He went into his room, grabbed the M-4, and waited for a knock on the door. The high-impact combat ammo would slam through the door at high velocity and take out anyone foolish enough to be standing on the other side. The thought of it lifted his spirits and he felt like a kid waiting for the party to begin. Images of the dead cops made him happy and he fingered the trigger, eager to fire. The safety was off.

Ossening and the chief walked into the motel office and looked around. There was no one there. The door to a back room was open and they heard someone making noises.

"Hello? Anyone back there?" the chief called out.

Silence, then a rustle. A young man came out looking angry and frustrated. He was buttoning his fly. An older woman, who appeared to be in her late forties, was behind him, combing her hair with her fingers. The young man wore his "Shit Happens" tee-shirt. He was not wearing shoes. His anger was replaced by a look of fear when he saw the chief and Ossening, who had F.B.I. written all over him.

"Hello. How may I help you?" He looked from the chief to Ossening and back again. "Is anything wrong?"

The chief held up the photo of Segal. "Have you seen this man?"

"What's he done?"

"We just want to know if you've seen him."

The young man examined the photo, holding it close to his face in the manner of someone who normally wears glasses that have been misplaced for the moment. "No, no one like that around here. What's he done?" He gave the photo back to the chief.

"You're sure you haven't seen him or anyone who looks like this." Ossening examined the young man's face.

"No, not that I recollect. Lots of men look like that but we don't have anyone here that does."

"Do you mind if we knock on some doors to see if some of your guests have seen him?" Ossening studied the young man's reaction, which was apprehension.

"I don't, no. But some of these folks aren't exactly friendly, if you get my meaning."

"Maybe you could explain it to me." The chief put his hands on his hips.

"Folks who live here aren't the upstanding type. We got a few homeless families but we got more of the dropping out from life type. But, sure, knock all you want."

Most of the doors remained closed without any response from inside. The few that were opened were unproductive, with the people who answered the door saying they hadn't seen Segal or anyone else and didn't know anything about anyone anywhere and just kept to themselves. No one made eye contact with Ossening and the chief.

Segal heard them coming and understood that they had no idea he was there but were on a fishing expedition. He moved to the back of his room and hid behind a partition that created a small closet near the bathroom. He aimed the M-4 at the door and waited. *If they came through the door they're dead.* Ossening and the chief knocked on the door, got no response, and left.

Chapter Twenty-eight

Dave's phone made a chirping noise, alerting him that a text message had arrived. He was sitting at a table in a coffee shop, admiring Elena's large brown eyes, when it came in. He was in a moment of certainty about his life, a rare moment for him, and he didn't want to give it up to see who had sent him the text. He was resolving to commit to her, to devote his life to something besides the street and stories and high highs and the low lows, in the words of Jim Russell. *To be a more complete person, that was it.*

"Go ahead, see who it is," she said, sitting back with a small smile.

"Fuck them," he said. "They can wait."

"You won't be able to think about anything else until you look at it."

He sighed and looked down at his phone, which was resting near the edge of the table. "Call my office." It was from Jerry Finegan. Dave looked up at Elena. "Finegan wants me to call him."

"He's defending Prewitt. You were right." She had abandoned the smile and had a look of resignation on her face. Her arms were crossed. "Go ahead. Make the call."

"It won't take long." He went outside and stood under an awning to avoid a light rain and pressed the number that would ring at the law firm.

"Mr. Finnegan's office, how may I help you?" The voice was male and young.

"Dave Haggard returning Mr. Finnegan's call."

Thirty seconds later Finegan picked up. "I'm sitting here with an excellent bottle of scotch and no one to drink it with. How'd you like to come by for a chat about this and that?"

"Right now?"

"No time like the present, Dave. You're first on my list. If you're not available I can move down to number two."

Fifteen minutes later he was sitting by the fire in Finnegan's office, swirling a very expensive single malt around in the bottom of a glass. Elena had been cool but there were no fireworks. She had gone back to her own place in Adams Morgan to "be alone", as she put it.

"So, Dave, let's play you show me yours and I'll show you mine." Finegan was in full lawyerly attitude, all flags flying. His face was both friendly and threatening and his voice was low and well modulated.

"Forget the Redskins and football, this is the most popular game in town," Dave said. "Everybody plays it and nobody knows the rules."

"It's simply an exchange of information, tit for tat. Scratch mine and all that."

"You know mine, Mr. Finegan. It's been on the air."

"Every reporter who's worth his or her salt knows things they don't or can't use. You must be privy to information that hasn't made it into your reporting."

"It's not considered good journalism to open your notebook to anyone who wants to see it. You know that."

"It's not considered good lawyering to have chats like this with reporters."

"As I understand it, that depends on what's said."

"True." Finegan sat in silence playing the lawyer's game of allowing the silence to create discomfort in the other party. The two men stared into the fire for a full five minutes. Finegan had other plans for the evening and didn't have the time or the patience to play a game that clearly wasn't working. "I've been retained to represent Congressman Prewitt."

"I already knew that. Can you elaborate as to just what you're representing him about or against?"

"You have a pretty good idea. Oddly, he has not received a target notice from Justice, even though everyone knows they're after him."

"What would trigger such a notice?"

"My guess is they're close to it and probably would have sent it had Judge Beechum not been killed. Once a request is made to the court, they send the notice. Sometimes sooner. Sometimes never. Depends on who's the target." Finegan turned to Dave. "Now you."

"You still haven't told me anything I didn't know."

"I confirmed that I'm his lawyer. That's quite a development, I'd say."

Dave wondered at the ego of big shot lawyers. It was a fact that some attorneys were so outsized in their reputations that they outshone their clients, no matter who those clients were. "I think the corruption probe is small potatoes if they connect Prewitt to the killing of Beechum, which they're trying to do."

"There is no connection."

"Tell that to the F.B.I. They link Prewitt to Cole, Cole to the shooter, the shooter to Judge Beechum, and so on. You're the expert here, not me. You tell me how it goes down."

"They don't have anything, no case, nothing. They're using you to stir up the mud, that's all. My advice to you would be to walk away from this. You're being played."

Dave knew a play when he saw one and this was a play from Finegan that both men knew wouldn't work.

"So, I've got the other side telling me to turn left and you're telling me to turn right."

"I have a lot of experience with this kind of thing, Dave, and I know smoke and mirrors when I see it. You're going to look very foolish when this thing blows up. People will say you were a lapdog for the government prosecutors. This could spell the end of your career."

"Thank you for the advice, Mr. Finegan. I would be happy to hear anything you have to say regarding this case or any others you have on your desk."

Finegan stood and offered Dave his hand. "I have another engagement and I'm afraid I'll have to send you on your way. Please think about what we've discussed."

"One more thing. When do you plan to go public with this?"

"I just did." Finegan smiled as he escorted Dave to the door. "Have a good evening."

"Any chance I can get a quick recording, a thirty second statement?"

"Not tonight. Call my office in the morning and we'll see what we can work out."

Dave went back to Now News and wrote and recorded two versions of the story, each one containing the news that Finegan had confirmed that he was representing Congressman Prewitt in the Justice Department investigation into corruption regarding the Oak Ridge cleanup money and Finnegan's assertion that the government had no case and that Prewitt had done nothing wrong. It was boilerplate stuff that every reporter in town knew contained nothing new, but they all would also understand that the government was tightening the screws on Prewitt to the point where he had retained a supernova lawyer to defend him. The city was now on notice that a major league legal game was underway.

Dave's reporting went up on the Now News website at three o'clock in the morning and the audio was available to anyone who wanted to listen. It went out to member stations on the five o'clock feed. It was the lead on the morning drive time newscasts, although the television morning shows played it down because it was not seen as a major story, more of a "Congressman hires lawyer" item. Ho hum.

For Prewitt, who was asleep when his radio came on to wake him up, it was news. Finegan had taken the case. For Prewitt, it meant two things: Finegan thought he could win, or at least get some major publicity out of it, and the government's case was serious. He ran to the bathroom and threw up into the toilet.

Chapter Twenty-nine

Sid was at his desk, pondering his coffee mug, and waiting for Dave, when his phone rang. It was Sheila Futterman at the AP, a rising star who was seen as a big thinker. "Sid here." The new greeting had replaced "Yeah," which had been viewed by the upper management as ungracious.

"Sheila here. How's it hanging?" She had learned the crude greetings that seemed to please the older male lions of the news business.

"How goes it?"

"Your boy is working up quite a story."

"He has no other life that I know of. I think he walks around with his recorder on twenty four hours a day. What can I do for you?"

"He blew us off on working together on whatever is going on with Prewitt, Beechum, and everybody else. We need to talk about this, Sid. We lost a man here. We're not going to stand around waiting to see what happens next."

"Dave doesn't play well with others, Sheila. Good reporters don't. You know that."

"Sometimes the grownups have to get involved."

"He hates your guy."

"Why, because Adams is smart and ambitious?"

"Could be. He says Adams is an asshole."

"He is. So is Dave. What else is new?"

"So what are you proposing?"

"We're not just sitting around over here. We have something to trade."

"Dave will be here in a few minutes. Why don't you catch a cab and come over for a chat."

Thirty-minutes later the three of them were sitting in Sid's office. Sid was leaning back, his bottom drawer being used as a footstool, and he was chewing on a thin, black, unlit cigar, watching Dave. Dave was clearly not in a mood to share. Sheila was wearing her best management face and trying to look above whatever hostility was in the air.

Sid broke the ice. "We're competitors. You go after your stories and we go after ours. You guys are a thousand times bigger than we are and we all know that most of the day to day stuff we put on the air comes off the wires. But now and then we get to snatch a prize and we don't want to give it up."

"Sid," said Sheila, "We're a member organization. We work together, all of us, as one giant news gathering group. Every newspaper, every broadcaster, every everybody who signs up for the AP is part of it. We share."

"So, Sid says you have something for us?" Dave tried to smile but it was forced.

"Are we playing nice?" Sheila's tone was cool.

"You know what we have, Sheila," Sid said. "We've had it on the air."

"Right. So there's no reason for this meeting because you all have been up front about the whole story." Her voice had moved from cool to cold.

"We have sources, probably the same as yours."

"Okay. A guy was killed on the Appalachian Trail recently. You may have heard about it. Beaten to death. Just another hiker mysteriously killed by person or persons unknown. We've heard it before."

Dave looked down at his hands. "Okay."

"Would you be surprised to learn that Ossening at the F.B.I. thinks it's the guy who killed Cole, beat up Captain O'Neil, shot Judge Beechum and killed Peter

Deutch, who, I would like to add, was a very fine human being?"

"The guy who was killed?"

"No, I'm sorry. The guy who killed the hiker. It was near Front Royal. Ossening went out there to look around but didn't turn up anything. That doesn't mean the killer is not around there somewhere."

"You're talking about Edward Segal." Dave's voice was a whisper.

"Yup."

"Ossening told you Segal is in Front Royal?"

"He didn't use his name but he gave us everything else. He's playing us, Dave. You, us, somebody else, it's all the same to him."

"Is he talking to other reporters?" Sid sat forward and chomped on the wet cigar.

"Who knows? If so, they haven't made any noise about it, but something could break any time."

"What exactly did Ossening tell you?" Dave asked.

"He told Adams that forensics had linked the judge's killer to a murder on federal land along the Appalachian Trail and he was going to Front Royal to look for the guy."

"Did Adams go with him?"

"They're not that cozy."

"Have you considered that it might be bullshit or just some random information to see what happens and who goes after it?" Sid was making a mess out of his cigar.

"Of course. They can claim some national security reason and track all of us like we're rats in a maze. They probably are." Sheila losing patience. "Are you in or not?"

"Dave has been invited to appear on Jim Bohannon's show. It's open-ended. He can accept and bring Adams along with him. The two of them can throw out what they feel comfortable talking about and we'll see what happens after that. That's the best I can do right now." Sid sat back and tossed the web glob of black tobacco into his trash can.

"When are you thinking?"

"I'll call Jim's producer and see what he says," Dave said, glaring at Sid.

An hour later Ossening got a secure email with a transcript of the meeting at Now News. He liked the phrase "rats in a maze" and thought it fit. He drove to Charles County and paid a visit to Captain O'Neil, who was feeling much better but was still eating through a straw. He laid out the search for Segal and used the rats-in-a-maze line to explain his own personal media plan. Both men agreed that men like Edward Segal have trouble with loose ends and, one way or another, need to resolve them. Dave was a loose end and Segal would be tempted to make it right, whatever that meant to him in his current state of mind. His options depended on how near to reality he was. That was an open question.

At that moment, Segal was driving east on I-66, heading for Washington.

Chapter Thirty

The Philadelphia House was on Massachusetts Avenue near 17th Street, a few doors down from a high-level think tank and across the street from buildings housing foreign legations that enjoy diplomatic immunity and protection. Also on the block is a world-class school for international studies. Mixed in are late 19th century townhouses occupied by the gray residents of a city where things are not as they appear to be. Because of the diplomatic presence on the block, there was a noticeable security element consisting of men and women of uncertain nationality wearing everything from business suits to rock and roll tee-shirts.

Dave liked the feel of the place. It was close enough to Dupont Circle to experience what passed for a counter culture in Washington, with the occasional blue hair and heavy leather and studs devotee strolling by. There was a strong gay culture but it tended toward an establishment look, distaining the flamboyant signatures of San Francisco or New York. And it was international, with a mix of languages and clothing on the street.

The Philadelphia House's lobby often rang with many languages and looks. One look that did not fit in was hillbilly redneck. Hunting hats, sleeveless sweatshirts, work boots and chewing tobacco were not common sights along that portion of Massachusetts Avenue. A swaggering man in a five thousand dollar suit would not be remarked upon. A guy who looked like he made whiskey in the mountains would be noticed immediately.

Edward Segal did not want to be noticed and it occurred to him that while he blended in in Front Royal, he did not fit the profile of Embassy Row or Dupont Circle. He made what he considered a compromise. He stopped at Tyson Corner and went to department store in the giant mall there and bought himself khaki pants, a button-down shirt, a light windbreaker, and a pair of penny loafers, assuming that he would look preppy enough to disappear into the street traffic. He had a soldier's sense of fashion and had no real grasp of what other people were wearing. He trimmed his beard until he was satisfied that he appeared to be somewhat literary and he purchased a Washington Nationals baseball hat. The team was doing well early in the season and the hats were common in and around Washington, even among people who normally wouldn't be caught dead in a cap.

He found a small café on 19th Street and ate a Greek salad as the sun set. He was one of the most wanted men in America and he was hiding in plain sight two miles from those who were hunting him. To the local people he appeared to be a middle aged, middle class tourist in a Washington baseball hat. No one matched the man in the windbreaker with the face that had been on television and identified as a professional killer.

He had been trained to observe and spot targets and he used that training to watch for Dave. He was patient and appeared to be just another man on the street. The sunset brought a chill to the air and he walked faster to get his blood moving. His limp became more noticeable in the cold and he put a smile on his face to avoid generating any sympathy from passersby who might remember him. A cheerful face is less likely to stick in the mind, he believed.

Dave arrived in a taxi and walked up to the front door of the Philadelphia House, inserted his security card, and opened the door. Segal was right behind him.

The Cameroonian behind the desk saw them and waved to Dave and assumed that the man behind him was Dave's guest. The two men walked to the elevator and stood silently while they waited for it, got in, and rode to the third floor. Dave was lost in his own thoughts and didn't pay attention to the man next to him, who appeared to be just a generic guy.

They both got off on the third floor and Segal walked behind Dave as he made his way to his door, inserted his key, and stepped inside.

"Hold the door," Segal said.

Dave turned around and saw that Segal was holding a handgun. There was something familiar about his face. "Is this a robbery?" He briefly considered slamming the door but saw that Segal had placed the tip of his cane in the door jam.

"No, Mr. Haggard, this is not a robbery. Let's just go inside." Dave heard the same East Tennessee accent he had grown up with.

"Are you Edward Segal?"

"That I am. Now let's get inside where we can talk." Segal motioned with the Glock toward the interior of Dave's apartment.

The door was closed and Segal locked it and inserted the chain into its slot. He walked to Dave's dining table that also functioned as a desk and sat down. "I've been doing a lot of walking. I hope you don't mind if I take a load off."

"What are you doing here?"

"Like I said, I've come for a talk. You have any water?"

"Half the country is looking for you, you know. Every cop from here to Knoxville is edgy, thinking you're going to open fire or smash their faces in."

"I know. Now, about that water."

Dave went into his kitchen and filled a glass with water from the tap, came out, placed the glass on the table and waited for Segal to drink.

"Have a seat. We might be awhile." Dave sat down.

"I've seen you on television. Where do you get your information?" Segal seemed genuinely curious about how Dave had come into the details of his stories.

"I have sources."

"Who are they?"

"You know reporters don't reveal their sources."

"They do when there's a gun pointed at them." Segal lost his friendliness.

"Why are you here? Are you going to kill me?"

"Somebody paid me to do that already. I'm sorry I hit that other fellow. Right now I'm not sorry I missed you. You're lucky as hell. I don't usually miss."

"You didn't answer my question."

"I don't have any plans to kill you but that might change depending on how this goes."

"What exactly are you looking for?"

"I need to know what you know, all of it, not just the stuff in your news reports. I want to know who you've been talking to and what they're saying. All of it, even the stuff you don't think is important, even the rumors."

Dave began with the Justice Department investigation into missing money from the Oak Ridge cleanup, Prewitt's possible involvement, Arnott Cole, Bud Ossening and Captain O'Neil. He spent the next half hour walking Segal through it, going over his conversations and phone calls, the possibility or even likelihood that other reporters in the city were pursuing the same leads and getting bread crumbs from Ossening and other sources. He found himself saying things he didn't mean to say and the more he said the more he began to understand how the parts fit together.

Segal grew agitated at the details and then his face got red and he began to grind his teeth. "So this guy Prewitt is the one who's the shitbag," he said, "him and this guy Cole and a bunch of others. They hired me to kill the good guy, this judge."

"Looks that way," Dave said, wondering why a professional killer would classify anyone as good or bad. "Please don't be offended, but I didn't know people in your line of work made those kinds of judgments about people."

"I live down there, Mr. Haggard. I see what's happened. Hell, you can't even eat the danged fish out of the Tennessee River anymore, not even the fish caught back up in there. We've been poisoned. It ain't right. I'm not sayin' I ain't done bad things, I have. Mostly I've done bad things to bad people, so I don't lie awake nights. I thought this judge was one of them and now you're sayin' it's this Prewitt."

"Most people would say it's best to leave these things to the authorities. The government will get Prewitt and his friends so you don't have to."

"There's justice your way and there's justice my way."

Dave took a deep breath. "I think you should turn yourself in."

Segal smiled. "I'll bet you do. It ain't my way, Mr. Haggard." He stood, pulled up his shirt, and unwound thin nylon rope from around his waist. "I'm afraid I'll have to restrain you. It won't kill you but it will keep you from making any phone calls for a while." He was an expert at such things and soon had Dave bound to his chair, which he laid on the floor and tied securely to the table. He went to Dave's dresser and removed a pair of sox, rolled them into a ball, and stuffed them into Dave's mouth, secured by a duct tape. "You'll be okay. Somebody will find you before you die. Tell Captain

O'Neil I'm sorry I broke his face. I'm happy he survived. Most don't." He walked to the door, turned out the lights, and left.

Dave's phone was in the front pocket of his jeans and the monitoring station in Virginia picked up only muffled noises. A computer program noted that Dave was at home.

Chapter Thirty-one

Dave's apartment was locked down as F.B.I. forensics people went about the task of dusting every surface for any bit of evidence that would tell them anything about Edward Segal. Swabs, special vacuums, spectrum cameras, sterile plastic bags and items from equipment kits were scanning surfaces, furniture, the water glass Segal drank from, and everything else in the place, including Dave. His clothing had been removed and taken away for analysis. He had been questioned for hours by Ossening and a detective from D.C. police.

Sid had called a half-dozen times demanding that he file on his face-to-face meeting with Segal. Ossening had nixed the idea but later relented after he conferred with a lawyer from the Justice Department.

He had lain on the floor of his dark apartment for twelve hours after Segal left. He had come within minutes of pissing his pants. Elena had trouble sleeping and came to see him in the early morning to have a "talk" about their relationship. The Cameroonian at the desk told her he was in. He did not answer the door. The desk gave her a key and she found him bound to the chair, making muffled shrieking noises. Now, it was dark again and Elena was huddled on his bed against the wall, weeping and dazed.

She wondered what it would be like to be dating a normal man, one who went to work and came home and watched television. What would it be like to be with a man whose excitement consisted of the Fourth of July fireworks and spotting a celebrity on the street? No guns, no knives, no brass knuckles, no being tied to a chair and left in the dark by a professional killer.

She asked herself if she had the strength to be one of those women whose husbands risked their lives for a living. A war wife, a cop's wife, a firefighter's wife, a woman like that. Goodbye dear, have a nice day. Survive, okay? She idly wondered if Dave had it in him to be the husband of a woman who went to war or ran into burning buildings. Could he take it as well as he dished it out?

She felt weak. It was a physical thing, it was spiritual and emotional. It had to do with her image of herself and the life she had always imagined. In truth, she had always seen herself as a princess to be cared for and pampered. It was not something she was proud of but it was the way she had always seen her life. She had always been beautiful and her beauty had given her certain advantages. Men liked to give her things and take her to the best restaurants to impress her. How she became attracted to Dave was a mystery to her. He was nothing like the men she normally went out with. He had no money to speak of. He didn't even own a car. He was afraid of commitment and made a habit of disappointing her.

What was it? She laughed in spite of herself when she admitted that she loved him because he had a backbone and she knew he would give up his own life for hers if it came to that. He was no metrosexual who fussed over his clothes or his actions. He could not care less what was politically or socially correct at the moment. He had a sense of honor. But, all of these things stacked against a wall still put her at a distance from his center. That is how she saw it. She had no way of knowing, because he could not express it, that she was at his center, as clumsy as it was.

Ossening saw her on the bed and thought she was stoned. She had a dazed look and appeared to be unfocused. "Are you all right?" he asked, leaning down to look into her eyes.

"Yes, I'm fine. I was just thinking about something."

"I'd like to go over this again. Tell me why you came here."

She went over her story again with the weary air of someone who was repeating a word over and over. For her it was repeating a nightmare, something she wanted to forget. She had the name of a therapist in Bethesda who specialized in "women's issues" and she thought it might be a good idea to give her a call. Elena was not drawn to therapy and had, in fact, developed a disdain for her friends who spent an hour a week picking over the details of their lives and relationships. *I don't need a thermometer up my ass*, is how she put it. Maybe it was time to take her temperature. She felt she was losing her grip. It occurred to her that she had felt this way ever since she woke up to the fact that she was in love with Dave.

Dave was in his small kitchen, drinking coffee and making small talk with a uniformed officer whose job was to keep him there. It was a small apartment and the scene had the feel of a crowded social event, with people scurrying here and there. Finally, the specialized items that snared DNA here or fingerprints there were packed up and the experts left. Ossening looked around and offered his hand to Dave.

"He's long gone by now," he said. "Half the population of the country is within a twelve hour drive of Washington. He could be anywhere from Maine to Detroit to Atlanta or even Florida. Maybe we'll get lucky. You did all you could."

"He could be waiting in the lobby," Dave said. "He's better than you guys."

"So far, Dave. He's not the type to run and stay gone. He's got an agenda. His little talk with you wasn't just a way to kill an evening. He's after something or someone. If I had to guess I'd put my money on Prewitt. We'll put a detail on him and warn him but you might want to have a talk with him and explain that our friend Segal seems to have a special interest in the gentleman from Tennessee."

"I suppose you could say Mr. Segal has turned on his employer," Dave said, hoping for an answer he would like.

"One never knows, Dave."

He didn't care for the answer but it was a long shot going in, so nothing ventured, he thought. "I need some rest and I have to satisfy my own employer, but I'll give him a call if he's still around."

"He hasn't left town."

Elena watched the exchange and thought both men were crazy. There was only one rational course of action, in her mind, and it was to get in a car and drive to a safe place far away. Dave had no plans to go anywhere with the possible exception of Tennessee, which was not what Elena had in mind.

At that moment Segal was standing at a bus stop on Maryland Avenue Northeast, a few blocks from the Capitol, watching the front door of a federalist-style rowhouse. Inside, Congressman Prewitt was slowly getting drunk on a special batch of Tennessee whiskey that the distiller produced for a select group of men in high places. The group was all male because high-level women had rebuffed the distiller's offer, assuming there were strings attached. Prewitt was representative of the males who had no such misgivings.

The whiskey was amber and smooth and went down easily as Prewitt sat in a wingback chair and enjoyed a moment of satisfaction. He had no idea why he felt this good and he had no desire to explore the feeling but he allowed himself to savor it, despite circumstances that would send most men to their beds in panic. It occurred to him that he might be cracking up. *Screw it,* he thought.

Segal was wearing a trench coat and a fedora he had purchased at a men's store on F Street, Northwest. It was misting and the outer wear was appropriate for the weather and the neighborhood. People out walking their dogs or hurrying home paid no attention to him. He was just another guy waiting for a bus in a neighborhood where using public transportation was as fashionable as it was practical. Save the planet by riding Metro.

Segal had no plan. He watched Prewitt in the way he had watched his targets in Iraq. He would first study his habits and his movements. He would wait until he knew for certain where Prewitt would be and under what circumstances. He had yet to decide how to kill him, quick and easy or slow and painful. Judge Beechum had gone to eternity with a smile on his face, unaware of the transition from life to death until he was on his way to wherever souls go in that moment. But there are other ways to send people to that place, ways that make the journey longer and more difficult.

Some societies consider a quick death merciful, even for miscreants, and define themselves as humane in a sentence of beheading or a quick bullet to the brain. Did Prewitt deserve such mercy? Segal imagined the congressman in a vat of mercury and wondered how he would die from it. There were many such powerful toxins polluting his beloved hills, so it was possible to submerge him in a cocktail. His reverie was interrupted when Prewitt stood in a window overlooking the street and appeared to be looking directly at Segal. He was wearing the trousers from the suit he wore that day, a white shirt with the collar open, and a tie that was loose at his neck. He stood there for several minutes, taking sips from a glass. Segal imagined that he had an M-14 aimed at Prewitt's forehead and he saw the image of the congressman's skull exploding. It would be quick but would it be justice?

Prewitt reached into his pocket and took out his phone. He put it to his ear and spoke to someone, walking away from the window. Segal stood in the mist and studied the house, noting the low, wrought iron fence in front and the budding azaleas and blooming tulips in the small garden. A thin brick walk led from the street to the front door. The garden would be soft from the rain and anyone walking in it would leave tracks that would tell a great deal to a seasoned investigator. He was making mental notes of all of this when a taxi pulled up to Prewitt's door and Dave Haggard got out and rang the bell.

Chapter Thirty-two

Prewitt's good mood shattered the moment he opened the door. Dave was not smiling and he was not offering his hand in greeting.

"We have to talk," Dave said.

"Come in, please." Prewitt stepped back into a small vestibule that led into a formal living room that appeared to have been furnished in 1900. Antique furniture, oriental rugs, formal paintings of long-dead serious-looking men, cut crystal decanters and other reminders of days gone by were scattered around the room. Prewitt was unfocused and appeared to be drunk. "May I offer you something?"

"No, thank you," Dave said. "May I sit?"

"By all means." The conversation had taken on the formality of BBC costume drama.

Dave sat on an armless chair whose seat and back were covered in red and gold brocade. The seat cushion was hard and uncomfortable but he remained where he was to avoid looking like a man who spent time looking for the right piece of furniture to sit on. Too late, he realized he had not removed his wet raincoat.

"So, what's so important that you find yourself here at this hour?"

"I had a visitor last night, someone you may know, or know of."

Prewitt put on his arrogant face. "And who might that be?"

"I believe he's known as Edward Segal." Dave let that news sink in.

"Which Edward Segal?"

"The Edward Segal, the one who's been identified as the professional killer who shot Judge Beechum, killed Peter Deutch, and probably beat up and killed several others that we know about and, in the bargain, badly injured Captain O'Neil. It's been in all the papers."

"You don't have to be a smart ass, Dave. I find it hard to believe that this fellow would take the time to stop by for a visit." Prewitt's hands began to shake and he was trying to maintain his composure.

"It wasn't a social visit. He came to ask me some questions, mostly about you."

"Me? Why me? What do I have to do with anything in this man's life?"

"That seems to be the subject of some discussion, isn't it?"

"Please don't go into that again. There is nothing to these rumors and I hope you didn't fall into the trap of spreading them to this alleged visitor of yours."

"I wouldn't say it was alleged, Congressman, he talked to me and he tied me to a chair. He's not all that stable, in my opinion, but he's not stupid, either. I'd say he thinks you're a bad guy."

"That's a good one, a known killer calling me a bad guy. I serve my constituents, well, I might say. I perform a public service and what do I get for it? Rumors and snooping around by my own government and you and your kind spreading false rumors and now this fellow, this hit man, allegedly, and yes I use that word, coming to you and making accusations. It's a house of lies, the whole thing." Prewitt's voice was rising and he paced the room, drinking the whiskey and waving his arms.

"I don't mean to be rude but...Wait, I take that back. I do mean to be rude. There are many in this town who think it is you who have created a house of lies,

Congressman. My guess is the F.B.I. thinks so and if they do, can the Justice Department be far behind? Have you talked to Finegan lately?"

"Just today, in fact. I can't divulge our conversation but I will say he would not have accepted my commission if he believed for one second that I am in jeopardy. Did you hear me? Not for one second."

Dave wondered what the words "my commission" meant. He decided that Prewitt was too drunk to fully understand what he was saying.

"Who hired Segal?" Dave went for it.

"How in God's name would I know? Cole handled all of that." He stood staring at a portrait of an ancestor, lost in thought, unaware of what he had said.

"How did he do that?"

"You know Cole. He knows people who know people. How does anything happen?"

"Did you know?"

"Know what?"

"That he was going to have Judge Beechum killed?"

"Killed? He never said killed. He said it would be taken care of." At that Prewitt came to his senses despite the alcohol and turned to face Dave. "I didn't admit anything. I've obviously had too much to drink and I don't know what I'm saying. Now you'll have to leave." He looked stricken. "Get out."

"Congressman, you have admitted to me that you were part of a conspiracy to murder a federal judge."

"I admitted no such thing. Everyone knows I had contact with Cole. Everybody in this town who is anybody had contact with him. That doesn't prove anything." He moved to the door and opened it. "Leave or I will call the police."

"That would be interesting, don't you think."

"You're a son of a bitch and a backwoods yahoo grits eating bastard and I don't have to spend any more time in your company."

Dave brushed past Prewitt and stepped into the misty night. Segal watched from a dark spot under a tree across the street and noted that Prewitt was breathing hard and his face was red. Dave had a small smile on his face and stopped at the corner to take the phone out of his shirt pocket to check the recording he had made of his conversation with Prewitt.

Fifteen minutes later Bud Ossening at the F.B.I. was reviewing the recording that had been picked up at the listening station in Virginia and uploaded to a secure website. He played it several times and used software to transcribe it. He used a secure email account to send the transcript to Captain O'Neil. Ossening placed the recording and the transcript onto a flash drive and taped it to the inside of a file folder marked "Prewitt Investigation". It was one of a dozen such flash drives in the file, along with a considerable amount of paperwork and photographs. Ossening weighed the file in his hands and smiled. He felt enormous satisfaction when cases such as this came to an end and the perpetrator in question came face to face with the justice system. He allowed himself a moment to imagine the despair that would come over Prewitt when the weight of the government's case became clear to him and his fancy lawyer. *Fuck you*, he thought.

Chapter Thirty-three

It was rare for Sid to be invited to a meeting of the Now News board of directors, most of whom were fans of public broadcasting but not experienced in the ways of broadcasting or journalism. The meetings were usually social affairs with the members telling each other how wonderful it was to be associated with such a fine product. The men and women who gathered that day in an upstairs conference room were either rich or connected in some way to substantial funding sources. They understood their roles. Or they did until Dave Haggard upset every apple cart in sight.

Sid hated the board. It wasn't personal. He barely knew any of the members. He was troubled by the unstated control the board had over everything at Now News. He saw the news operation as his "shop" and resented any intrusion and was known to have insulted several board members who dared to offer suggestions about coverage of stories or the tone of the news product, even if he had privately admitted only to himself that they were good ideas.

He considered his options. He could ignore the invitation and deal with the fallout, which could, in theory, result in his firing. He didn't think that was a likely outcome but other issues were at play, including money to expand into new media and hire more staff. He accepted Jim Russell's, The Program Doctor's, assessment about the future, which meant he had to get into new forms of audio and video distribution and increased Web presence. That would take money. The board controlled the purse.

He stood up, straightened his tie, put on his jacket, and went upstairs. The board members were sitting around a polished wood stable sipping from plastic water bottles and nibbling on organic grapes. They all wore unhappy faces and looked stricken when Sid walked in.

The chairperson was a tech company executive named Elaine Fuller whose career had pinballed from one startup to another. She had a reputation as a great idea person who had no follow through. It had served her well enough to amass a fortune and positions on various boards. She was in her mid-forties, fashionably thin, and suitably grim.

"So, welcome Mr. Slackey. We're glad you could join us." She waved in the direction of the only empty chair. The other board members sat in silence and watched as Sid took his seat. "We've invited you here to get a clear explanation of the situation with Dave Haggard and your assessment of the story that has exploded around him."

What a load of crap, he thought, scooting his chair closer to the table. He looked into the face of each board member and acknowledged to himself that they had no idea what was happening in the newsroom. *It's like explanting brain surgery to a group of carpenters.*

"You all know pretty much all there is to know," he said. "Dave's chasing a major story."

Fuller raised her hand. "What we're looking for is a bit more than what's been on the air, Mr. Slackey. For one, is his life in danger? Are any other Now News staff people in danger? Do you think it would be advisable to spread some of this risk around, possibly with the AP. I hear they've made overtures."

"What Dave does, and others like him, carries some risk. But he's not in a war zone or chasing guerrillas in

South America, so his risk is minimal compared to other journalists. Yes, he was shot at and the death of Peter Deutch was horrible, but there was no way to predict that attack. As for working with another news organization, yes, there have been discussions but nothing has been agreed to." Sid sat back as though he had said all that needed to be said.

"I don't mean to be rude, Mr. Slackey, but we're not children here. We have a right to probe this and know more than we do at the moment." Fuller's face was even more serious than its normal sour presentation.

"Dave is working his sources and is reporting the story. I don't know what else there is to say."

"Well, how about the visit of a professional killer to his apartment. How did that come about?"

"You're referring to Edward Segal. Yes, he's been identified as the assassin who shot Judge Beechum and the likely shooter of Peter Deutch, in addition to other grisly crimes. How he came to know where Dave lives and why he went there is not something I can explain, nor can Dave."

Fuller slapped the table. "Mr. Slackey, each one of us here on the board has received numerous emails and phone calls about this story. It's not that Dave is reporting on the story. Dave is the story. That's our concern."

"Well, I beg to differ. Dave is reporting a huge developing story and he's out front on it and therefore is getting attention. It's happened before with other reporters. You may have heard of Watergate."

Fuller's face faded from concern to disgust. "I don't need a lesson from you. But you must understand our concern. We've discussed it and the board believes that another reporter or maybe a team of reporters should be assigned to this story."

"And Dave?" Sid's face was red.

"Dave can assist and act as a consultant."

"A consultant? On his own story? How do you think his sources will react to that?"

"He can introduce his sources to other reporters. It's called networking. It happens all the time in business."

"This isn't business. This is news. We don't have meet and greets to make our circle wider. We have secret meetings to make our circle smaller. This is Dave's story. He works it. I assign others to help out when necessary and they do and have made significant contributions, but it's Dave's story. He's put in the time and he has the sources."

"This may be out of your hands, Mr. Slackey." Fuller and the other board members stared at him.

"You'll do what you have to do. So will I. And so, I suspect, will Dave Haggard." Sid stood up and walked to the door.

"Is that a threat, Mr. Slackey?" Fuller glared at him.

"I'm a newsman. I deal in facts."

Sid was ripping off his tie as he walked into the newsroom. The staffers nodded to each other to acknowledge that he was in one of "his moods", which meant that he was considered radioactive until it passed. There would be no knocks on his door until the mood was eased. In a worst case, it would be days.

He stopped outside his office. "Dave around?" His voice was loud and gravelly.

"Not yet," replied a desk assistant who didn't raise her gaze from the computer screen she was reading.

"Get him in here!" He walked into his office and slammed the door.

Dave was home having coffee with Elena, who was working the evening shift and still groggy from sleeping late. He had been working all over the clock and hoping for some rest when the phone rang it's dobro riff.

"Smash that damn phone!" Elena said, her voice soft and sleepy.

He looked at it and saw that it was Gabriel, the news assignment manager at Now News. "It's the desk. Who do you think they want, me or you?"

"It's not my phone that's ringing."

He picked it up and pressed "answer". "Dave," he said, it was nearly a shout.

"Gabriel here, Dave. Our lord and master is summoning you into his venerated presence."

"What does he want?"

"He's in a mood. He didn't say."

"Anything going on I should know about?"

"Not that I'm aware of. Nothing on your stories. No calls. No meetings. Just Sid pissed off."

"Great. I'll be there. I have to shower and get organized. Maybe an hour."

"That might be pushing it. He's pacing his office right now."

"He can wait."

An hour later Dave knocked on Sid's door and was met by a growl. "Where have you been? Has it occurred to you that this is a work day?"

"Sorry. I've been working around the clock and I need some rest now and then." Dave was on edge.

"We have a problem. It seems our esteemed board of directors has made a decision about something, for once, and they've decided to take over the newsroom." Sid glared at Dave.

"And that means…?"

"They want you off the story."

"What story?"

"The one you've been breaking and nearly got shot over. That story."

"What do you mean they want me off the story? Have I done something wrong?"

"You've been a little too public for their taste. They think you're not just covering the story anymore, you are the story. That, in their expert opinion about these things, compromises your journalistic integrity. They want a quote team effort. They want you to brief this so-called team about your sources and what you know so this so-called team can advance the story into whatever greatness these idiots have in mind." Sid sat back, looking disgusted and angry.

"You're not going along with this!"

"Hell no. But I have to tell you about it in case anyone asks. We already have a team on it. You're leading it. Others at the desk are following up and working their own leads. If a board member, and I'm thinking about Elaine Fuller, asks you about anything associated with this story or this blatant interference, tell them to talk to me. Board interference in the news operation is strictly forbidden in the bylaws and they won't get away with it."

"Are they going to fire you?"

"They might."

"If you go, I go. I'd bet Elena goes. The desk might empty out. They'd have a problem."

"They don't see it that way. They think you and I are the problem. They don't like any kind of heat and they're getting it from people who think reporters should be seen and not heard, at least not as the subjects of their stories."

There was a knock at the door and Gabriel opened it and came in before Sid could respond. "Dave, you should know that somebody just took a shot at Congressman Prewitt. He was not hit but he took off and police don't know where he is."

Sid broke into a wide smile. "God, I love this business."

Chapter Thirty-four

Congressman Prewitt was on Route 211 in Virginia, staying off the interstates as long as possible, avoiding the areas where he thought his pursuer might be expecting him. His temples were pounding and his ears were ringing and he was making small, animal-like noises that he didn't hear. He was driving a ten year old Mercedes that he kept garaged behind his Capitol Hill rowhouse and rarely drove. It had officially been a gift from his father, who had received it from a major donor to Prewitt's campaign. When new the car had come with an all-expenses paid vacation to Paris. And an expensive Swiss watch. The donor was a developer who wanted in on the cleanup money at Oak Ridge and had been handsomely rewarded. All in all, the car had been pocket change in the deal.

Prewitt was not thinking about the car or the donor as he drove through the beautiful landscape of Rappahannock County. He was nervous and looking into his rear view mirror for any sign that someone was following him. He had a cut on his cheek that had bled down to his chin from the chip of brick that had blown onto his face when the round hit the front of his house. He was stepping out the door at that moment and had turned to lock it when the shot rang out. *One shot. Inches from my face! Segal! Jesus! He could have killed me!* He felt like he was going to pee his pants and he pulled over and quickly relieved himself by the side of the road, frantically looking around for signs of his would-be assassin. A pickup loaded with bags of feed drove by, the driver and his passenger staring at Prewitt and laughing at something one of them said.

Prewitt found I-81 at New Market and headed south. He hoped that by picking up the interstate farther down in Virginia he would avoid Segal, whom he believed was hot on his trail, possibly waiting around the next bend in the road. Prewitt was again near the edge of his reasoning power and he would have been hard pressed to answer any question more complicated that who was he. He need not have worried about Segal at that moment, but his concerns about his future were justified.

Edward Segal was behind him but not on pursuit. He had aimed the M-4 at the spot near Prewitt's head hoping to scare him and drive him to leave his home. The chip of brick that cut Prewitt's face was an added bonus, in Segal's mind. It would remind the congressman that he was vulnerable to a bloody end. Prewitt had run like the coward he was, hurrying in a panic to his car and driving away without even locking his front door or calling the police. A neighbor walking her dog dialed 911 and screamed that someone was shooting up the neighborhood. Police were looking for the shooter and for Congressman Prewitt, who was being described in media reports as "panicked."

Segal's plan had come together as he watched Dave leaving the rowhouse. More than anything he wanted Prewitt to suffer. A quick death was not justice. The people back in East Tennessee who were dying of cancer and other horrors caused by toxic government waste were not given an easy or quick death, so why should Prewitt be given such a grace? No, Prewitt's end would take time.

Segal saw it as a game, like running an animal to a spot where it can be shot. He would first drive Prewitt south in a state of panic, looking over his shoulder, expecting a bullet at any minute. He wouldn't sleep. He would have trouble eating. His stomach would cramp. His hands would shake. He would run like a rabbit with a fox behind it, darting and screaming and knowing the darkness was at hand. He would go to where he felt safe. He would go home to the farm that chicanery had built. The white columned mansion, the magnificent old trees, the lake, the hills, the horses, all of it stolen from the people of Tennessee. There he would suffer his last moments.

Segal was content as he drove south. He had no intention to interdict Prewitt on the way to Tennessee. It was an eight hour drive and he wanted his prey to feel panic on every mile of highway. Experience had taught him that the threat of pain is a greater torture than the actual pain, at least to a point. The real pain would come later. He contented himself with his fantasies and he fondled the brass knuckles as he drove.

Congressman Prewitt stayed in the left lane and grew impatient with the heavy traffic that kept his speed at seventy miles per hour, five miles above the speed limit. He was eager for the safety of his farm. *If only I can have a moment of peace to think things through. It's going to be all right.* Tractor trailer rigs dominated the right lane and travelers in cars and SUVs were stacked in the left lane, vying for road space. He honked his horn and gave the finger to other drivers, who shouted unheard obscenities at him.

The traffic cleared going into Harrisburg and he pressed the accelerator, increasing his speed to eighty five just as the speed limit lowered to fifty five where the interstate went through the small city. It was common for drivers to ignore the lower speed limit and, for the police, such drivers were low hanging fruit. Speed traps produced needed revenue.

Prewitt saw an officer standing in a group of cops and their cars, pointing at him and waving him over. He had no intention of stopping for the police or anyone else. He pressed the gas pedal to the floor and zigzagged his way through a knot of other vehicles in an effort to get away from the police, assuming that they would know who he was, realize the gravity of his situation, and let him go on his way. In his panic, he had begun to levitate above reality.

The police had long experience with speed traps and expected the occasional runner, so other officers were stationed one mile south to intercept those who fled. Prewitt was travelling at nearly one hundred miles per hour, weaving in and out of truck traffic, when he went past a Virginia state trooper whose roof lights were already flashing. The trooper called for a backup and within minutes three police cars were chasing Prewitt, who, in his delirious state, thought he was being given a police escort.

He was not a skilled driver and nearly lost control of the Mercedes each time he changed lanes at high speed. The police cars were right behind him, flashing lights and using all of the sirens and alarms that modern technology offers. Cars and trucks ahead of the chase saw the flashing lights and pulled over, opening the traffic lanes to even higher speeds. Prewitt began to feel intense elation and began to laugh hysterically and believe that he had reached a point of divinity, a state where he was invincible.

An officer pulled up next to him and used the car's public address system to order him to pull over. He waved at the officer and laughed. He sped down hill toward a bridge that was being rebuilt over a rural road. The construction had created temporary lanes that forced traffic to slow and move to the right around a line of barrels that warned drivers away from a portion of the bridge that was closed because the road surface had been removed as part of the bridge work. Prewitt was still laughing at the trooper when he plowed through the barrels and onto the portion of the bridge where the pavement was missing, leaving only the steel support grid between Prewitt's Mercedes and the road below.

The front wheels of the Mercedes were caught in the grid and were ripped off, sending the car's underbody skidding along the steel bars in a display of sparks and screaming metal. The car angled into a Jersey wall on the far side of the bridge, coming to a stop almost on its side with the driver's door pinned shut. A fuel leak sent a stream of gasoline down the side of the engine and onto the hot steel support rods of the bridge and then onto the road below.

One of the troopers had run off the road and up an embankment but managed to stop before his cruiser fell off a small cliff. The other two stopped in the traffic lane and ran to Prewitt, who was still smiling and wondering what had happened. They noticed that smoke and steam were coming from the front of the car and knew that a fire was going to consume the Mercedes at any moment. One of them grabbed a fire extinguisher from his cruiser while the other man climbed up on the passenger door and tried to open it. It was locked. Prewitt was inside, bleeding and laughing.

The troopers used the fire extinguisher to break the passenger window and spray the area where smoke was rising. It took five minutes to get Prewitt out. It would have taken only one minute if the congressman had been cooperative, but he kept saying he liked where he was and didn't want to leave.

A fire and rescue team arrived form Harrisburg and Prewitt was taken to a hospital while police tried to sort out what had happened. Southbound traffic on I-81 was backed up for four hours and the jam was so great that it made the national news.

By then Prewitt had been identified and was isolated in a VIP room where he could be assessed and questioned. He was diagnosed as suffering from a nervous breakdown—"severe emotional trauma"—and the F.B.I. assumed responsibility for getting him to a facility where he could receive the proper care. Prewitt refused to speak to anyone who was not wearing a police uniform. He tried to run away when Ossening walked into his room, screaming, "He's trying to kill me!" at the top of his lungs and throwing his paper cups. He was given a sedative.

Edward Segal spent his hours in the traffic jam, wondering what was happening up ahead.

Chapter Thirty-five

"Good evening and welcome to the Jim Bohannon Show from the Dial Global Radio Networks. We're joined tonight by two men who are right on top of the biggest story in Washington, the murders of Judge Alexander Beechum, Associated Press reporter Peter Deutch, and Beltway insider Arnott Cole. They are Bill Adams of the Associated Press and the man who was with Peter Deutch when he was murdered, Dave Haggard of Now News."

Dave and Bill Adams were sitting next to each other in studios in the CBS Bureau on M Street in Washington. Sid had made it clear that the invitation to appear on the Bohannon Show was to be accepted, despite his feelings about Adams and his attempts to "share" the story. He was to answer the questions without revealing his sources or anything he could not verify. Adams was his arrogant self as he arrived at the studio at the appointed time of 10:45pm for the one-hour interview that would be heard by several million people, many of them in cars and trucks on the highways of God-knows-where.

Bohannon was a large man with a booming voice, a beard, and a reputation as one of the most well-liked men in broadcasting. He was a member of the National Radio Hall of Fame and was one of the few broadcasters of his generation to remain employed in a business that consumes its young.

"Dave, we've got to start with you." Bohannon's voice boomed the question. "There are reports that the prime suspect in these killings, former army sniper Ed Segal, has actually gone to your home. Is that true?"

Dave had reported it on Now News but had been warned away from any details by Ossening. "It is true. He came to my home. He followed me into my apartment and, ah.." He struggled with what to say. He saw that Adams had his notebook on the table and was set to take notes on anything Dave said. "He, ah, tied me to a chair. We haven't released many details yet at the request of the F.B.I...."

"Did he try to kill you?"

"No, I don't think he did. It didn't seem that that's what he was after. He seemed to be after some information. As you know, I've been working on this story for awhile and he seemed to want to know if I had any inside information about Congressman Prewitt, who's been in the news as a target in a federal investigation..."

"Well, yeah," Bohannon jumped in. "That's another story that you've been following and I was going to ask you about that. Are we now to assume that the murders of Judge Beechum, Peter Deutch, and Arnott Cole are related to the investigation of Congressman Prewitt. I mean, this is like the all-encompassing story."

Dave felt like he was being dragged under a bus. Bohannon was probing deeper than the other news types who had interviewed him. "Well, my sources have indicated that that's the case and one of them is at the F.B.I. This sources believes that there's a link to Judge Beechum and the others and it may have had something to do with Congressman Prewitt."

Dave felt light headed as though his mouth had somehow run off on its own and he, along with the others, was waiting for what would come out of it. "As you know, Congressman Prewitt has hired one of Washington's premier defense attorneys who isn't saying anything and is not allowing Prewitt to say anything other than, you know, the standard line that his client hasn't done anything wrong." He took a breath and looked over at Adams, who was writing his notes in shorthand. "But, yes, my sources tell me investigators are looking for a link."

Bohannon turned to Adams. "Bill Adams, what about this hitman, or alleged hitman, Ed Segal. There reports that he might have been responsible for other attacks, fatal beatings. D.C. Police Captain Daniel O'Neil sustained series injuries in such an attack. He is said to be recovering. Is that somehow connected to this entire web of intrigue and possible conspiracy?"

Adams glanced at Dave with a look a frat boy would give to a towny, a smirk that dripped of contempt. "I will share something with you that I haven't shared with Dave, but I feel comfortable sharing it now. Our sources tell us that it was Captain O'Neil of the D.C. Police Department who first identified Edward Segal as the primary suspect in the killing of Judge Beechum and the shooting of Peter Deutch and that the identification was made from images captured by street cameras. So, a link could be made that this was some kind of retaliation for that."

"Segal going after Captain O'Neil?"

"That's right."

Adams was telling Dave that Ossening was playing both sides and had probably given Adams everything he gave Dave. He wondered if either side any secrets left.

Bohannon pressed Adams. "How would Segal know that?"

"I don't know. That's a big question. Maybe Dave can answer that."

"We can speculate all night, I suppose, but the obvious answer is some kind of leak from the inside to Segal. I, for one, don't know where the leak is. Do you?" He looked at Adams.

"Not yet." Adams appeared to be gloating.

Bohannon looked at both men. "I'm hearing reports about you two working together. I've talked to a lot of reporters over the years but I don't recall hearing about a reporter committee. Is there some kind of joint investigation here? I wasn't aware that the two organizations worked that closely."

Dave jumped in before Adams could answer the question. "We are not working together. This is not a joint investigation. As you know, this is a big story and every reporter in the city is pursuing some aspect of this." He glanced at Adams. "He has sources. I have sources. Some of the information is similar." Dave used the word "similar", hoping Adams would assume that it was not identical and that he still had some cards to play.

Adams leaned closer to the microphone. "It's not unusual for reporters to share facts now and then."

"Yeah," Bohannon jumped in, "but I don't recall two news organizations sitting down together like this and jointly discussing an ongoing story they were working on. I don't recall that happening during Watergate. So, at the end of the day, do you both go home with half a scoop?"

Dave and Adams were silent, waiting for the other to say something.

Bohannon filled the dead air. "We'll take a break and be right back." The studio went silent while hundreds of radio stations played the commercials that filled the break.

Dave wanted to leave but he had committed to the rest of the hour. Adams wrote in his notebook. Bohannon got up and opened the studio door to relieve the stuffiness of the small room. His producer brought in Styrofoam cups of water.

Sid sat at his laptop and listened to the show online. He hoped that the Now News board was listening and would know that Dave was in a race with Adams and probably other reporters in D.C. and pushing him away from the story would have the effect of giving up and handing it to a pack of wolves.

Elaine Fuller was listening at home and was surprised to learn that the story had many tentacles. She was relieved to hear Bill Adams on the show because it meant that Dave wasn't the only journalist in the spotlight. She missed the finer points of the exchange with Bohannon because she had no experience as a street reporter.

Edward Segal listened to the radio in his truck in the parking lot of a motel in Roanoke. He felt that Dave had betrayed him. He had assumed that there was some kind of bond or understanding between them that would keep their conversation private. After all, he had spared Dave's life. He would have to rethink his opinion of Dave and what was to become of him

Captain O'Neil listened at home and was shocked that Dave and Adams were releasing so many details of the case. He assumed that most of the information came from Ossening and that could only mean there was much more to be learned from and by him and the other investigators.

Special Agent Ossening listened on his office computer and took notes. He was pleased. As he listened he reviewed the transcript of recordings made from the phone tap on Adams smart phone, both during his calls and while he was having what he thought were private conversations with his boss and others. He felt good. It was always a good feeling when a plan came together.

Chapter Thirty-six

Congressman Prewitt was transferred to a small private hospital in Leesburg, Virginia, a few miles outside Washington. It was a psychiatric facility owned and operated by a celebrity psychiatrist who regularly touted his books on afternoon talk shows and presented himself as a kind of mental health guru. He was tall, thin, wore expensive tailored suits, and monogrammed French cuffs. He also had an expensive cocaine habit that he kept hidden from the rest of the world. He took his vacations in foreign countries where sexual activities that were illegal in the United States could be indulged for the right price. As a younger man he had undergone intense analysis and had found, to his uncomfortable delight, that certain rooms in his psyche were dark and dangerous.

He was a closet sociopath. As such, he was also charming and could read others and determine their weaknesses. His name was Gavin Leland Andrews. He signed all of his correspondence "GLA" and preferred that his staff address him in that manner. He cultivated the rich and powerful and often suggested that a few days "away from the light" might do them some good. He peppered his advice with vague spiritual references and often referred to "life spirit" and "higher power" in his sessions. He had never been known to disagree with a wealthy client or "patient", as he called them. His hospital's going rate was three thousand dollars per day, plus another two hundred fifty for a one hour session with him. Sedatives were extra. Gourmet meals were available for additional charge. In-room movies were free.

GLA didn't know what to do with Congressman Prewitt. On the one hand, Prewitt was a powerful member of Congress and well-connected and wealthy. In that regard, he was GLA's prime target market. On the other hand, there was a cloud hanging over Prewitt and the very strong odor of scandal and even corruption, given the reports in the press. And, worst of all, Prewitt was clearly out of his mind, something GLA preferred not to deal with in any of his patients. Crazy people needed more attention that he was prepared to give. He saw his hospital as a kind of psychiatric spa, not a psychiatric facility in the more traditional definition.

And so he reluctantly walked into Prewitt's room to assess his patient. The congressman was standing by his window, gazing out at the rolling countryside as it greened in the spring sunshine. He was not at his best. The sedative had dulled his mind and he had a dazed look. He was bruised from the accident and his face was swollen and he had a black eye. To GLA, he had the look of a man who had lost a prize fight.

"Good morning, Congressman Prewitt. How are you today?" GLA used his friendliest tone, the one designed to put the other person at ease.

"Huh?" Prewitt didn't recognize GLA.

"How are you? Are you feeling better?"

"Who are you?"

"I'm your doctor. I'm Doctor Andrews but everyone just calls me GLA."

"Okay. Where am I."

"You're someplace where you can get some rest so you can feel better."

"Where are the police?"

"Why do you want to know about the police?"

"Someone is trying to kill me. I need police in here."

"Oh, sir, you're quite safe here." GLA was offering the smile he would present to a toddler or an idiot.

"Get me the police!" Prewitt began to look around for something to throw and settled on his pillow, which was within arm's reach.

Five minutes later Prewitt was unconscious, having been injected with a powerful sedative. GLA was on the phone to Prewitt's family in Tennessee, announcing that the daily fee would have to be doubled, given the serious nature of the congressman's condition. They thanked him for his care and agreed to pay any fee that GLA deemed appropriate.

Ossening was waiting in a small anteroom when GLA got off the phone. "How's our boy?"

"Not good, I'm afraid. He's resting now."

"Meaning you've knocked him out and I can't talk to him."

"He's in no condition to discuss anything with anyone, I'm afraid."

"How long?"

"Give him another twenty four hours. I'll try to have him alert enough tomorrow at this time?"

"Has he said anything about what happened to him?"

"No, he's still screaming for the police. He thinks someone is trying to kill him."

"Doctor, someone is trying to kill him and damned near succeeded."

"Then why don't you have officers protecting him?"

"Who says we don't?"

"As I look around, I don't see any police officers."

"Would that make you feel better?" Ossening thought GLA was a martinet and he had read his file and knew that he was not the paragon of mental health that he presented himself to be.

"I think it would make Congressman Prewitt feel better." GLA's patrician face tilted back into arrogance and he looked down his nose at Ossening. "I'll see what I can do."

"Has he had any visitors? Any phone calls?"

"Not that I'm aware of, other than some calls from the press. We have not returned those calls nor have we issued any statement to anyone about any of our patients, as is our policy."

"So someone knows he's here," Ossening muttered, not looking at GLA.

"It seems so."

"We'll have him moved, probably tonight."

"That won't be necessary. He's perfectly safe here." GLA was concerned about the inflated fees he was looking forward to and what it would mean for a future vacation in Costa Rica.

"I have a different opinion about that. He was safe as long as no one knew where he was. If you're getting calls it means that there's a leak somewhere and it's only a matter of time before you have television trucks on your lawn. Under the circumstances, you don't want that and we don't want to risk any more attempts on his life."

"Is that so you can prosecute him?" GLA's glare was challenging.

Ossening ignored the remark. "Keep him under until we can pick him up. I'll ask you not to discuss this with anyone, including your staff."

Edward Segal's truck was parked under a copse of pine trees two hundred yards from the entrance to the hospital's front door. He was wearing a gardener's jump suit and digging a hole with a shovel he had lifted from a maintenance shed. He had been there for five hours

204.........Larry Matthews

and had driven to Leesburg immediately following a phone call that lasted less than ten seconds.

He watched Ossening leave the hospital and get into a government issued, American made sedan that all but shouted F.B.I. Ossening had the serious look of some-one who had received bad news. Segal assumed that Prewitt was either dead or not doing well. That meant he would be leaving the hospital, either in a bag or on a gurney, most likely through a back door. He moved his truck and settled in for surveillance, his sniper training was serving him well.

Ossening took the Dulles Toll Road back to Washington and reviewed the facts. Who knew where Prewitt had been taken? Too many people. Harrisonburg Police, Virginia State Police, EMS crews, the ambulance driver, staff people at GLA's hospital, and who knows how many others? It was time to button him up. But where? He could go to St. Elizabeth's, the federal government's go-to psychiatric hospital. It was where John Hinkley went after he shot President Reagan, along with other real or would-be presidential assassins. It was where Father Darius was sent after he stabbed the priests. Even the poet Ezra Pound had been kept there after he was declared insane following his pro-fascist broadcasts for Italy during World War Two.

St. E's, as it was known, would be secure, but could it be kept secret? No, he thought. There are too many people who would be in the loop. Phone calls would be made and a media circus would erupt. It had to be somewhere small and private. He made a few calls to discrete mental experts at George Washington and Georgetown Universities and got the name of a high-end retreat for the emotionally fragile in West Virginia's panhandle, a three hour drive from Washington. Very few of the patients were there under their own names.

The list was impressive and included a former President, Secretary of Defense, Forbe's top fifty CEOs, and a few actors who had not bothered to conceal their identities.

The challenge was getting Prewitt into a room without anyone knowing who he was. That would not be a problem if Prewitt could be kept sedated and quiet. The plan had the added bonus of keeping the congressman on ice until the case was ready.

He called a private medical transport company that had been cleared by the F.B.I..

Chapter Thirty-seven

The ambulance backed into a space at the end of the concrete ramp at the rear of the hospital, a few feet from the loading dock where supplies and furniture were delivered. The attendants wore blue E.M.S. uniforms designed to look like the clothing worn by local firehouse personnel in any community. The ambulance bore a red cross and the words "Emergency Response", but no other identifiers. Discretion was the only word on the company's mission statement. Its vehicles had transported the powerful, the famous, the feared, and the occasional terrorist.

Congressman Prewitt was in a stupor and could not have given anyone his name under intense torture and there was no chance that a probing orderly or nurse would get anything out of him. His eyes were partially open but all he saw was a haze of moving lights. He could have been on the moon for all he understood. He was wheeled out of his room and down a hallway to the security doors that opened onto the ramp.

GLA was fretting about his patient and was trying to talk Ossening out of moving him. The agent ignored the doctor and escorted the attendants to the ambulance. Ossening paid no attention to the people whom he assumed were staff members as they stood watching or assisting in the movement of the stuporous patient. The staff members wore scrubs in bright colors with active patterns, the idea being that this would stimulate patients who were depressed or lethargic. The effect was more like a preschool but GLA thought it worked and so the staff had a cartoonish appearance.

One of the cartoon characters standing helpfully by the ambulance was Edward Segal, wearing a lime green set of scrubs with large frogs wearing sunglasses. Segal wore a net head covering and reading glasses he had purchased at a drug store. The glasses made his eyes appear to be large and a casual observer would see a hospital orderly with bad eyesight, not a trained killer. Ossening was busy ignoring the pleas of GLA and he was focused on getting Prewitt out of the hospital and into the ambulance and he did not pick Segal out of the others.

Segal held the ambulance's rear doors open and watched as Prewitt's gurney was placed inside. He held a small medical case in one hand and helpfully placed it into a corner at the rear of the ambulance. He stood back and watched as the doors closed and the ambulance drove away. Then, like the others, he walked away, glancing at Ossening and several agents as they got into their cars and left. GLA stood looking bewildered and wondering how he had managed to lose a patient that could have brought him a great deal of money.

Segal walked behind a dumpster and removed the scrubs under which he was wearing black pants and sweatshirt. He quickly went to his truck and drove out onto the highway. He pulled into the parking lot of a supermarket and opened an application on his smartphone. He looked at the screen and saw a moving, blinking dot. The GPS tracker was working. He would follow it to its destination.

Three hours later he parked on the side of a two lane blacktop road at a gate that bore no address or name. The gate was eight feet high, steel, and was closed. There was a call box embedded in a stonework column where the gate joined a security fence that was topped with coiled razor wire. Segal wondered whether the fence was there to keep intruders out or "guests" in. A paved driveway wound into the woods and disappeared. He drove a quarter mile down the road, turned around, and waited in his truck, lights out and engine off. It was not long before he saw the ambulance pull up to the gate and wait until it opened, then roll onto the highway for the trip back to Washington. Congressman Prewitt was nicely buttoned up, for the moment.

Ten hours later, Ossening received a secure message from the Virginia monitoring station. Segal was on the hunt. The GPS device had been discovered. *Clumsy,* Ossening thought. *Amateurish. He's better than this.* He briefly considered that Segal was playing a game but rejected the idea in favor of the assumption that Segal was as unstable and acting on blind emotion.

He went to visit Captain O'Neil and explained what had happened to Prewitt and what Segal was doing. O'Neil listened and wrote on his notepad, "Segal is leaving breadcrumbs. Be careful."

"You think he's playing us?"

O'Neil nodded and wrote, "He's playing Prewitt. Could have killed him...didn't."

"Well, he knows where Prewitt is now and I'd bet he's around somewhere. We can get thermal surveillance on him and flush him out."

"He was trained at Ft. Benning. Knows how to evade." O'Neil's sloppy hand writing was all over the page and it took Ossening a minute to decipher it.

"We've been trained, too."

"Dave know?"

"Not yet."

O'Neil chuckled through his wired jaw and winced. He picked up his pencil. "Tell him."

"Soon."

The two men sat back and watched Fox News. Ossening made an observation. "Have you ever noticed that conservative women look better?"

O'Neil wrote, "more makeup," and smiled.

"More something."

The men were silent when O'Neil's wife walked in with a tray of crackers and cheese.

Chapter Thirty-eight

The federal court in Washington, like other such centers of American justice, is encouraging journalists and others in the media to open an account for electronic case filing and to engage in other such online activities to move into the digital world. The idea is to get nosy reporters out of the files at the courthouse, where they can use whatever interpersonal skills they might possess to establish relationships with court personnel and perhaps glean information that would be best left confidential. A computer is not personal and a reporter cannot ask an electronic file who showed up from which law firm to file documents or inquire about certain judges. An e-file is only able to provide what is on the screen.

Street reporters know that rule number one is to establish relationships with people who might one day be in a position to offer information. It is accepted that this is a two-way street and that the user is occasionally the used. It was not unknown for Redskins tickets to change hands under this system. At times sources had a score to settle and called a reporter with some "insider" information. At other times the source liked the feeling of importance that tipping a reporter offered. But it all required relationships. The electronic file does not want to attend a Redskins game and has no feelings, positive or negative, for any of the players in any given story.

That is not to say the electronic filing account is useless. It provides emails to reporters about case filings, docket activity, written opinions, case lists and court schedules. Dave had such an account and it saved time once spent going after the paper versions of these things. But it also kept him from doing "maintenance" on the men and women who worked at the courthouse and knew the rumors and gossip.

So he decided to devote a few hours to trolling through the offices where he could legitimately be expected to show up now and then. His search of the electronic files did not turn up any mention of Congressman Prewitt. He didn't expect it to, at least not at this point in the investigation, but the Justice Department had been known to spring surprises and given the high intensity interest of the story, a quick drop-by might be a dramatic way to get the ball rolling.

The courthouse at midday is packed with lawyers, prosecutors, investigators, defendants and their families, people who've been called to jury duty, and courthouse employees. One of them, a woman named Bertha Alberta, was a supervisor in the records department. She had been working there for over two decades and had, in her own mind, seen it all. She was large, black, devoted to "her Jesus Christ," and under no illusions about the word "justice" as it was applied in the world she could see and hear.

In her private moments she had confided in those she trusted that neither the crooks nor the cops had a corner on good or bad. She had seen bad people go free and good people get locked up. She had seen evidence enhanced to convict and incompetence displayed to acquit. In her younger days she had enjoyed a period of idealism about the goodness of man. Those days were gone. Her faith had taught her that Satan was real and she believed he revealed himself daily at the federal courthouse.

She saw in Dave Haggard a fellow traveler. He, too, had the look of someone whose illusions had been ground by the feet of bitter experience and disappointment. They had shared sweet tea breaks on summer days and exchanged stories of life in the rural South, where she had been raised. The racism had driven her north, but the tone and sweetness of life was different in Washington and not as healing.

She believed that Dave was an agent of truth, or as close to truth as could be found on this side of Heaven. She had been warned against becoming his friend for obvious reasons and a note about their tea times had been placed in her file. It didn't concern her because she believed she had never compromised herself or the court, even though she had, at times, mentioned this attorney or that meeting. She had not seen him in weeks but knew he was around because he was in the news almost every day. She was delighted to see him walking the hall on the first floor, reading posted notices.

"Well, if it isn't Mister Famous Reporter himself," she said, sneaking up behind him.

He turned and smiled, giving her a hug to the stares of those passing by. "Hello, Bertha, my favorite courthouse person."

Fifteen minutes later Bertha was in possession of two good tickets to that night's Wizards game and Dave knew the name of the judge who would be handed the Prewitt file. She was a semi-retired hard ass who was universally feared for her dislike of every lawyer who walked into her courtroom and had the temerity to believe that ego and a gift with words could trump evidence and the law. Senior Judge Janet Blancett had been appointed during the Carter administration and had been one of the first African American women to sit on the court. She had enjoyed a long and successful career as a civil rights attorney and law professor. Her formative years had made her skeptical about the legal system and what she believed was its lopsided tilt toward those who already had power and position. Her appointment to the

Prewitt matter was bad news for the gentleman from Tennessee.

Dave wondered if Prewitt or Finegan knew. Who else at the courthouse knew? He had to be careful what he did with the information. It was possible that the circle was so small that Bertha Alberta would be an easy answer for someone probing the leak. In any case, it would not be long before Finegan was told and the wheels of justice would begin to crank again. He went to Now News to have a chat with Sid.

"Call Finegan and run it by him," Sid said, chewing on a gummy cigar. "Ask him if he's heard anything and run some names by him. We can't go with a single source on this anyway, so what's to lose? And this is not something that has a long shelf life. I'd be surprised if it's not in the Post tomorrow. If your source knows and is talking, other people at the courthouse are also talking. You're not the only reporter in town with a pair of shoes, if you get my drift." Sid was in an unusually good mood and it worried Dave.

"How're things with the board?"

"Fuck 'em."

"How do I read that?"

"The she dragon seems to be breathing less fire."

"Meaning?"

"We're in a let's-see-what-happens-next phase of our little drama. Your appearance on Bohannon's show let a little steam out. She's allowing herself to believe that we are actually cooperating with Bill Adams. I am not disposed to tell her otherwise. So, we go our merry way."

Finnegan's office took Dave's number and claimed the lawyer was in court. Finegan called back two hours later and Dave could hear traffic noise in the background. "I'm outside the federal court, Dave. What can I do for you?"

"Get a judge yet?"

"For?"

"The gentleman from Tennessee." Dave tried to make his voice light and friendly.

"Funny you should ask. May I ask you why you're interested at this particular moment?"

"I won't bullshit you. I have some names to run by you. My sources tell me the case is moving forward again."

"No need for this little charade, Dave. If you called me you have one name. Let's hear it."

"Blancett."

There was a pause and Dave heard a bus pull away from the curb where Finegan was standing. "You need a second source on this and you're hoping it will be me."

"Is it Blancett?"

"You know, Dave, I could hang up on you and call Bill Adams or a half dozen other reporters and invite them over for a little chat in my office. That would make your source at the courthouse worthless."

"Or you could confirm or deny."

"I'm concerned about leaks, Dave. The sanctity of our justice system depends upon trust that some things will remain confidential."

"Judge's names are not state secrets."

"I'll do this. I'm on my way to meet with my client and inform him of whatever new developments are in the works. Let me talk to him."

"I hear he's in no shape to discuss much of anything."

"That's a complication that merits special attention."

"Mr. Finegan, you and I both know that by the time you get back from wherever they've got him locked up the news about the judge will be all over town."

Another pause. More traffic noise. A door slamming. Quiet. "Sorry about that. I was waiting for my car. I'm going to need to get our side of the story out, Dave. The government is going to crucify this guy in the press and make their usual somber-faced announcements in an attempt to influence the jury pool. Will you agree to hear our side and give us fair reporting?"

"Always."

"Call my office tomorrow and we can talk on the record. For now, yes, it's Blancett." The call went dead.

Dave stared at his phone. Advance the story; that was the goal. Put one foot in front of another. It was only a name but it was an important name that would set the course for what was to follow. He logged in and wrote his story. Another lead. Another scoop that would put his name on the lips of other reporters.

One question was answered but others were still hanging in the air. Where was Prewitt?

Chapter Thirty-nine

Representative John Prewitt, Jr. was, to use the medical jargon of the day, "resting comfortably," meaning he was semi-conscious. His dreams were vague and fog bound. He would have no recollection of them when he came around. He was in a private room that was decorated in the style of a high end mountain lodge, with allusions to logs and antlers. High thread count sheets and quality reproductions of Western sculptures added a note of class to the room. An antique quilt hung on the wall opposite the bed and was there to offer reassurance and hominess. Large windows presented a mountain vista to inspire spiritual reflection. Prewitt was unaware of any of it.

His doctor was a tall, elegant man who catered to the privileged but fragile psyches of a certain economic class. He was Dr. Bernard Helmut, trained in Switzerland to recognize and treat the ailments of the orchids of civilization. More than a few of his patients were happily back in the world, medicated to a state of personal joy and a sense of balance.

Jerry Finegan stood at Prewitt's bedside and shook his client. "Can you wake him up?"

"We believe it's best for him to rest," said Dr. Helmut, using the perfect tone of arrogance for which high-end psychiatrists are known. Its purpose was to convey a message that the listener had no qualifications to weigh in on anything of importance regarding the patient at hand.

Finegan had some ego issues of his own. "I don't care what you believe, Doctor, wake him up."

"He is highly agitated and is susceptible to instability."

"I am highly agitated and I have a matter of great importance to discuss with my client. Wake him up."

"It's not possible at the moment."

"Let me make myself clear on this. I will go before a federal court and accuse you and this facility of holding my client against his will and I will not hesitate to seek criminal kidnapping charges. This man has no idea where he is or what is happening to him. He has not been party to decisions made on his behalf. There has been no ruling of incompetence. Wake him up."

"I beg to differ with you, sir. This man is here by order of the F.B.I. He was brought here under federal protection. You have no authority to override those orders."

"Is he under arrest?"

"I have no idea."

"No, you don't." Finegan was furious. Prewitt's status amounted to federal custody without the customary legal protections. He was being held as a drugged confinee without his permission or even his knowledge.

"Whatever you need, Mr. Finegan, I am not in a position to give it to you. I suggest you take this up with the proper authorities."

Fifteen minutes later Finegan was on the phone with an assistant U.S. Attorney for the District of Columbia, who informed him that whatever issues were related to Congressman Prewitt were to be brought to the attention of the U.S. Attorney for the Northern District of West Virginia in Wheeling. The man helpfully offered the number of the office, which was closed for the day. It took an hour for Finegan to obtain a private number and another hour for a call to be placed to Dr. Helmut.

Dawn was coming over the mountains when Prewitt began to come around. The new day brought a gray and rainy light that added gloom to the room and hid the mountains. Prewitt, himself, was a bit gray and rainy as he struggled to find his way to reality, looking like a dazed animal as his eyes searched the room for something to remember. Finegan drank stale coffee with a pasty powdered cream product clotted in it, trying to decide whether to drink it to help him wake up or pour it down the sink and demand something better. His coffee machine at home had cost several thousand dollars and required gourmet beans. This stuff was swill. He reassured himself that he was man enough to drink it and he gagged on the clots of creamer.

Prewitt smacked his lips and licked them, looking over at Finegan. "Water."

Finegan poured water from a pink plastic pitcher into a Styrofoam cup and held it to the congressman's lips. Prewitt took several sips and laid his head back on the pillow, staring at Finegan.

"Where am I?"

"You're in a kind of hospital. You were in an accident. Do you know who you are?"

"I'm John Prewitt." There was no hesitation.

"What is your job?"

"I am a member of Congress."

"Excellent. I'm going to get you out of here. Do not allow anyone to give you any medication, even something for any pain you might be experiencing. Do you understand?"

Prewitt nodded and stared into Finnegan's eyes. "Thank you, Mr. Finegan."

"Stay here. Do not get up. I will be outside in the hall." Finegan stood guarding the door while he called the chairman of a company that operated a chain of boutique urban spas where the well-off could spend a day or two drying out and eating healthy food, and engaging in a few low impact yoga classes and spiritual discussions. The places were adult time-outs. One of them was located on Wisconsin Avenue in the upper addresses of Georgetown and was known for its discretion. A Supreme Court Justice was at that moment lying on a small cot listening to soothing music and trying to conjure the image of his inner light. Finegan didn't want Prewitt in Washington and he arranged for his client to be placed in a facility in the mountains, but this time in a place where the F.B.I. was not in charge.

Finnegan's second phone call was to Dave. "Be at my office at noon. No recording and no pictures."

Prewitt was dopey but mobile as Finegan walked him down the brightly waxed hallway to the exit sign. Dr. Helmut clucked and advised against removing the congressman from the safety of the hospital but Finegan ignored him and helped Prewitt through the doors and into the misty light. Visibility was limited to a quarter mile and to Prewitt the world was black and gray and ended at the trees near the edge of the parking lot. He was able to identify the moment but it had no context. He knew he was with his lawyer but he could not recall why he needed one. He was like a child being led by an adult.

Finnegan's expensive German SUV was capable of speeds in excess of one-hundred-fifty miles per hour in comfort. Finegan was a cautious man and rarely exceeded the speed limit, but the implied speed of the vehicle appealed to him just as the implied power of the law in the hands of a skilled lawyer appealed to him. He believed that the credible threat of action was more intimidating than action itself.

The engine issued a throaty, muffled roar as it started and Finegan lost no time driving away. He wanted to be clear of the place before the federal court or the F.B.I.

could think of a reason to detain his client any longer. The pieces of the puzzle were moving into place and nothing was guaranteed, especially his client's freedom.

He was cautious as he navigated the winding road out of the hospital grounds to the highway, keeping his SUV in the middle of the road to avoid losing traction on the wet pavement. He passed a small herd of deer eating by the trees. The animals looked up as he passed and soon went back to their chewing. He rounded the bend that led to the gate and was pleased to see that it opened as he approached. He pulled up to the highway and looked right and left into the mist to see if other vehicles were approaching. He saw an indistinct vehicle on the side of the road but paid no attention to it.

He turned toward Washington and kept his speed down because of the mist and wet road and settled in for the three hour drive. Prewitt nodded off in the passenger seat and his face was pressed against the window. Finegan leaned his elbow against the arm rest on the driver's door and reviewed the case against the man beside him.

The government clearly had enough to bring a case. What was the delay? Prewitt was obviously guilty of something, but what? Did he take millions of dollars from federal environmental cleanup funds? Who else was involved? Was he somehow tied to the murder of Judge Beechum? Prewitt was, like most of his clients, a lying, deceiving, self-interested man who could never bring himself to come clean even with his own attorney. He did not understand that revealing everything to his counsel, even the most embarrassing, humiliating details, was his best chance of beating the charges. Only then could Finegan plot an effective defense. He would take Prewitt to his office to explain to Dave Haggard how the government had, in fact, kidnapped a member of Congress, and hope to generate enough smoke to provide cover long enough to dig deeper. He paid no attention to the truck following him at a discreet distance. Pickups in West Virginia are not unusual.

Chapter Forty

Dave couldn't believe what he was hearing. It sounded like the plot of a bad movie. A member of Congress was, to believe Finegan, kidnapped by the F.B.I., drugged, and taken to a private psychiatric hospital to be kept quiet; all of it under the umbrella of "protecting" him from an assassin who had already killed a federal judge, a reporter, and others.

Finegan had laid it out in the way a lawyer of his skills would present an argument to a jury, one step at a time in clear, concise, easy to understand language. He left no room for ambiguity or consideration of alternative narratives. It had been staged in his office, with the victim, Prewitt, sitting quietly while Finegan stood and outlined his case. Dave had been commanded to sit by the fireplace, which was cold, and listen without taking notes or recording what was being said. After an hour, Finegan sat at his desk and waited for Dave to speak.

"If what you say is true…"

"Every word of it," Finegan cut him off.

"If what you say it true, then the whole thing takes on an even grander scale. What's the F.B.I. saying?"

"Nothing. The U.S. Attorney's office is acting like it doesn't know anything about anything, either here or in Wheeling, where the guy I talked to acted like I was having hallucinations. I think that's why he had no trouble authorizing the Congressman's release. I'll bet the guy was humoring me and thinking the Congressman could leave any time he wanted, so what the hell."

"Have you talked to the F.B.I.?"

"They don't really talk to defense attorneys. They leave that up to the prosecutors. My guess is the prosecutors didn't know what was going on and went merrily about their way to put their case together against Congressman Prewitt. I would further state that this will be the shit that hits the proverbial fan at the U.S. Attorney's office and will have the effect of delaying whatever legal action they plan to take against my client."

"They'll have to clean this up before they move ahead." It was the first time Prewitt had spoken and his voice was thin and reedy. He had the manner of a man who was floating up near the ceiling. His face was still lumpy from the car accident and the bruises were blue and yellow. No one would have judged him to be distinguished or important.

"How are you feeling?" Dave asked.

"I'm not sure. Ask him." Prewitt waved a weak hand toward Finegan.

"He's not well at all, as you can see. The man has been through hell in the past few days. My God! Someone tried to kill him. He was in an automobile accident and injured. He was kidnapped by his own government, drugged, and kept confined in a stupor. How do you think he feels?" Finegan was wearing his best lawyerly outrage.

"Okay, let's talk about what I am going to report. I assume you didn't bring me here to share secrets to be kept in this room. You said I couldn't take notes or record your comments but there were no other ground rules. So why did you bring me here?"

"We want this story to get out. We want America to know what their government is doing. We want you to tell the tale."

Dave picked up his phone and pressed the icon that would begin recording into his "memo" file. "Let's

begin. Tell me what happened to Congressman Prewitt."
He held the phone to Finnegan's face.

The lawyer took a deep breath and glanced at
Prewitt. He began firing sentences at Dave's phone,
each one a sound bite. He had been dealing with reporters long enough to understand that there was no room
for nuance. Simple, declarative sentences were the only
form of communication that penetrated the thick layers
of resistance between the source and the end user, the
news consumer, who was probably not paying attention.

It was an edited version of the story he had told
Dave and much of the background was left out, replaced
by a tone of outrage and a demand for a full explanation
and apology. Even so, it took Finegan a full five minutes
to fire off these sound bites, each one under twenty seconds. When he was finished he looked at Dave, expecting questions. He had covered everything and Dave had
no questions so he put the phone away.

"You could give a master class on how to speak to
the media," Dave said.

"I have," Finegan replied with a weary voice.

"So, what's next for your client?"

"That will remain confidential, I'm afraid, for obvious reasons. I will ensure that he is taken somewhere
that is safe from everyone who wishes him ill. Please
feel free to contact me if you need anything else."
Finegan walked Dave to the door.

"Once this gets out your phones will be burning up
with calls from every news organization on Earth."

"There may be a news conference in my future, depending what happens in the next twenty four hours.
Let's see how the government responds to your reporting. Have a good day."

Dave was in a reporter's golden moment. He had
exclusive information about a story that earlier generations of newsmen would describe as "blowing the lid off

this town," and he was on his way to file it. He sat in the back seat of a cab and listened to Finnegan's words. It was, to be sure, unbelievable. But so was the whole dramatic series of events, beginning with the murder of Judge Beechum. It was so explosive that Dave doubted if Sid would have allowed it on the air without the recording of Finegan. He needed reaction from Justice or the F.B.I., if only to say they had no comment.

He placed a call to Ossening who, as usual, picked up on one ring. "Dave, the scribe, how are you?"

"Scribes are the print guys, ink stained and all that. We're the ones who aren't smart enough to work for the papers and we can't spell, so we're in broadcasting. I have a tale to tell. Do you have a minute?"

Ossening had been waiting for the call. The monitoring station in Virginia had just sent him a transcription of what had been said in Finnegan's office. Bugging an attorney's office is as illegal as kidnapping a member of Congress. Technically, it was Dave who was bugged and not Finegan. Ossening didn't think Judge Blancett, who was about to review the file on Prewitt, would appreciate the difference. "Sure, what's on your mind, Dave?"

Dave laid out what he had been told by Finegan and Ossening remained silent during the recitation. "Reaction?"

"I think I may have mentioned in the past that we don't comment on ongoing investigations, even to something as outlandish as this."

"So you're denying it?"

"I am neither confirming nor denying anything. Frankly, what you are presenting isn't something that would be commented on at this level in any event. You'll need to go to Justice on this. I'd start at the AG's office." His voice was cold. "You know you're carrying water for him, don't you?"

"I've been carrying water for you, too."

"Things are getting dicey, Dave. Watch your step." The line went dead.

His next call was to the Attorney General's office, where an aide answered and told him to hold. By the time the line was picked up Dave was in the lobby of Now News, having paid the cabbie and taken the elevator. The line was picked up by a serious-sounding woman who identified herself as an assistant Attorney General.

"This is Dave Haggard of Now News. I'm looking for a response to a claim being made by Jerry Finegan that his client, Congressman John Prewitt, has been confined against his will by the F.B.I. at a psychiatric facility and during his confinement was medicated to the point of unconsciousness."

There was no pause. "We have nothing to say about that allegation."

"Will you be issuing a statement?"

"We have no plans to address the allegation."

"So, when I report the claim, I can say the Justice Department has no response?"

"You can report whatever you like. I have been instructed to tell you that we have nothing to say and there are no plans in this office to issue a statement."

Dave could hear breathing on the other end and wondered who else was on the line. "I will report that the Justice Department is aware of the allegation and has not responded."

"As I said, report what you like. Goodbye." The line went dead.

Dave walked into the newsroom and sat at a work station, logged in, and plugged his phone into an audio source, where he transferred Finnegan's statement into an audio file that he could edit. Finnegan had done a fine job of editing his own material and it was easy for Dave to chop it into short sound bites for his pieces. Half an hour later he had three two-minute reports and two one-minute spots ready to record. He sent a top of the line message to Sid to check his scripts. Five minutes later Sid's door opened and he jumped into the newsroom.

"Are you fucking kidding me! When did you get this? Did it occur to you to give me a heads up? Can you verify this?" Sid's face was red and he was waving his arms. "The lid's gonna blow in this fucking city. Kidnapped? A member of Congress? Jesus H. Christ!"

The newsroom staff sat stunned as Sid went through his rant. They didn't know whether to look at Sid or stare silently at their computer screens.

"Do I laugh or cry," he said. "Do I tell the board? Dave, go record these pieces and sit on them until I figure this out." He looked at the staff and pointed at each one of them. "Do not, I repeat do not, call anyone or post anything on this for at least five minutes. We're sitting on a bombshell here. I can't believe I just said that."

Dave was fascinated by Sid's behavior. Normally a hard-boiled newsman, Sid was like a kid who didn't know whether to laugh or cry over his new Christmas bike. "We have to get this on the air, Sid. Fuck the board."

"This place is going to go nuts when this gets on," Sid said. "Are you absolutely positive about this?"

"We have audio of Finegan and no denial from Justice. We're not making any assumptions and we're not speculating. Everybody had a chance to tell their side. That's all we're saying. You and I know that this exclusive has a short shelf life. Bill Adams will be all over this in a couple of hours. Finegan is not one to sit on a case when he wants to make a point. We go now or we watch somebody else break it." Dave spoke in a soft voice as everyone else remained quiet. The only sound in the newsroom was the small fans that cooled the computers.

"Record your pieces and we'll alert the stations for a special report." Sid's eyes were bright. "Goddam it! Let's do it!" He walked to a small room where the website people maintained the Now News Internet presence. "Get out here!"

Dave's first report was a special feed that was picked up by the major market stations on the network. The report was simultaneously put up on the website along with a script of the piece. In less than ten minutes alert sounds came from the newsroom computers as other news organizations, including wire services, ran bulletins crediting Now News as the origin of reports that Congressman John Prewitt of Tennessee, rumored to be the subject of a federal probe into kickbacks and other crimes, had been kidnapped and drugged by F.B.I. agents following an attempt on his life and a traffic accident in Virginia. The F.B.I. had no comment. Neither did the Justice Department.

The phone lines in the newsroom lit up with questions from the wire services, major newspapers, television networks, the Now News board, and the usual assortment of crackpots who call newsrooms to report spacemen on their roofs.

Chapter Forty-one

It had been a long time since Edward Segal had laughed so hard that he fell down. But that's what he was doing, on his side, in a cheap motel along Route 1 in Alexandria. The aging television was on, its big tube glowing with the stock footage of Congressman Prewitt from some past event, as the anchor woman delivered the news. *Son of a bitch! It just gets better!* Segal's plan to drive Prewitt out of his mind had never included the F.B.I. angle. *Who could have thought that up?* He laughed so hard his stomach hurt.

He had checked into the motel after he had followed Finegan and Prewitt back to Washington. He had watched Finnegan's SUV drive into the underground garage at his office building on 9th Street. He was disappointed. He had hoped to find a way into the hospital in West Virginia and take a few shots at Prewitt, not fatal shots; shots to wound or frighten and drive him further into hysteria and madness. He was disappointed until he saw the television story about Prewitt, a story that was broken by Dave Haggard. Segal was glad he hadn't killed him. His feelings about Dave were still up and down. He was up at the moment. How could he not like the reporter? He seemed to know more than anyone about what was going on. Segal had no knowledge of the news business and how sources and reporters lived their strange arrangements.

The cable news channel he was watching could not stop talking about it. The anchor woman introduced a lawyer who hosted a talk show about legal issues and she speculated about whether the Director of the F.B.I. would be forced to resign or even whether the Attorney General might fall victim to what she described as "reckless and lawless behavior" on the part of the F.B.I.

A panel was introduced to discuss it and each panel member seemed to be concerned only with inserting his or her opinion, baseless though it was, into the discussion. The segment degenerated into an argument over the role of the Executive Branch in the affairs of the Legislative Branch and what Thomas Jefferson and Alexander Hamilton would have thought of what was happening to Congressman Prewitt.

"What about what he did?" Segal shouted at the television. "He's Satan!"

Segal's mood collapsed into a seething hatred of Prewitt, the news media, the F.B.I. and the grand conspiracy he thought of as "those in charge." This included the Defense Department, which had trained him to kill, the high school where he had graduated despite a pitiful academic performance, and even the church where he had learned that his immortal soul was stained and probably doomed to an eternity of fire and suffering.

His head began to pound and he had trouble breathing. He grabbed the M-4 and some ammunition, fondled the brass knuckles, and went to his truck. He drove over the 14th Street Bridge into the District and turned right at New York Avenue, driving northeast past North Capitol Street and into a neighborhood of working class African Americans. New York Avenue was lined with small strip malls, gas stations, tire stores, and relics of a time when people patronized neighborhood shops.

He searched for a pay phone, now another relic, and it took three stops before he found one that worked, the others having either been disconnected or vandalized. He dialed the number for Now News and was enraged when he was forced to maneuver through a voice message system that required that he either leave a message or dial in the last name of the person he was calling. His hand was shaking as he pushed the buttons for Haggard.

Dave didn't have an extension of his own. Calls for anyone who worked in the newsroom went to the desk, where it would be picked up by the desk editor on duty. Gabriel was working and had been fielding the calls that came rushing in after Dave broke the Prewitt/F.B.I. story. It took a dozen rings before the call was picked up.

"Now News. Gabriel speaking. How may I help you?" His voice was weary and distracted.

"I want to talk to Dave Haggard."

"He's busy at the moment. Who may I say is calling?"

"Tell him it's Ed Segal and I need to talk to him right now."

Gabriel was reading an item on his computer screen and wasn't paying attention. "What's this in regard to?"

"Tell him it's Ed Segal. He'll know."

"Just a moment." Gabriel pressed the "hold" button and stood up, looking for Dave, who was having a private talk with Elena. "Dave, some guy named Ed Segal is on the line for you." Gabriel's face showed recognition as the entire newsroom looked up, then at Dave. "Holy shit!"

Dave ran to a studio. "Get someone to roll on this!"

Gabriel pressed an intercom button and told an engineer to record the line Dave was picking up. Seconds later the engineer nodded to Dave.

"Dave Haggard."

"What the hell is going on, Dave?"

"Hello Mr. Segal. Where are you?"

"I asked you a question. What's going on?"

"Are you asking about Congressman Prewitt?"

"You know I can pick him off any time I want. You too, Dave."

"Why don't you go to the police, Mr. Segal. You know they're looking for you."

"You know what I think, Dave? I think you and the F.B.I. made this up. I think you made it up to make the F.B.I. look bad so they don't have to make Prewitt pay for what he's done. I saw the television. They're not talking about what he's done. They're talking about what the F.B.I. has done and I don't think that's even real. You're in it with them, Dave. Don't think I don't know what's going on here."

Segal's voice was rising and there was a hint of hysteria in it. A young black man wearing coveralls bearing an auto repair shop patch walked by, smoking a cigarette. He stopped to look at Segal during his rant. The face looked familiar to the young man but he couldn't place it. He didn't make the link to the stories he had seen on television. He assumed the guy was a customer at the shop. Segal noticed the young man and let the phone dangle from its cord, he raced to the young man and attacked him with the brass knuckles. The victim's cheek bone collapsed with the first blow and he went down, enraging Segal, whose prosthesis twisted on the uneven sidewalk, sending him off balance.

Two men who were sitting on folding chairs outside a liquor store saw the attack and came to the young man's aid, pulling him up and away from Segal, who was making animal-like noises as he adjusted his prosthetic leg.

One of the rescuers saw the blood rushing from the young man's face and turned to Segal. "What the fuck's wrong with you, man? You outta your mind?" The man opened his cell phone and dialed 911.

Segal's first thought was the M-4 but it was locked in his truck a half block away. He would never make it. He saw a small crowd gathering, every face black and, to his mind, angry and murderous. He limped and ran to his truck and sped away up New York Avenue and into Maryland. It would be hours before police put the pieces together. By then, Segal would be in another cheap motel, hiding behind his bed, the M-4 aimed at the door. He vowed to obtain an M-14 as soon as possible because he would need long range accuracy the M-4 Carbine couldn't offer. It was best for close in shooting. What he had in mind would require skill at longer range.

Chapter Forty-two

Elaine Fuller walked into the newsroom accompanied by an older man in a well-tailored pinstripe suit. As chairperson of the Now News Board of Directors, she felt it was her right and duty to be in charge anywhere and everywhere in the building. She affected a look of contempt mixed with pity for anyone who came into her line of sight.

"Where is Sid?" she asked of no one in particular.

Gabriel was running the desk and, as usual, was double-tasking by working a source on the phone and checking the wires on his computer screen. He ignored her. Elena was doing a phoner in a booth and so she paid no attention to Fuller. An intern who was devoting her life to getting on full time at Now News sat at a work station and tried to become invisible out of fear that to be noticed by Fuller was to be dismissed forthwith. Other staffers acted busy and stared at their screens.

"I said, where is Sid?"

Gabriel looked up and pointed at Sid's closed door, then went back to his call.

Fuller didn't knock. She opened Sid's door and walked in, accompanied by the suit. Sid was hunched over his desk, diagramming the Prewitt story. The Congressman was at the center with lines growing out to his subcommittee in the House, to Ossening, Segal, Cole, and then to his district, to Oak Ridge, and several question marks. It took him nearly a minute to notice that Fuller was in his office, glaring at him. When he looked up, he glared back.

"Something I can do for you?"

"This is David Feinman. He is our general counsel. He and I met privately this morning and we are here to share our serious concerns about Dave Haggard and this Prewitt story."

"I thought we discussed that," Sid replied.

"Oh, did you? That was before the shit hit the fan, as they say in your circle."

Feinman stepped forward, looking very lawyerly and officious. "Our concern is this: Mr. Haggard is under federal court order regarding his role in the capture of Father Darius in the priest killings and the various aspects of that story that he is not allowed to report until certain matters are resolved. Now, he is involved in a very serious series of developments and has been making claims which the Justice Department is now disputing, drawing into question not only his sources but his journalistic integrity. Have I made myself clear?"

"Not in the slightest. Perhaps you would like to translate that into English." Sid sat back and glared at Feinman and Fuller.

Fuller spoke first. "Let me put it this way. Justice now says Dave is full of shit about the kidnapping of Congressman Prewitt and questions his sources. It seems the F.B.I. denies in the strongest term that it did anything but protect Prewitt after the assassination attempt and the subsequent traffic accident. He is, after all, subject to federal protection."

"Dave's source was Prewitt's lawyer. Justice and the F.B.I. were given an opportunity to respond. There's nothing below the water line here."

"There are those in this town who now view Mr. Haggard as irresponsible, Mr. Slackey. A loose cannon, if you will. We can't allow the integrity of this news organization to be tainted by a wild man." Feinman's face displayed a thin, sinister smile.

"He's a hell of a reporter who has been scooping the shit out of everyone else in this town," Sid's voice dropped to a dramatic and sarcastic tone, "and that's why those people you're talking about are saying the things they're saying. He's not irresponsible, Mr. Feinman, he's damned good at what he does." Sid stood up and put his hands on his hips.

"Allow me to wrap this up, Sid. Dave is off the story. Period. No more scoops. Put someone else on it." Fuller's tone was the bloom of authority.

"No can do," Sid said.

"How much do you like your job?" Fuller shot back.

"Not that much right now."

"You're on dangerous ground."

Sid and Fuller were leaning into each other and Feinman, never comfortable with emotion of any kind, stepped between them. "Let's take a break. Mr. Slackey, please consider what we've said. We'll be in touch. Perhaps we can all have a meeting with Mr. Haggard."

"Dave is busy," Sid said. "He's blowing the lid off this town, as they used to say."

Sid's door had been open during the exchange and work in the newsroom had stopped so the staff could listen to the back and forth. Not even the clacking of keyboards broke the silence outside Sid's office. Fuller and Feinman issued one last serious look at Sid and walked out to the stares of those who had heard everything. They watched as Fuller strode past the desk not bothering to look at them. Feinman was behind her taking tiny steps and looking anxious. "Hello, hello," he said in a thin little voice that made Gabriel smile.

When the two were gone the entire staff gathered at Sid's door and stared at him.

"Sorry you had to see that," he said. "Dave's not going anywhere." He sat down and shuffled some papers on his desk.

"We could be looking at a mutiny if the board starts running things," Gabriel said.

"This is my shop." Sid didn't look up.

No one noticed Dave walking into the newsroom. "Something happening?" he asked.

The staff parted to let him into Sid's office. "The board thinks you're a pussy and you need to be more aggressive," Sid said, sitting back and smiling.

"What's really going on?"

"We're gonna rent you a car. It's about time you got off your ass and went to Tennessee to look into whatever the hell is going on down there. Leave tomorrow. Take your time about getting there and don't worry about rushing back. You know what to do."

Sid waved him away and closed his door. Elena, who had been watching from the door of a studio, walked up behind Dave and wrapped her arms around him.

"Do what he says," she whispered.

"What's going on?" Dave looked at the faces of the staff members who were looking back at him."

"Elaine Fuller and some suit came down to demand that Sid take you off the Prewitt story. It's what happens when you get too far out in front of the others. If you leave town you won't be in their face every day when they wake up." She tweaked his nose and he wondered why she was being playful. "And you'll be out of harm's way. Bring your fishing pole and catch up with your family while you're down there."

"I don't have a fishing pole and most of my family is dead. Hell, I'll just be chasing the story there instead of here."

"Rent the car, pack your bag, and go." She had the soft, serious look of a woman who was happy to be making a point. Dave wanted to take her home with him and make love all day.

"Out!" Sid's shout boomed through his door. "Don't say hello to anyone on the board when you leave!"

Sid was already dialing Fuller's cell phone to inform her that Dave was going out of town for a few days. She didn't pick up, so he left a message. It was perfect. He wouldn't have to explain anything to her and he didn't expect her to call him back for details. Neither of them wanted a conversation at that moment. Everyone could make believe that everything was fine.

Chapter Forty-three

Jerry Finegan was trying hard not to loathe his client, John Prewitt, Jr., member of the United States House of Representatives and chairman of a powerful subcommittee. "Do you know what it takes to be a successful defense attorney?" he asked, swirling his expensive Tennessee whiskey around the tumbler in his hand.

"Law school, I'd imagine," said Prewitt, slouching in a leather loveseat.

"Intellect, to be sure, but what's more important is a strong stomach."

"I suppose you get your share of loathsome characters in here." Prewitt was drunk and the booze had loosened his already tenuous grip of reality. He was having trouble focusing on anything but his glass.

"Have you ever heard of a lawyer named Melvin Beli? He was quite famous in his day. He represented Jack Ruby, for free, after Ruby shot Lee Harvey Oswald, the guy who killed President Kennedy. Big case. He tried to prove that Ruby was nuts. Ruby was a pretty low end guy. Anyway, Beli is supposed to have said, 'There is never a deed so foul that something couldn't be said for the guy; that's why there are lawyers.'"

"So?"

"That's where you come in, Congressman Prewitt. I'm searching for the something to be said for you."

"That's your job, to get me off."

"I want you to be honest with me, if you're up to it. What was your deed so foul?"

"What do you mean?"

"Let me ask you a question. When you look in the mirror in the morning, what do you see?"

"What kind of question is that?"

"What's your answer?"

"I see me, goddam it!"

"Are you satisfied with this you?"

"Of course! I'm an accomplished man. I am a substantial man. I'm a man who matters. I'm not like these bums who go through life being told what to do."

"Did you steal money from the United States?"

"How do you define steal?"

"Take what wasn't yours."

"Then, no, I didn't steal it. It belonged to me because I had control of it. Finders keepers."

"How much finders keepers are we talking about?"

Prewitt began to giggle like a child. "I'll never tell."

"It's better that I know everything now, before the Justice Department starts dropping discovery documents all over the place. I need to know what to prepare as a defense."

"What you need to do is make this go away before there's any more trouble." Prewitt was becoming belligerent.

"Did you have anything to do with the murder of Judge Beechum?"

"Of course not! That was Cole's job. He knows people who know people."

"Do you know who these people are?"

"I tried to find out but the F.B.I. already had the files, I think."

"What does that mean?"

"I thought I could get files from Cole's house but I was too late."

"I'll be honest with you. The worst case here is you become the first sitting member of Congress to be strapped to a gurney and executed by your own government. That would be bad for my career. So try to jog your memory."

"I don't need to sit here and listen to this. I have friends in high places."

"Your friends aren't exactly stepping up to support you. The House leadership has been pretty quiet. All we've heard so far is along the lines of let the wheels of justice turn and we wish him well. I wouldn't expect these folks to be character witnesses at your trial."

"I don't remember much."

"Let's agree on this, then. You need to get control of yourself. That means no more booze. Go home to Tennessee, dry out, get your head together." He gave Prewitt a soft leather briefcase onto which had been glued a white piece of paper that read "Confidential legal documents." "I want you to take this with you. When you are sober and alert I want you to write down everything you can remember about all of this and place the documents in this briefcase. Do not leave them on your desk or out where they can be seen by someone who happens to walk into your office. Do you understand?"

Prewitt looked at the briefcase and nodded.

"I am going to have someone drive you to Tennessee. If you need anything from your home here in Washington I will arrange to have it sent to you. You will not be going there for a while. The car is downstairs. The driver is also a trained bodyguard. He has instructions not to allow you out of his sight. You are not to go into any bars or stop along the way for anything other than relief of bodily needs and fuel. Am I clear?"

"Am I your prisoner?"

"You are my client and you are in very big trouble."

"People keep telling me that." Prewitt was pouting like a small boy.

"People are correct."

Finegan escorted Prewitt to the underground garage where a car was waiting. It was a gray Mercedes sedan, a vehicle that would not be noticed at all in Washington and in Tennessee only because of its nameplate. The driver was a tan-skinned man of uncertain ancestry wearing a military-style haircut and a dark suit. His face was non-threatening but blank. He appeared to be very fit.

"This is James. James is your driver. If you need anything just ask him and he will provide what you need. As I said, he is under instructions to get you to your home as soon as possible without any unnecessary stops or distractions. There is a cooler in the back with bottled water and fruit. You have had your last drink until further notice. If I am informed that you have been drinking I shall no longer represent you and, frankly, I doubt if you will find any top flight lawyer willing to take you on. Please, Congressman Prewitt, do yourself and favor and get yourself together." With that, Finegan closed the door of the car and James drove up the ramp and headed for the George Washington Parkway to the Beltway and eventually down Interstate 81 to Tennessee.

Chapter Forty-four

Edward Segal was shaking. He was on the floor on the far side of the bed, rolling ammunition between the palms of his hands, and trying to decide what to do. He had not slept and he was aware that his thinking was foggy and unfocused. He couldn't decide whether doing something was better than doing nothing. Nothing meant remaining where he was and waiting for whatever came through the door. He was rational enough, in odd moments, to understand that what was most likely to come through the door was a maid. In his less rational moments he was prepared to shoot anyone, even the maid, for violating his space.

His breathing was heavy and drool was dripping from his chin. He had flashbacks to scenes in Iraq and saw grotesque images of bodies blown apart and heads exploded by the .50 caliber rounds he had sent into them. His dreams were filled with these people, men and women, coming for revenge, shouting Islamic verses as they cut him to pieces. But his dreams were only there in sleep, and sleep was nowhere in the room, so the images seemed real. He screamed at them and the sound made them go away and he was left with the feeling one has after waking from a nightmare, nothing but the breathing and the looking around at reality.

He managed to stand up and hurry into the bathroom, where he relieved himself and climbed into the shower still dressed. He sat in the tub and felt the cold water slowly warm and then become too hot. He adjusted the water temperature and sat under it for a long time, forcing his mind to work. What was he doing here? Who was he after? What was his mission?

Prewitt. Yes. Him. Dave Haggard. What about him? No, Prewitt. Prewitt must die. How? He remembered shooting at Prewitt and following him. Where was he now? He went with his lawyer.

Where does the lawyer live? Maybe Dave Haggard would know and tell him. Where was Dave Haggard? He was at his apartment. Where was the apartment? Am I safe here? Should I leave?

Slowly, Segal went through the details and they came back to him, if only in pieces. He got out of the tub, turned off the water, and changed into dry clothes. He field stripped the M-4 and placed it into a canvas carrying case. He gathered his things, placed them in the truck, and drove away. The traffic and the people along New York Avenue helped bring him back to what was left of his senses and he realized he had not eaten. He pulled into a fast food chicken place and ate three orders.

He drove to Suitland and found a working class neighborhood of small brick bungalows that had been built in the fifties, a community where low level government workers and mechanics who drove Harleys lived side by side; the blacks as churchgoers and the whites as long haired dopers. He cruised the streets until he found what he was looking for, a pickup truck with current plates that had been parked at the end of a driveway that was near a backyard fence. He removed the Maryland plates and swapped them for plates he had stolen in Florida. The pickup was dirty and Segal assumed that it was not driven every day. The owner might notice the swapped plates within hours or maybe not for days. Segal would steal another set when he got to Tennessee.

He felt much better. He was able to create a to-do list in his mind and placed obtaining an M-14 at the top of the list. It was ideal for the long range shooting he planned. He would trade the M-4 Carbine for the M-14 and an ammo box of 7.62 high impact bullets. He smiled as he drove. Two hours later he pulled into the yard of a farmhouse in Culpepper County, Virginia, where he was met by a large bearded man whose black baseball cap displayed the wings of an army paratrooper. A few beers later Segal had what he needed and his mind was clear.

He was south of Roanoke before he stopped for fuel and a bathroom break. He kept his speed just above the limit and allowed faster vehicles to pass him. He had travelled the road enough to know that Virginia State Police maintained speed traps in areas where travelers were tempted to mash down the gas pedal to make better time. He cruised through Bristol and crossed into Tennessee, taking I-81 to its end and picking up I-40 toward Ashville, getting off the interstate at Tennessee route 411 and driving up towards Gatlinburg, staying on state routes through the mountains and small towns.

He found a low end motel a few miles from Gatlinburg and pulled his truck onto the gravel parking lot to a spot in front of the small office where a "VACAN-CY" sign was blinking and buzzing. There was one other car in the lot and he assumed it belonged to the owner of the motel.

The man behind the desk was very tall and thin and wore a full beard and bib overalls. Segal wondered if the fellow was acting out a hillbilly fantasy. The man wore a nametag that read "Hello I'm Bob."

"Hello, I'm Bob," he said, standing nearly to the ceiling. "What can I do you for?"

"I need a room," Segal said. He had pulled the bill of his baseball hat down low so most of his face was hidden.

"We got 'em," Bob said. "Just happen to have a bed or two." He stuck his fingers behind the overall's shoulder straps in the manner of a farmer looking at a heifer.

Segal noticed that a woman, probably Bob's wife, was in the back, working at a sewing machine.

"Emma's making curtains," Bob said, noticing Segal's glance. "She keeps the rooms looking real nice."

"How much?" Segal asked.

"Room's twenty-eight dollars during the week and ten dollars higher on weekends. We only raise it when we're full. That's in the fall when the leaf lookers come around, so I wouldn't worry if I was you. How long you planning to stay?"

"Not sure. I'll pay for two nights." He handed three twenties to Bob.

"You from Maryland?"

"Moving back." Segal felt bad that Bob had noticed the tags on his truck. It would mean painful trouble for Bob and the woman in back. He could not risk questions.

"Never been there myself and don't have a desire to. Too close to Washington if you ask me." He handed Segal his change. Segal waited for Bob to hand him a registration card but Bob just stood behind the desk smiling. "Have a good stay. We close up around ten at night so if you need anything call the desk before that. You want to be on the end or in a middle room?"

"End is good," Segal said.

He parked his truck behind the motel and settled into his musty room, which was furnished with cheap furniture, homemade curtains, a worn linoleum floor, and two scratchy towels. A hand printed sign over the dresser announced, "Folks don't come up here to watch TV so we don't have any." There was a pay radio next to the bed that offered one hour of listening for fifty cents.

It was a dump even by the low standards Segal had set. He locked the door and closed the curtains. He opened a long canvas bag and removed the M-14 and field stripped it so it could be cleaned and examined. He reassembled the weapon, wiped oil on a dozen rounds of 7.62 ammo, loaded the weapon, set it beside him on the bed, and fell into a deep sleep.

Chapter Forty-five

Dave drove into Oak Ridge in the late afternoon, passing a college and a shopping strip anchored by a big box store. The town is a community of people who live, literally, with The Bomb. Nuclear weapons are its reason for being. The federal government swept into Bear Valley in 1942 tacking eviction notices on the modest homes of the people who lived in the valley, forcing them out to make way for the Manhattan Project. It was ideal. It was rural, remote, had water from the Tennessee River and electricity from the Tennessee Valley Authority, a Depression era program to electrify the South. It was renamed Oak Ridge, declared a secret facility and populated by people who had the skills necessary to develop and build nuclear weapons. Oak Ridge is a place of secrets, rumors, and poison.

Dave drove past the sites with their odd government names: K-25, now decommissioned, where uranium was enriched; Y-12, electromagnetic separation of uranium; X-10, graphite reactor; strange looking, windowless buildings in massive complexes where instruments of mass death were designed; here and there a historic marker. To Dave, it was a charmless town that could have been the setting for a horror movie.

He had an appointment with Bob Alford, the sheriff of Roane County, which is home to part of the Oak Ridge complex. Alford had been a law officer for nearly thirty years and knew the back roads as well as any moonshiner. He knew where the stills were operating and where the crystal meth labs were cooking. He had known and worked for or against all of the politicians in East Tennessee and he had a good idea where every bone was buried, even if he had decided that some are best left that way.

Dave pulled into the gravel parking lot at the Midtown Restaurant and parked near the door, which displayed a sign proclaiming "The 4th Best Hamburger in East Tennessee". He laughed as he got out and wondered where he could find the top three. Alford was sitting in a booth, wearing a short sleeve white shirt and a brown tie. He had the look of a man who had no illusions about human nature.

"How you doin', Dave? Long time since we've seen you down here."

"Good, Bob. How's life in the hills?"

"Nothin' ever changes around here. Well, that's not exactly the way it is. We can't eat the fish from the river or drink the water anymore, but other than that…" He let the words drift away.

"How's your wife?"

"She's the same. Chemo seems to be working. I went by your people's graves on Sunday and told them you were coming down. You should go by."

Dave's family was buried in an old church yard in Rockwood. He rarely visited the spot, which caused him to shut down his emotions to a point where he couldn't talk to other people for days. "There's too much cancer in these hills," he said.

"Hell, it's in the air. It's everywhere. You know what? I poured some tap water into a clear glass and let it set on the counter to evaporate just to see what would happen. It turned into an orange gel, then it turned black. The government tells us it's okay to drink. 'We put chemicals in it,' they say. I say, yeah, they sure do. Poison chemicals."

A young couple sitting in the next booth overheard the conversation. The woman held up a glass of water the waitress had put on the table. "I ain't drinkin' this. Anybody that drinks the water in Oak Ridge is crazy."

The man with her nodded. "The air smells funny around here. I don't know what it is, but it ain't healthy."

"People around here are mean," the woman added, "and they don't talk to anybody."

Alford raised his eyebrows and leaned over to whisper. "I locked them up awhile back. Dope heads."

"What're people saying about Prewitt?"

"Nothing. Nobody talks much about him. To be honest, most people around here assume that everybody in Washington is crooked, so they go about their business and let the crooks have their day."

"Congress appropriated billions of dollars to clean up Oak Ridge and the Tennessee River after the potash spill. Has anything been done?"

"Not that I can tell. If you read the papers they'll tell you that all sorts of things are happening but I can't see it." Alford drained his coffee and laid a five dollar bill on the table. "Let's take a little drive."

Alford drove into the older part of the town, the section that had been built by the government in the early days of the bomb's development. Small, ill kept houses in a neighborhood that had worn out written all over it. He drove to an overlook where a historical marker noted the bomb development that had taken place across the street, where a tall fence protected acres of whatever was taking place at that moment. Cars, trucks and people were over there doing their secret work. Dave wondered whether a security camera was taking his picture. He took out his smart phone and took a picture of his own.

"See that mountaintop over yonder?" Alford pointed to a treed hill southwest of where they were standing.

"There's a quarry up there. It's been filled with water for years. Kids swim in it every summer. A few years back we had a drought and the water level went down, way down. And, lo and behold, what turns up? Equipment and old cars and trucks, radioactive as hell. It seems that when these things got contaminated the dang government just dumped them into the quarry. That's what they did back then, they got rid of things that became too radioactive to be around. Some of it got dumped in the Tennessee River. It's a wonder we're not all walking around with two heads."

"But there's got to be something that's cleaned up, Bob. That money went somewhere. They're building new houses around here, so things can't be all bad."

"Local people ain't buyin' them, Dave. Retirees come down here and get the pony show about how safe everything is. Hell, man, would you buy a house across the street from where they make nuclear bombs?"

"Prewitt says it's being cleaned up. He crows about how much money he got for it."

"Have you seen his place? I'll show you where heavy money is being spent." Alford walked to his cruiser and waved Dave over.

It was a forty-five minute drive from Oak Ridge to the Prewitt estate, a two thousand acre mountain paradise of streams, meadows, polo grounds, tennis courts, and houses big and small. A gate guarded the paved drive that disappeared behind mature trees.

"I know his daddy made a lot of money but there's been a ton of construction up in there and I don't think a Congressman's salary is enough for what's been built. I know people who've done the work and you would be shocked at the things he's built. Luxury ain't the word for it. He's living like a king. He's got himself a half acre heated indoor pool. It's got waterfalls and grottos that would make Hugh Hefner jealous. He's got a bas-

ketball court and a full theater. Somebody paid for it."
Alford's cadence was staccato like a man reading from a
list.

"And nobody's mad about it?" Dave asked.

"What good will it do? He'll get re-elected. Nobody
around here'll vote him out. He spreads just enough
honey around to keep the bees coming back."

"Have you heard the news reports about him? He's
under investigation, you know. The Justice Department
thinks he's involved in kickbacks and all kinds of
things."

"Sure, we've heard it. As for the Justice Department, don't get me started on them, Dave. Or the F.B.I.
They called me this morning to say they'll be down here
keeping an eye on Prewitt. Yeah. The cavalry's here."

"Prewitt's down here?"

"Seems so."

"How long?"

"Beats me. He doesn't call me with his schedule. It
can't be long or the F.B.I. would have called sooner. I
got the feeling they called so I wouldn't be keeping an
eye on him. It was a courtesy call that had the smell of a
warning. We're here so you don't have to spend any
time look at his place. That was the message I got."

It was getting dark and Dave wanted to get some
rest. It had been a long drive. "Is Uncle Danny still up
and around?"

"I already called him. He's expecting you. How
long has it been?"

"A long time," Dave said.

"Damn, boy. You need to keep in touch. He's all
you got left."

"How is he?"

"Three bouts with the cancer and two heart attacks.
How would you be?"

"Pissed off, I guess."

"Too late for that."

An hour later Uncle Danny Haggard was standing in his doorway, looking frail and small. He wore an oxygen line into his nose. His hair was gone. His skin was pale. He was a shadow of the man who had carried Dave on his back in happier years. His house smelled of sickness. Dave saw that his kitchen faucet was taped closed with a warning sign. Bottled water was placed by the cupboard.

Chapter Forty-six

Congressman John Prewitt, Jr. was in his heated pool, naked. He sat in one end and stared at the other. James, his bodyguard, stood by the side of the pool in a business suit, looking uncomfortable. Prewitt had been in the pool for hours and had finally quieted down after shouting orders for James to get him a drink, a tumbler of fine Tennessee whiskey. James had offered only bottled water, the kind flown in from faraway places.

"You know I'm a powerful man," he said, staring straight ahead. "Down here people of my station matter and what we say goes. There was a time when we could have people shot or hanged if they didn't jump when we said jump." He looked up at James.

"Would you like some water, sir?"

"I'm sitting in some damned water. I'd rather be sitting in some whiskey. At least I could get a taste."

The pool was enclosed in a building whose walls were glass coated to reflect the sun and prevent the structure from becoming unbearably hot during the southern summer. At night, however, the glass walls offered no protection against those on the outside who wanted to look inside. It was not considered a serious problem because there were acres between the pool house and the nearest road and many trees and hills to provide privacy. In the reasoning of Prewitt's class, intruders were unthinkable. Who in their right mind would risk intruding on the property of a Southern grandee? As Prewitt himself had put it, such a thing would once have been a hanging offense.

Edward Segal was a product of this society and he had contempt for it. He had long ago given up any respect for it and no longer felt bound by its rules or etiquette. He had walked these hills all his life and had no trouble negotiating what passed for security fences around Prewitt's property. He had scouted the area during dusk and saw the F.B.I. agents at the gate, looking at maps. He knew it meant they had not stationed themselves at security points and were still planning their mission, whatever it was.

Segal was lying on his stomach in the prone position. He had attached a bipod to the M-14 to stabilize the barrel and he was using a high quality, commercial grade scope to plan his shot. He was wearing black clothing and had smeared burnt cork on his face to darken it and prevent a reflection on his skin. He felt good. He felt in control. He was ready.

He set the bipod on firm ground under a large Virginia pine whose branches offered cover. He scanned the grounds near the house and saw lights in the windows of the main house. To the left he saw the glow of the pool house and adjusted his scope until he had focus. He saw a man's head sticking out of the water at what appeared to be the shallow end. He could make out Prewitt and he considered the odds of hitting him at this angle but rejected the idea because the target area was small and the glass and the water would affect the bullet's trajectory. He would wait until Prewitt exited the pool and offered a better target.

Segal saw the other man standing on the pool deck. He assumed the man was a guard or a servant. He scanned up to get a closer look but the man's back was turned to him. He waited for the man to turn around and considered the wisdom of taking him out before shooting Prewitt. The fellow took his time with whatever he was doing and when he turned Segal saw that he was holding a plastic cup and liquid was spilling from it. Prewitt looked at the man's face and froze.

The man with Prewitt was, like Segal, a professional killer. Segal didn't know his real name. Names were not freely offered within the organization that hired the ones who did the wet work, but he knew the man's reputation. He was known as an inside man, a killer whose specialty was working from the inside, unlike Segal, who was an outside man, a killer who took lives from a distance. This man worked for the same agency that employed Segal, not that any of the contractors who worked through the agency had any idea who ran it or where it was headquartered. It was a small world and the prime players knew each other by sight, whether their employer approved or not.

Segal assumed that the man with Prewitt knew that he was out there and planning the shot. If so, he was cool. There was no sign of nervousness or concern. The man handed the cup to Prewitt and went back to his place on the pool deck, his hands behind his back. Segal had to stifle a laugh. Whoever was setting the rules of the game had a sense of humor. Prewitt was a dead man walking. Who else was on the list? Segal had no doubt that his name was there.

He could strike first and take out the man, but that would likely send Prewitt back into the arms of the F.B.I. and another hiding spot. He had the skill to take them both out but the odds were lower and his window was closing fast, so a miss on one or the other could be his last chance. And there was the matter of Dave Haggard. He had called Now News from the motel and was told that Dave had gone to Tennessee, so he was here and had to be found. There was no room for mistakes. He judged his chance of survival at no more than fifty-fifty.

Segal watched through the scope for another hour as Prewitt sat in the water looking glum. The man with him stood nearby and did nothing. *He's waiting for me to make a move*, Segal thought. He made his way to his truck and drove back to the motel. He would spend the next twenty four hours looking for Dave Haggard.

Prewitt was losing patience. He had led a pampered life and assumed that this man James would succumb to the congressman's obvious superiority and power and get him a drink, a real drink, something with hair on it, not this stupid water.

"Look, James. This has gone on long enough. Get me a goddam whiskey and be quick about it."

James's face remained without expression. "I'm sorry, sir, but I have my orders."

"I'm giving you new orders. I'll make you a deal. You get me a bottle, a whole bottle, and I'll give you anything you want. I can get a beautiful girl here in half an hour and she'll do whatever you want. I can get you drugs. You name it." His voice contained more desperation than authority.

"What kind of drugs?" James had a small smile on his face.

"Whatever you like. You want pot? I can get it for you."

"I want heroin. Can you get that?"

"Heroin? My god, man! You don't look the type."

"Get me a good shot of heroin and I'll open the bar for you. That's the only deal I'll make."

Prewitt stood up and climbed out of the pool. His pasty body was dimpled from the time in the water and his lack of personal discipline had given him a lumpy appearance that betrayed bad eating habits and too much whiskey. He showed no embarrassment as he stood naked and made a phone call, whispering something that sounded like code to James, who was trying to appear disinterested.

"Go down to the gate in fifteen minutes. Someone will hand you what you want. I'll get dressed. We'll both have a good night." Prewitt had the self-satisfied look of a man who has found and exploited another man's weakness. He went to his bedroom suite and dressed in silk pajamas. He looked at himself in the mirror, smiled, and saluted. He inserted his feet into soft leather slippers and went down to his den.

James arrived back at the house bearing a small package that had been handed to him by a young woman who appeared to be barely conscious. She was in the passenger seat of an old, rusty Japanese car driven by a young man with long, oily hair and a glassy, straight-ahead stare. The car had only slowed, not stopped, and the woman held the package out to James and the car sped away. Two F.B.I. agents wearing camouflage suits witnessed the handoff and noted the car's license plate. They took photos of James and uploaded them into a database for identification.

James found Prewitt in the den, sitting by a gas fire, holding a glass. "So, my fine friend, I believe you owe me a drink."

James went to a mahogany cabinet and inserted a key into a brass lock, opening the ornate door and removing a bottle of Tennessee whiskey, which he opened and held out to Prewitt. The congressman poured three fingers into the glass and drank it down, expelling a burst of air like a punctured tire. He poured and drank another, then another. He face grew red and arrogant. "Well, aren't you going to use what's in the package?"

"Later," James said. He stood by the fire and watched Prewitt drink.

When the bottle was empty, and Prewitt was incoherent, James knelt by the chair and looked into his eyes. "I think it's time for you to sleep." He picked Prewitt up like a baby and carried him to his room. He did not put him to bed. Instead, he removed the silk pajamas, folded them, and put them back where they were stored. He did the same with the slippers. Prewitt, nude again, mumbled something that James could not make out.

James carried Prewitt back to the pool house and laid him on the deck. Prewitt's stomach protested the large volume of whiskey by expelling some of it. James did not bother to clean it up. He opened the package and found a syringe loaded with a cloudy liquid. He smiled. Prewitt had ordered a hot shot, a killer dose. "What goes around..." he whispered, inserting the needle into Prewitt's left arm. The congressman was right-handed and he wanted the F.B.I. agents to assume that Prewitt has injected himself. He plunged the drug into the drunken man and left the needle in his arm. He slipped Prewitt into the shallow end of the pool and left him to die.

Prewitt would not be found until morning. By then the man called James would be in a room in Knoxville, checking his account for payment. He had one more task.

Chapter Forty-seven

Uncle Danny was a gun lover. He had rifles and shotguns displayed on wall racks and rejected the idea of gun safes, believing that guns should not be hidden away. When he was asked about burglars who could break in and steal his guns, he replied by saying he never went out anymore and kept loaded guns all over his house, so a burglar's chances of surviving a break in were zero.

Uncle Danny also liked beer, which he drank out of shot glasses, one swallow at a time, poured from quart bottles. It had been a habit ever since Dave could remember. When the rest of the family was alive Danny's drinking habits had been the subject of discussion, but now that Dave and Danny were the only ones left, it was not mentioned.

"You recognize that one up there," Danny asked, pointing to a 30.06 propped in a wooden rack that held three other long guns. "Your daddy had that made out of a Springfield he picked up for twenty dollars. He had that stock put on and the barrel blued. Single shot but man it's a good gun."

"That thing used to knock me down when I was a boy," Dave said. "My shoulder would be sore for days after an afternoon in the woods."

"You don't get to be a man by popping BB guns." Danny was an old-style Southerner who believed that being a man meant living by an honor code that required a skill with firearms and fists.

"Not much call for guns like that up in D.C."

"That's a matter of opinion, it seems to be. There are those of us who believe that a good shootout could do wonders for the country, if you get my drift." Danny tried to laugh but it was a weak effort and sent him into a coughing fit.

"How you feeling?"

"Hell, who knows? Day to day. Tell me, what's this I've been reading about you and all you been working on up there?"

Dave sipped a glass of beer and told Uncle Danny about Congressman Prewitt, Edward Segal, and the details of the story. He held nothing back. In the Haggard family, secrets and confidences were held to be sacred and Dave knew that Danny would never reveal what was said under any circumstances, even the threat of harm or prison. It was a quality that had brought grief to past Haggards but had also bonded them.

Danny listened and drank his beer one shot at a time, closing his eyes at some points in the story and nodding at others. When Dave sat back, Danny got up and slowly walked into his bedroom, returning with two handguns. "This is your daddy's .357. He carried it for years. It's old fashioned by today's standards but it will knock a man down. Here's my KelTec .32. It's small but it will do the job. Keep the .357 on your belt and the KelTec in your pocket."

Dave was moved by Danny's generosity. "I can't have guns in D.C., but thanks."

"Boy, you're not in D.C. right now and from what you've told me, you need all the protection you can get. Nobody will give you grief for being armed around here."

"You know the Segal clan?"

"I know of 'em. They're up in Sevier County and some of them live across the border in North Carolina. Some good, some bad, like everybody else. I don't think

I know Edward personally but I believe his daddy was a state trooper that died of cancer. And I recall he had an uncle that was a guide in the Great Smoky Mountain National Park. Big hunters and fishermen, like half the folks around. Like us, they're not folks to trifle with."

Dave knew the type. Southern boys, good with guns, long on slights and short on patience. "Are you up for a little shooting?"

"Always."

Uncle Danny's back yard was thirteen acres of woods sloping uphill. It was a natural gun range. Danny handed Dave a sack of cans and bottles and watched as Dave placed them away from the house at distances up to a hundred yards. For two hours the men fired handguns and rifles and it was not long before Dave had his shooting eye back and could pick off a can and bounce it up hill or shatter a bottle and then pick off the larger pieces. He felt good and even the ringing in his ears gave him a sense of peace and home. They spent the evening cleaning the guns and talking about family. Dave knew that soon Uncle Danny would be gone and he would be alone in the world. He thought about Elena and how she fit into his life. He had no answers.

He had left these hills to get away from the demons of his childhood and to see the big city. He could write and he liked excitement, so he fell into the news business. If someone asked him how he had become a reporter he had no ready answer. Journalism students often asked him for advice and he was a loss for words, so he offered platitudes about working hard and showing up on time. He pondered the direction of his life as he watched Uncle Danny cleaning the guns and the scent of the gun oil brought back the happy moments of his childhood when he had sat at the kitchen table with his father and oiled the revolvers, rifles and shotguns that were part of his family life. It occurred to him that anti-gun Yankees would never understand the gun culture of the South. It was not about violence or robbing banks. It was tied to the past when firearms were part of survival. He wiped down the .357 and gently inserted it into a leather holster. He held the .32 in the palm of his hand. In the world of gun owners it would be described as a "ladies gun," small and easy to use. It fit into a man's front pocket or even a sock. It was solid. It was useless at distance but effective in close.

Dave and Uncle Danny went to bed that night with warm family feeling that comes over people who haven't seen each other in a very long time. Danny slept with oxygen tubes in his nose and a nest of medicines beside his bed. Dave slept in a spare room that had become a repository of items that Danny didn't see fit to put away or dispose of, so Dave had to clear a spot on the bed. His mind was far from the story of Prewitt and Segal and what was happening at the Justice Department. He breathed the air and felt the nudge of his childhood as he fell into a deep sleep.

The sun was shining through the old lace curtains when the dobro ringtone woke him. He answered with, "Yeah," and rubbed his face.

"Prewitt is dead. Did you know that?" It was Sid, sounding angry.

"What? Where?"

"I imagine you can smell his corpse from where you are. He was found this morning at his home around the corner from you. The F.B.I. isn't saying what caused it, only that it's under investigation. What have you found down there?"

"Nothing, I just got here. No one seems to be talking much about him. And Prewitt's place is not exactly around the corner."

"Time to get to work. Half of the Washington press corps will be down there by tonight, so you can get a jump on them if you move fast. And file. Use that fancy phone of yours."

It took Dave nearly an hour to drive to Prewitt's estate and television crews from Knoxville and Chattanooga were set up outside the gate as he pulled up. He didn't recognize any of the reporters but they recognized him and two identical-looking blonds with big hair and heavy makeup pushed microphones into his face as he walked to the gate.

"Dave, Dave! What do you know? What can you tell us?"

"I'm just a reporter like you. I don't know anything."

"Please, Dave. You've been working on this story. Tell us what happened."

What kind of world is this? Reporters interviewing each other? "I don't know anything." He walked away from the blonds and their microphones and heard one of them say, "He's lying. Asshole."

The gate was closed and guarded by a Roane County sheriff's deputy and a woman who had the appearance of a federal agent, stern and businesslike. Dave didn't know the deputy and he doubted it would have mattered if he had, given the power vibes coming from the agent.

"Ossening around by any chance?" he asked, hoping the name would impress her. He assumed that Ossening was in Washington or on his way to Tennessee.

"Inside," she replied. "Who are you?"

"Dave Haggard. I'm from Washington."

"Wait one." She walked away and spoke into her wrist. "He says wait here."

Special Agent Ossening was wearing jeans and a fleece vest when he walked up the gate. He smiled at Dave, opened the gate, and waved him in as the television blonds ran up shouting questions and demanding to be allowed onto the grounds with Dave. Ossening didn't acknowledge them and ordered the female agent to close the gate. The two men walked up the long drive to the main house.

"How did he die" Dave asked.

"Officially or off the record?"

"Both."

"Officially, it's under investigation. Unofficially, it looks like he got drunk and injected himself with heroin."

Dave laughed out loud. "Yeah, right. I buy the drunk part but heroin is pretty wild."

"That's what we're thinking. Our lab guys have more tests to run but they've run some analysis at the scene and it's heroin. Pretty pure. Enough to kill him."

"You think he did it to himself?"

"Just between us, we think he had help. Whether he was willing is another matter."

"Suspects?"

"We have a person of interest, as we say these days."

"In custody?"

"Not yet."

"Do you know who he is?"

"Again, unofficially, we believe he is one of Mr. Segal's colleagues, a professional killer."

"Name?"

"Not yet, for you, anyway."

They had reached the main house and Ossening walked Dave around to the pool house where technicians, F.B.I. agents, and local police were examining the scene and taking photographs and making videos. A Skype call was underway between an agent at the scene and someone in Washington and images were being uploaded.

"I need you tell me what the rules are here," Dave said, surveying the scene.

"You can say he's dead and we're investigating. You can say he was last seen in the company of another man who is being sought. Here." Ossening handed Dave an eight by ten photograph of the man who called himself James. It was one of the images captured by agents when James picked up the heroin packet. "Person of interest. We'll be handing these out later today but you get it first. You can say you were at the scene and investigators are processing it. Would you like to do a quick recorded interview with me?" Ossening had an odd smile on his face.

Dave was surprised. "Okay, who are you and what have you don't with Agent Ossening? Why the cooperation?"

"This is a new ball game, Dave. Suddenly, the missing money isn't our top priority. Justice will get to that and I expect we'll all be shocked at how much this guy stole, but right now there are bigger issues. Some very bad people are loose."

Dave set his smart phone to record and Ossening went over his talking points. He asked for the public's help in identifying and capturing the man in the photograph. The recorded interview was over in five minutes. Dave had sound bites for several reports, all of which would contain information exclusive to Now News.

"You've got this for one hour, Dave. By then everybody else will be howling for it. The AG will be holding a news conference to say what I just said. Go get em, cowboy." Ossening pointed down the driveway to the gate. "The clock is ticking."

Dave sat in his rental car as he listened to Ossening's words and wrote his pieces, each two minutes long. *Thank you, Neal Augenstein*, he thought, as he used the phone to edit, mix, and record the reports that he uploaded to the Now News server. He was thankful that Augenstein had taken the time to show him how to file from the smart phone. Dave was only in his thirties but he felt old and out of touch with the technology that was changing the way the news world worked. *Well, this will keep me in the game, for now.*

Chapter Forty-eight

Edward Segal was walking to his truck when the motel owner shouted at him. "You hear about that congressman? Killed himself, I hear."

"Who?"

"Prewitt. Found him dead this morning over at his place."

"What do you mean killed himself?"

"It ain't official or nothin'. Just what folks are sayin'. Found him in his swimming pool. It's on the TV."

"I don't have a TV in my room."

"Well, just wanted to let you know. It's all over, the story."

Segal felt a surge of energy and he was oddly happy. It was on! He knew he was next. It would be a contest, a death match. He believed he had the advantage. After all, he could kill at distance. All he had to do was find his opponent and take him out. Where? Bees go to honey. Where was the honey? He smiled. Dave Haggard was the honey and he knew where Dave was. It like trapping a fox. Put a rabbit in a box and wait.

There weren't many Haggards left in that part of Tennessee and Segal had no trouble finding Uncle Danny's place. It was up a rural blacktop road and was, like the houses around it, set back from the road and several acres from the nearest neighbor. To Segal it looked like the area where he had grown up. He imagined that the moonshiners in the hills still lit their fires at night and boiled the mash that stank and produced a clear, powerful liquid.

He drove past the house and pulled his truck into a copse of black walnut trees that were coming into bloom. Husks from the previous year's output were still on the ground and crunched underfoot as he walked away from the truck. He carried binoculars but no weapon. He was scouting his target and was provisioned with water and granola. He had a rolled up army poncho on his belt. He was prepared to spend time on the ground, if that's what it took.

He walked up a game path and stepped gingerly through the kudzu that was greening, wary of snakes that were active in the spring warmth. They were hungry and in a bad mood. The path zigzagged to the top of the hill overlooking Uncle Danny's place and he kept low because the trees had not leafed out enough to afford much cover. The sun was high in a clear sky and the air was warming. Segal began to sweat and attract gnats that crawled into his eyes and ears. He found a spot under a chokeberry bush, spread the poncho, and lay down. He watched the house until the sun began to set and Uncle Danny turned on the lights in the kitchen.

Dave drove his rental car up the drive as Segal was making his way back to his truck. He stopped to watch Dave walk up the steps to the porch and open the front door. He glanced at his watch to note the time and carefully made his way down the hill, stopping every fifty feet to watch and listen. It was an old habit. He knew the natural sounds of the mountains and he was alert to noises that were manmade.

His truck had been parked for hours and it was possible that someone had come upon it and had stuck around to see who came back to it. It might be the landowner or a hunter curious about a stranger. Trespassing could be dangerous in these hills. He saw the silhouette of the truck under the trees and squatted against the hillside to listen before he came down to drive away. That's when he heard it. It was faint, but it was unmistakably a man walking on the walnut hulls near the truck, a crunch that would not be made by a deer or a fox. There was no movement to see and no outline of a man. It was someone who knew how to hide.

Segal knew who it was and he admired the man for his skill in tracking him. The man who had called himself James and had acted as a bodyguard for Congressman Prewitt, and who had accomplished his contract to kill him, was waiting for Segal in the dark. *You're not that good. I heard you.*

Snipers are trained to move silently without being seen. The darkness offered Segal cover but the ground was covered with the dry leaves that had fallen the previous autumn and small sticks and hulls, making his movement difficult. He knew that the man by the truck would be patient. He had time. Segal moved one foot at a time, slowly, sliding his boots along the ground, silently pushing the leaves and sticks out of the way, feeling his way downhill. It took him twenty minutes to cover fifty feet. The moon was rising when he reached the copse of walnut trees and began to move on his hands and knees toward the truck.

He could not see his enemy, the shadows swallowed the man and the steel-colored light from the moon only made the scene more abstract. He stopped and closed his eyes, trying to imagine where the man would be waiting. He slowly slid his right hand into his front pocket and extracted the brass knuckles, satisfied that the flat black finish would prevent a reflection that would give away his position. He squatted and saw himself as a tiger ready to leap at a meal.

He remained motionless, listening and waiting. He heard a small crack and turned in the direction of the sound when the man was upon him, pummeling him with his fists. Segal sprang up and swung his right hand at the place where he thought the man's face would be, anticipating the feel of the brass knuckles breaking bone. Instead, he felt air and a sharp pain at the man's fist crashed into his kidney, sending him to his knees. The man's hands were around his throat, squeezing his windpipe, and pressing him down to the ground.

Segal managed to turn his back to the man and reach his left hand between the man's legs, grabbing his testicles and squeezing, producing a scream from his attacker, whose grip on Segal's throat weakened for a second, long enough for him to turn and smash the brass knuckles into the man's nose, producing an explosion of blood and snot. The attacker was strong and determined and he came at Segal with a combination that connected on his face and in his stomach, causing him to bend over and wretch. The man pressed his hands together and clubbed Segal on the back of his head, sending him to the ground. The man then stomped Segal's spine, producing a howling pain from Segal. He grabbed his attacker's legs and jerked him up, causing the man to stumble against the truck.

Segal closed his eyes against the pain and exhaustion, rose up to his knees, and slammed the brass knuckles into the attacker's crotch, crushing his testicles and causing him to cry out an animal noise that could be heard down on the highway. Segal managed to get to his feet and slam the brass knuckles into the man's face again and again until he felt the attacker's skull collapse.

In the quiet after the violence the only sound was Segal breathing and the wind through the trees. There was no sound or movement from the man on the ground. Segal waited until he felt strong enough to move before he dragged the body away from the truck, climbed in, and drove away.

Dave Haggard had been sitting on Uncle Danny's porch, sipping from a Mason jar of moonshine, when he heard what he thought was a rabbit caught by a fox. He didn't think anything of it.

Chapter Forty-nine

Segal parked his truck behind the motel and spent the day assessing himself. He was not seriously injured but he was not fit for duty. His throat was sore and he could barely speak above a whisper. His back ached and sharp pains bent him over when he walked. He needed rest. He lay down on the bed and looked up at the ceiling, following the water stains to the spot where the wall and the ceiling met, idly pondering the location of the leak in the roof. He imagined climbing up a ladder with new shingles and repairing the roof. *What would it be like to own a place like this? It's probably a simple life. People come and go. Make the beds. Take the money.*

He glanced at the door and grabbed the M-14, checking to make sure a round was in the chamber. If they came through the door they would be hit by a bullet travelling at twenty-eight hundred feet per second. He visualized the jacketed round travelling through their bodies. It was the wrong ammo for close quarter fighting. The M-4 was ideal for that but the mission had changed. Now, Prewitt was already dead. It was Dave Haggard's turn, but he had to move fast. They were coming, he knew it. He, too, was a dead man.

He would take a day to recover and find his resources to do what he had to do. He fell into a troubled sleep and his dreams brought him images of death. Faces of black-haired, dark skinned men, women, and children, bloody and crying out to him. He twisted the sheets and hugged the rifle and dreamed that he put the muzzle into his mouth and pulled the trigger, sending a torrent of brains onto the wall over the bed. He woke up crying and rocked himself, holding the rifle like a child. He was sweating and breathing hard.

He began to sing an old Methodist hymn that his mother had taught him when he was a boy.

I come to the garden alone,
While the dew is still on the roses,
And the voice I hear falling on my ear,
The Son of God discloses...

He felt comforted in the garden alone. He sang in a soft whisper.

And He walks with he, and he talks with me,
And He tells me I am His own

He knew how it would play out and he was at peace. He fell into a deep sleep and woke when the sun was high. He was stiff and his back hurt when he stood, but he managed to get to the shower and stood under hot water for a long time, allowing it to sooth him and relax the muscles that had been battered in the fight. His throat was still sore but he could drink. He had no desire for food. The couple who ran the motel had to be dealt with, although Segal couldn't remember why. The man and woman would be found hours later by a swarm of sheriff's deputies, F.B.I. agents, and assorted investigators.

By dusk he was in position above Uncle Danny's place, wrapped in his army poncho against damp ground, watching. He had a restricted view of the porch, which faced the highway, but he could clearly see the kitchen through the window over the sink. Danny was at the stove, stirring something in a pot. There was no sign of Dave.

Segal scanned the terrain around him and saw no sign of anyone else. It would take a few days to replace the man who had come after him, the man who called himself James before he killed Prewitt. A replacement would have to be found, contracted, and sent to Tennessee. It wasn't like a basketball game where a coach could snap his fingers and insert another player into the game. There were protocols to follow. Discretion took time. But the clock was running.

He had been trained to wait. He would lie motionless, relieve himself in his pants if necessary. Darkness fell and the moon rose.

Dave Haggard had spent the day working the Prewitt angle, interviewing key supporters and listening as they offered somber reflections about a man no one really liked. He found no one who would comment on Prewitt's potential legal troubles, now less urgent, given the mortality of the would-be accused. The ruling class in Prewitt's District, the aristocracy that had either inherited or bought influence over public affairs, rallied in a formal but cool manner to their slain chosen Member.

"He was a fine man who watched over us in Washington," was a typical comment.

"Always had a kind word for the common man," was another, even though it was groundless. Prewitt had contempt for ordinary people and never tried to hide it.

Ordinary people, for their part, offered comments along the lines of, "I never met the man."

For Dave, the air had gone out of the story once his reports on Prewitt's death had been filed. It was clear that the story's center of gravity had shifted back to Washington, where reporters were screaming for news about the Justice Department's investigation into his death, his finances, his alleged kidnapping by the F.B.I., his state of mind, and anything else that might turn up in a tip to a reporter.

Reaction pieces, known in some news circles as "neighbor tape," were never the lead. Reaction pieces always followed the real news. Dave's pieces, if they ran at all, followed whatever late developments had turned up in the Prewitt mix and were topped with something along the lines of, "Meanwhile, the voters in Congressman Prewitt's Tennessee district are shocked by what has happened. Now News reporter Dave Haggard has more."

The lead-in was not entirely accurate. It appeared that the good folks in Tennessee were clueless about whatever chicanery their elected member of Congress was up to. And, they didn't seem to care, assuming that simply being in Congress was evidence of criminality.

It was time to head back to Washington, if only to catch up to the other reporters who had been working the phones, coffee shops, bars, parking lots and every other venue where information could be exchanged. The Justice Department was Dave's beat and it was there that the news was being made, or would be once the F.B.I. put together whatever it had.

Dave drove his rental car to Uncle Danny's to break the news that he was leaving. He didn't know if he would ever see him alive again, given the state of his health. Danny had told Dave he would inherit his home and land upon his death and Dave had suggested he leave it to his church. Dave already owned his parent's land and had not bothered to check in on it, fearful of the memories and emotions he would find there, so coming into another thirteen acres of ground was not something he relished. *Too many ghosts.*

For Dave, the trip home was sweet and painful, like a sip from a cup of milk that tasted like childhood gone forever, along with the laughter of loved ones whose love was warm and safe. He drove through the hills and felt them to be threatening and poisoned. His home ground had been disposable to others in faraway places; people who saw these mountains as closets in which to hide evil things, even if the evil was produced in the name of goodness and security. In that feeling, in that despair, he and Edward Segal were connected.

He would head back in the morning. He looked forward to an evening of drinking and story-telling, listening as Uncle Danny launched into his tales that began, "There was this old boy..." Danny had never bragged in his life. He was from a generation that believed that bragging about one's accomplishments was a sign of a weak character. The best jokes were told at one's own expense.

He pulled into the long driveway and saw the lights on in the house. Uncle Danny had promised to make fried chicken with white gravy for dinner. In the culinary standards of Washington, it was a dinner that came with a heart attack. To Dave, it was a tender reminder of a time that used to be. His mother had made it for him on special occasions like his birthday and his acceptance to college. His eyes were misty when he drove up to the house.

Chapter Fifty

Segal saw the headlights coming up to the house and adjusted the M-14. He was in the prone position, on his stomach, legs apart, left arm under the rifle, right hand on the trigger guard. He watched through the scope as the car pulled to the front of the house. He could not see Dave walk through the front door but he could see Uncle Danny turn and greet Dave as he walked into the kitchen.

Dave sat at the table while Danny stood at the stove, stirring something in a pan. It was a domestic scene that should have been mundane and safe, but this scene was malignant. Segal could not decide when to fire but it was not out of compassion. He was like a man staring at a slice of his favorite pie before he ate it, enjoying the anticipation and the flood of pleasant chemicals flowing through his brain. He decided to watch the men while they ate their dinner, chatting about the events of the day. He would make himself known while they cleaned the dishes.

Dave watched as Uncle Danny stirred the white gravy. The fried chicken was cooling on a plate and the grease on the crust was being absorbed by paper towels. Mashed potatoes were still in the pot, being kept warm. Danny had fried okra as a side dish. Dave was overcome by a feeling of love and comfort, gazing at the frail man who was making a meal that took Dave back to his earliest days. He missed his mother and father with an ache that he had learned to suppress. He knew that his feelings were still raw and fragile and he hoped he wouldn't break down. Feelings were something to be controlled, not indulged, he believed. They were too hard to control otherwise and could take him places he did not want to go. He had come to believe that life had more to lose than gain.

He helped with the table and sat in silence as he ate. The flavors of his childhood came flooding into his mouth and he could barely chew, not wanting the taste to leave him. Danny sat with his back to the window, slowing consuming the meal he had made. His face showed his sadness that Dave was leaving. The moment was sweet and bitter in its finality. They took sidelong glances at each other and smiled when they both looked up at the same time.

The chicken dinner that Dave had dreamed about ended with Dave's empty plate and Uncle Danny's best effort to get his meal down.

"I have pie," Uncle Danny said, struggling to stand, his voice shaky.

Dave took the plates to the sink and set them down. "I'll get it."

The pie was sweet potato and had been made by a woman at the church who wanted to do something nice for Dave, whom she hadn't seen in years. Dave took a large piece, about a quarter of the pie, and Uncle Danny took a small bite. They sat in silence and allowed the moment to take them. Danny seemed lost and stared at some unseen point in the distance. Dave looked at his uncle, the last of the clan, and felt like a man being launched into space, never to return.

Uncle Danny took a deep breath, stood up, and walked to the sink with his pie plate. He looked through the window and into the darkness, his eyes misty. Dave sat at the table and watched him. The 7.62 NATO round hit Uncle Danny in the throat and passed through him, severing his spinal cord. The round entered Dave's stomach and lodged there, its energy spent.

"Uncle Danny!" Dave screamed. He tried to stand but he fell to the floor as Uncle Danny's body settled next to the sink, his eyes still staring ahead. Dave was bleeding and he was overcome by a wave of pain that blinded him. He rolled onto his back and tried to force himself to stand but his body did not respond.

Outside, he heard a ferocious gunfight and a helicopter. It sounded to him like an army had arrived, all guns blazing. He heard shouting and the front door being knocked off its hinges. All he could see was the light over the sink and its whiteness as he tried to focus on what was happening around him. Sounds. Yelling. People running.

"Here he is!" He tried to place the voice.

"The other guy's dead," said another man.

"How's Haggard?" The first voice was closer.

Dave felt a hand on his neck. "He's still alive. I don't know for how long. Set that copter down and let's get him out of here."

"Get some photos." Voices were all around.

A man was kneeling next to him, inserting something into his arm. He felt himself being lifted onto a stretcher and carried outside. There was the sound of a helicopter's rotors and the feeling of lifting into the air. The lights in the cabin were red and the faces over him had a glow that made him wonder if he was dead and going to hell. A face came close to his and smiled.

"You okay there, Scribe?" Ossening's voice was friendly.

"Scribe's are the newspaper guys. You don't remember anything, do you." Dave managed a smile.

"Is that your uncle back there?"

"Yeah. What happened?"

"It was Segal. He got to you before we could get to him. I'm sorry. He's dead."

"Have you been watching him?"

"Not closely enough, it appears. We had him on and off and figured he'd go looking for you. We got that part right."

"Is this finally over?"

"Get some rest. We're coming in to Knoxville. They'll take good care of you."

Dave fell into a semiconscious moment of mourning for Uncle Danny and spent the rest of the night under the care of skilled surgeons at the University of Tennessee Medical Center. He regained consciousness in a recovery room as the sun was shining outside and by nightfall was in a private room arranged by Now News. He was sitting up, breathing on his own, when Elena and Sid walked in.

She stood in the doorway, staring at him, tears falling down her cheeks. She made small noises when she tried to speak and covered her mouth as she attempted to compose herself.

"I'm sorry," he said.

"Don't be. Just get better."

Sid stood next to the bed and tried to put on his best tough reporter face. "Jesus, Ace, hell of a thing. I'm very sorry about your uncle."

"Me, too. He was dying of cancer, so from his point of view it might have been better to go like he did. I don't know."

"How are you?"

"Sid, let me tell you something for once. It hurts like hell to get shot."

"I have good news and maybe not so good news."

"Okay, let's start with the good news." Dave waved to Elena to come to him. He looked at her and held her hand.

"The good news is you're the biggest thing in the news business again. Getting shot was a good career move, considering you were shot by the guy who shot Judge Beechum and went down in a hail of F.B.I. bullets."

"And the bad news?"

"Bill Adams at the AP scooped you on the end of the story."

"Which is?"

"The indictments. Twelve people were named, including Congressman Prewitt, who obviously isn't facing much of anything anymore. One of the names was familiar to you."

"Who's that?"

"Elaine Fuller, our own chairperson of the board. She was the money person in the scheme, paying off the hit men, hiring surveillance, doing the dirty work at the office, so to speak. She wanted you off the story because the group of them thought you were getting too close. Nice work."

"And Ossening?"

"He's on to other things."

Elena leaned over the put her hand over Dave's mouth. "Now, we're going to shut you up. You won't be chasing fire engines for a long time. Here's what will happen, Mister Hot Shit. You will be getting out of here in a week or so. Sid got Now News to get us, I said us, a condo in Ocean City for the summer. You will go there with me and get better. Got that?"

"I can't stand the beach."

"Shut up."

***

Coming soon from author Larry Matthews
and A-Argus Better Book Publishers:

Detonator
The next Dave Haggard thriller

Detonator
A Dave Haggard Thriller
By
Larry Matthews

Chapter One

Ikram Ali Ghazali hurried through Union Station and out onto Massachusetts Avenue into the light rain that made the summer heat steamy and close. To him, it felt like Pakistan without the smells and beggars. He had no time for sentimentality but he allowed himself a memory of the food stalls that had scented the neighborhood where he had attended the madrasa, learned to hate the West, and memorized every word of the Qur'an. He paused and recalled the first words of Al-Fatihah, The Opener:

1) *In the name of Allah Most Gracious Most Merciful.*

2) *Praise be to Allah the Cherisher and Sustainer of the Worlds.*

This man's heart was not most merciful. He seethed with a desire to watch his enemies suffer. He looked around and saw himself in the heart of the beast. He recalled the orders of his master, "Present a passive face to those around you and, when noticed, smile and appear docile. Strike with the venom of a snake."

The tourist bus was waiting in the circle outside the station and he could see the dome of the United States Capitol as he ran to join the line of other tourists, none of whom spoke English. The driver was a dark skinned man like himself, with straight black hair. The group had offered the cover of a tourist visit to the United States, arranged by an agency known for transporting Mexicans willing to spend money north of the border. Such tourists were always welcome in Washington.

"Prisa. Boleto por favor*" Hurry. Ticket please.* The driver looked past Ghazali at the next tourist in line. Ghazali was carrying a passport that identified him as a Mexican national named Juan Fernando Gutierrez of Mexico City.

He gave the man his ticket and climbed aboard, finding a seat next to a fat, middle aged woman.

"Es emocionante estar aquí." *It is exciting to be here.* She looked at the Capitol and smiled. "¿Es hermoso, no?" *It is beautiful, no?"*

"Si." He smiled with her. It was exciting, to be sure, after the years of study and planning. He had learned Spanish and had spent months in Central America, travelling and talking to anyone who would engage him, wringing the last of his accent out of his speech. He could speak high Spanish or low, Sonora or Oaxaca. He spoke English with a Mexican accent.

His trainer and master had told him about life in the West. Mexicans are common and accepted, in their own way, in America. Pakistanis are suspect. In many ways, we look alike to the whites and blacks in places like Washington or New York. And a man travelling on a Pakistani passport will be watched. A Mexican would be welcomed, so long as he goes home on time. A well-dressed Mexican will not be singled out at a concert at the Kennedy Center. A poorly dressed Mexican will not be noticed at a construction site. It is all about appearances." By the time anyone noticed the man who called himself Gutierrez, it would be too late.

He was an expert on electric grids and he had come to America to turn out the lights. *It will be a tribute to the martyrs when these dogs live in darkness,* he thought. *Let them live in caves and we will see how they survive.* The grid in America was like a child waiting to be taken in the night. *These people are fools.*

The bus drove past the usual tourist spots and stopped at a few like the Washington Monument, the Lincoln Memorial, and Pentagon, where it idled in a large parking lot while the tourist guide explained that it was the largest office building in the world and headquarters the most powerful military the world has ever known.

The man who called himself Gutierrez nodded in admiration and resentment. *You are fools. You lock the front door but leave the back door open. I have come to visit.*

He had no further use of the group. He told the driver he had business to attend to and would rejoin his fellow travelers in a day or two. He got off the bus 14th Street and Pennsylvania Avenue, not bothering to collect his luggage in the storage bin beneath the passenger compartment. He carried a backpack that contained with he needed. He checked into the Willard, went to his room, and studied the documents in his backpack. They contained the names of the Homeland Security employees who were tasked with protecting the American electric grid. All of them had the highest security clearances. Obtaining their information had been easy. Obtaining the weakness in the grid had been even easier.

He opened his laptop and logged into a program that provided him with the web identity of a man in Arizona who had no knowledge of Juan Gutierrez or his mission. A software program he had been provided put Gutierrez anywhere he chose. Once in, he opened a program that exposed the grid in the Washington area.

" Bismi-llāhi r-raḥmāni r-raḥīm." *In the name of Allah, Most Gracious, Most Merciful*. His voice was a whisper. He slid his finger over the touch pad and watched the curser slide to the point he had selected and, with a left click, he turned out the lights in north Arlington. *I am here. I have sent you a message.*

"Oh, crap!" Dave Haggard threw up his hands as others around him moaned and complained about the outage. "How long until the generator kicks in?" He was in the New News newsroom in Rosslyn, across the Potomac River from Georgetown. It was his first day back.

"One minute," came the reply from someone Dave could not see. "But it's about five minutes before everything boots up again."

"Goddam it! You'd think that if we can put a man on the moon we could keep the lights on." Sid Slackey ran Now News from a small office where his rants and ass chewings could be heard, and often, seen, by the staff. His office had no windows and he now sat in the dark, smacking his desk top.

"That was a long time ago, Sid." Gabriel was running the desk, as usual, and had been working the phones and checking the wires on his computer screen when the lights went out. "Nobody goes to the moon anymore."

"That's the problem with this country, we don't do anything anymore." Sid was sliding into one of his "moods" and Gabriel was pushing it along.

Dave was at his desk going through weeks of mail. He was spending the day back in the city after a summer-long recuperation from a gunshot wound he had suffered in Tennessee at the hands of a professional killer, who was now dead. News stories, no matter how important at the time, have a short shelf life and the one that had produced his wound was barely remembered, even in the news business.

"I'm bored, Sid," Dave said into the dark room. Now News had rented him and his significant other, a beauty named Elena, a condo on the beach in Ocean City, Maryland. "I hate the ocean, I hate the beach life and I hate seafood" He was trying to log on to a workstation when the power went out. "Sid, when can I come back to work?"

"When Elena says you're ready." Sid and Elena had formed a kind of alliance after Dave was shot, a pseudo-familial arrangement where Sid would play the father role to whatever role Elena chose; sister, mother, lover.

"She's not my keeper, Sid." They were yelling back and forth in the dark as the rest of the staff hoped they would shut up.

"We'll set up a test. I'll get a fire truck to speed by and you chase it. If you can run for forty blocks you can come back."

"I couldn't do that when I was in shape."

"Not my problem."

"Then I'll just sit here until I can hit the streets. I can't stand the beach another day. I need to smell some diesel and hear a Somali cab driver complain about immigrants."

The lights came on and a small cheer went up in the newsroom as the computers slowly came to life.

The man who called himself Gutierrez smiled and moved the curser on his laptop. The lights of Georgetown went dark. *Soon, you will all be like children screaming for your milk*

Meet our Author

Larry Matthews

Larry Matthews is an award-winning broadcast journalist whose thirty-plus years as a reporter provide the background material for his books. Matthews was a street reporter, anchor, news director, producer and editor for major radio stations, ABC Radio, and National Public Radio. He was a producer, host and reporter for Maryland Public Television. As a reporter he covered some of the major events of the late Twentieth Century in Washington, D.C. and other cities. He is the recipient of the George Foster Peabody Award for Excellence in Broadcasting, The

DuPont/Columbia Citation, The National Headliner Award, and national and regional awards from The Society of Professional Journalists, The Associated Press, United Press International, and other professional organizations and universities.

His memoir, *I Used To Be In Radio*, was hailed as "a must-read in journalism schools, especially for those who aspire to be investigative reporters" and as "a funny and moving page-turner".

Two of his novels, *Healing Charles* and *Saving Charles,* were praised as "outstanding works of fiction." The novels are about the life of one man, set thirty years apart.

Matthews is also co-author of *Street Business*, with Ernie Lijoi Sr., a police/crime novel based on real events in the career of retired Detective Lijoi.

Matthews's experience as an investigative reporter provides much of the background material for his Dave Haggard thriller series about a radio reporter in Washington, D.C. who finds himself at the dangerous center of major criminal investigations. The first in the series, *Butterfly Knife*, involves the hunt for a serial killer of priests. The second, *Brass Knuckles*, finds Dave chasing down leads in a murder/kickback scheme involving a member of Congress. The third, *Detonator*, is about the betrayal of national trust and high-level treason.

Matthews lives and writes in Gaithersburg, Maryland.

His website is www.larrymatthews.net.

Twitter @lawrencematthew

Facebook is larrymatthewsauthor.

www.ingramcontent.com/pod-product-compliance
Lightning Source LLC
Chambersburg PA
CBHW051526260626
47170CB00003B/805